THE CORMORANT

ALSO BY CHUCK WENDIG

CHUCK WENDIG

——————

THE CORMORANT

SAGA PRESS

LONDON SYDNEY **NEW YORK** TORONTO NEW DELHI

SAGA ꕥ PRESS
AN IMPRINT OF SIMON & SCHUSTER, INC.

1230 AVENUE OF THE AMERICAS, NEW YORK, NEW YORK 10020

+ Text copyright © 2014 by Chuck Wendig + Originally published in 2014 in Great Britain by Angry Robot
For information address Saga Press Subsidiary Rights Department, 1230 Avenue of the Americas, New York, NY 10020. + SAGA PRESS and colophon are trademarks of Simon & Schuster, Inc. + For information about special discounts for bulk purchases, please contact Simon & Schuster Special Sales at 1-866-506-1949 or business@simonandschuster.com. + The Simon & Schuster Speakers Bureau can bring authors to your live event. For more information or to book an event, contact the Simon & Schuster Speakers Bureau at 1-866-248-3049 or visit our website at www.simonspeakers.com. + Also available in a Saga Press hardcover edition + Cover illustration copyright © 2015 by Adam S. Doyle + The text for this book was set in New Caledonia LT. + Manufactured in the United States of America + First Saga Press paperback edition February 2016 + 10 9 8 7 6 5 4 3 2 1 + CIP data for this book is available from the Library of Congress. + ISBN 978-1-4814-5701-9 (hc) + ISBN 978-1-4814-4869-7 (pbk) + ISBN 978-1-4814-4870-3 (eBook)

TO THE DEAD,
WHO CAN TEACH
YOU A WHOLE
LOT ABOUT LIFE

PART ONE

FILTHADELPHIA

"And the Lord said, let there be light."

A flutter of black fabric, and the hood is gone.

Miriam winces. Blinks. A white wave bleeds in from the edges. The world presses through the blur: Shapes emerging from a puddle of milk.

The fat man who spoke sits across from her. Behind him walks the brittle woman, his partner—a boozy, tilted smile stitched between the moorings of two sharp cheekbones. Her hand is bandaged.

"You look like shit," Grosky, the fat one, says after a low whistle.

"You look like a track suit wrapped around a bunch of trash bags," Miriam answers. Her voice feels raw. *Sounds* raw. Like bare feet torn on broken shells, abraded by sand, stung by salt.

Ragged, ruined, roughed-the-fuck-up.

Grosky just shrugs. Laughs a little. He's got a soft voice. Though she knows he can turn the volume up when he needs to. The booming timpani in the barrel well of his chest.

He's got the box. *Her* box. Right there in front of him. He drums his sausage-link fingers on it. The lid rattles. The padlock judders.

The scarecrow—Vills, Catherine Vills—paces like she's nervous. Like she's got something to hide, which Miriam knows she does.

3

Miriam feels it in her feet as much as she hears it: The tide coming in. Not far away. The hush-and-boom of waves crashing. She looks around. This is just some ramshackle beach hut. Wood walls, leaning against one another as if for emotional support. Thatched roof overhead. Cobwebs hang and sway as a fishy breeze creeps in through open windows.

"Where are we?" Miriam asks.

Grosky doesn't answer her question. "You want anything?"

"Cigarette."

"You shouldn't smoke."

"You shouldn't mainline lard and melted cheese. Do you even eat the cheeseburgers anymore, or do you just inject them right into your man-tits?" She tries to mimic said injection, but remembers that her hands are cuffed in front of her, and the shackles are in turn cuffed to the leg of the table. The table is wood. Old. Rickety. She could bust it if she has to.

But she won't have to. Not yet, anyway.

"Funny thing about lard," Tommy Grosky says, "it's got a bad rap. Demonized with all the other animal fats in the Seventies. But the truth is, it's the vegetable fats that'll kill you. Crisco. Margarine. Those, eh, those trans-fatty acids will fuck you up pretty good." He squeezes a fist like he's angrily milking a goat's udder. "Closes your arteries off. Like with a clothespin."

"That is *fascinating*." She squeezes the words like a sponge, lets them drip sarcasm everywhere. "Thank you, Surgeon General Fatty McGee."

"I'm just saying, things aren't always what they appear." He pats his chest. *Boom boom boom.* "You look at me and think, *Hey, there's a blobby bastard right there. Like if Fred Flintstone ate Barney, Wilma, turned that purple dinosaur into dino burgers. Lift up one of his fat rolls, you'll see a couple Twinkies hidden away.* You think I got an expiration date coming up. That my heart's like a soup can in an old lady's pantry: sure to burst before too long. But see, here's the thing: I'm a forty-two-year-old guy who's as healthy as a sixteen-year-old. My good cholesterol is through the roof. My bad cholesterol, shit, I don't even think I *have* any. Great blood pressure. Perfect blood sugar—I don't even know how to *spell* diabetes. I eat well. I like a lot of greens. Chard. Kale. Spinach, obviously."

"Obviously."

"So maybe don't be so smug." His mouth hangs open. He waggles his tongue between the two rows of flat Chiclet teeth. It makes a wet, hollow sound. "Because maybe you don't know what you're looking at."

"Maybe you forget, I know how you're going to die."

His eyes sit tucked behind folds of flesh that look like someone is pinching the skin shut, but suddenly the eyes go wide and she sees something flash there in the dark of his pupils: anger, bright white, like light trapped in the steel of a knife blade.

"This again," he says. "Right. I'll play. So you're saying it's my health that kills me? If you can even do this thing that you say you can do."

"What time is it?" Miriam asks. Her turn to change the subject.

Here Vills looks down at a nice watch. A new watch. Movado. It hangs on her gaunt bone-knob wrist near a bandage. Miriam thinks, *We'll get to all this soon enough.*

"Five after noon," Vills says. A smoker's voice. A voice that's all rust flakes and precancerous nodes, all in the dry thatch eaves of the woman's scratchy throat. Then Vills drops a cigarette on the table between Grosky and Miriam.

Grosky gives his partner a look.

"Let her smoke," Vills says. "Let's get this over with."

"Fine," Grosky says. He flicks the cigarette over toward Miriam. It rolls and she catches it: a trap-door spider leaping upon its prey. Vills hands him a lighter but he doesn't give it over. He twirls it. Grinning.

Miriam screws the cigarette between her lips. Teeth on the filter. Tongue rimming the paper. She wants it. A nic-fit threatens to tear through her like a pack of starving dogs.

Grosky leans across. Strikes the cheap gas station lighter—*flick flick flick*. Just sparks, just empty embers, hollow promises, no flame.

He shrugs. Pulls the lighter away. "Oh well."

"Try again."

"I'm not breathing in your stink. I gotta do it with this one—" He jerks a thumb toward Vills. "But I don't gotta do it with you."

"I have had a *bad* couple of weeks," Miriam growls.

"Ooooh. Ho, ho. I know. We're gonna talk about that."

"I want my cigarette."

"You tell me some of the things I want to know, maybe you'll get that cigarette. And maybe I'll fix you a plate of greens—it's good for that sunburn. And—*and!*—maybe you'll get out of those cuffs, too. Or maybe not. Everything depends on you, Miss Black."

"Miss Black? So formal. Please. Call me *Go Fuck Yourself*."

"I want to know about this boy," Grosky says, grabbing a photo from a folder in his lap. He slides it across the table. Soon as she sees it, it's like someone yanks something vital right out of her. A child's hand jerking the fabric from a doll's chest.

The young man in the picture is dead.

Puffy green Eagles jacket spattered with blood.

Blood is black in the winter slush.

Outside the hut in the here and now, the tides rumble.

Somewhere, seabirds squawk and chatter.

Gannets, maybe, Miriam thinks.

Miriam draws a deep breath.

And she tells him the story.

ONE

PUT A RING ON IT

The engagement ring is burning a hole in Andrew's pocket. That's how it feels, like it'll burn through the fabric and drop off into the dirty snow of the sidewalk, maybe roll into the sewer grate and disappear into the slurry below. And if that were to happen, how would he feel? He'd feel horrible. He loves Sarah. He wants to marry Sarah. But he can't marry her with this ring. A ring too big for her perfect porcelain fingers. A big ring with a diamond too small. A ring he inherited from his mother.

Still. The ring's like a loaded gun. He's almost proposed five times in the last couple weeks. Part of him thinks, *Just propose; you can get the ring resized, get a new diamond later. Before the wedding. Which won't be for a year anyway. Oh, God, unless she wants to get married soon . . .*

But no. He has to do this right. Her father thinks Andrew does everything half-ass. And her father means the world to her. Andrew has to make this a good show. The ring has to impress her, but more important, it has to impress her father. The problem: Even Sarah doesn't know how bad Andrew's got it right now. He's got a good job at a brokerage here in Philly, but he's thirty thousand in credit card debt. Not to mention the car loan. And the student loans from b-school *and* from grad school. And the rent. The gas bill. The trash bill. The *this* bill. The *that* bill.

He's got a little money in his pocket but, really, he's broke.

Which is why he's out here now. In Kensington at quarter till eleven on a Wednesday night. Walking through a pissy wet snowfall—fat, clumpy flakes not drifting so much as *plopping* to the earth. His nice shoes white from the road salt. His socks wet from the slush.

Derek at work said, *"You want a diamond cheap, I know a place."* Derek said, *"It's in Kensington,"* and Andrew said, *"Oh, hell no, Kenzo? Really?"* He said that if he goes down there, he'll get stabbed. Or strangled. *"Isn't the Kensington Strangler still around down there?"* Derek just laughed. *"That's old news. Crime's down. It's fine. You want the diamond cheap, or you want to pay jewelry store prices?"*

Andrew thought but did not say, *I* want *to pay jewelry store prices.*

He just can't afford to.

And so, a pawn shop. Derek said, *"It's called K&P Moneyloan Pawn, except they don't speak a lot of English and they misspelled Moneyloan so it says Moneylawn, so at least you'll know you have the right place."*

Andrew thought he'd get there right after work, six, maybe seven o'clock. But suddenly the team of in-house lawyers demanded a new meeting at work, and meetings are like black holes: They eat up the hours, they suck in the light, they gorge on his productivity. Next thing he knew, it was past ten o'clock and he still had to get to Kensington.

The pawn shop was still open. Thank God.

The guy behind the counter—a guy Derek said was Indian (*"Curry Indian, not Wounded Knee Indian"*) but that Andrew thinks is Sri Lankan—showed him the diamonds and everything looked good; the prices were low enough he almost wondered if they were real, and then he had a small panic attack because wasn't he supposed to remember something about the three *C*s? Color, clarity, cut and . . . was there a fourth *C*?

Crap! Whatever. He's no expert. Neither is Sarah. He picked a princess-cut diamond that looked—well, it looked pretty. It caught the light. It felt heavy. Sharp, too, like it could cut a hole in the storefront window.

So there he stood in a dingy, cracked-floor pawn shop, the too-bright fluorescents above humming and clicking, neon lights trapped between the pawn shop window and the big metal grate just *inside* the windows, and finally he managed to argue the little Sri Lankan man down to a price he could afford (a price less than half of what he'd pay anywhere else), and then he whipped out his Visa and—

"No credit card," the little man said.

"I have a debit card—"

"No take, no take."

"But that's what I have."

The little man pulled back the small cloth with the diamond on it. "Cash only. No diamond. Only cash. No diamond."

So he asked, "Is there an ATM machine around?"

"Is just ATM," the little man said. "No ATM machine. ATM mean *Automated Teller Machine*. You no need to say extra *machine*."

This from a man whose store is named *Moneylawn*.

Andrew said fine, fine, just tell me where, and he thought—hoped—that the ATM was right across the street, but no, of course it wasn't; it was three blocks up and four blocks over and now the sky is really flinging the glops of wet snow down on his head as if to punish him for his bad money management—

So now here he is. Hurrying along. To an ATM in the middle of Kensington. A neighborhood no longer in decline because it can't decline any further—the car has already crashed, the wreck has already burned out.

Derelict storefronts. A lone pizza joint at the corner, still open. Eyes watching him from under a ratty overhang. Past an alley where a homeless guy in an overcoat sleeps in the shade of a dented Dumpster, using a blue tarp as a blanket. Someone yelling a block over—a Hispanic girl in a half-shirt and jeans, no jacket, no hat, bronze hair peppered with white flakes, and she's screaming at some little thug in a leather jacket, saying something about sucking his dick, something about someone named Rosalita. The thug's just laughing. Braying, even. Waving her off.

Andrew keeps his head down.

Turn around. Go home. The diamond will be there tomorrow.

No. Tomorrow is Saturday. He and Sarah are going to Wildwood Gardens. She loves that place. The orchid house. The Christmas lights. He's going to ask her there. Do the whole thing: down on one knee, ring up, maybe in front of a crowd so they have that story to tell.

Just walk. Hurry up. You need to do this. Man up, Andrew. What would her father say?

Her father would say nothing. He'd just stare at Andrew with those dark gray eyes, eyes like bits of driveway gravel.

Ahead—a basketball court. Tall fences. Three courts lined up next to each other. He can shortcut the block, he thinks.

But then—

Footsteps. Behind him. Crossing the street. Splashing in slush.

He casts a quick glance over his shoulder.

A shadow following. Hands in pockets. Dark camo. Hood up.

His heart starts kicking.

He hurries forward. Half a short block to the basketball courts. His foot catches on an uneven sidewalk—he falls forward, just barely catches himself, but he takes the opportunity to shift into a brisk walk, almost a jog.

But the person behind him is coming up fast now.

Faster than he is. A swift step.

The person raises a gloved hand. Points a finger-gun at him.

The thumb-hammer falls.

Andrew hurries. Grabs the pole holding up the chain link leading into the basketball courts. He ducks in through the gate—

"Hey!" calls a voice.

A woman's voice.

"Andrew!"

She knows his name?

Thud. Something hits him hard in the back.

Snow plops.

A snowball. She hit him with a snowball.

He wheels. Holds up both hands, palms forward. "I don't know who you are or what you want, but I don't want any trouble—"

The woman hooks her thumbs around the hood, flips it back. It's some white girl. She shakes free a shaggy ink-black pixie cut, the front bangs streaked with red. She stares at him from raccoon-dark eyes.

"You dumb shit," she says, baring her teeth from behind a fishhook sneer. "*What* are you doing out here?"

"Wh . . . huh?"

She sighs as snow falls. "I don't know why I'm yelling at you. I knew you'd be here. Isn't that why I'm here?" She taps a cigarette out of a rumpled pack of Natural American Spirits. Cigarette between lips. Clink of a lighter. Flame in the winter. Blue smoke.

He coughs. Fans the smoke away.

"I gotta go," he says.

"You don't remember me," she says. A statement, not a question.

"What? No, I—" Wait. The way she stares from under an arched and dubious brow. He knows that look. A look of unmitigated incredulity. A mean-girl look like she's saying, *You'd really wear those pants with that shirt?* Sarah gives him that look sometimes. Her judgey face. "Yeah. Hold up. I remember you. From the bus."

She gestures at him with the cigarette. "Got it in one."

A year ago. On the SEPTA NiteOwl route home to University City.

His stomach suddenly drops out from under him.

"You . . . told me . . ." He tries to remember. He was tired that night. No. Drunk. He was *drunk* that night. Not black-out-and-wake-up-in-Jersey drunk, but drinks with Derek and the other brokers . . . Did Sarah yell at him that night? No. They were only just together then. Not even living with each other. They'd just met.

The woman vents smoke through her teeth. "You have a ring in your pocket. Left pocket, I think."

His gaze darts down. His hand reflexively touches the pocket. There the ring is heavy. *The One Ring*, he thinks. On the way to Mordor. Absurd that he's thinking about that. He doesn't even like those books.

"How do you . . ." But then it all hits him. Ice breaking. Water rushing. The memory cold as the slap of the winter air.

On the bus. He'd seen her there before. Sitting in the back. Earbuds in. Then one day she came up to him. Sat behind him. Started talking. He'd had . . . what were they? A bunch of Long Island Iced Teas. How do they get them to taste so much like iced tea? They turned her into a smudgy blur, a Vaseline thumbprint on the lens of his life.

She just started talking. Like she couldn't stop, like someone karate-kicked the spigot right off the sink—words spraying everywhere. She was amped, jacked up in the same way he was slowed down, and she told him—

You're gonna die.

That's what she said.

She knows about the ring now because she knew about it then.

Didn't she? She told him he'd have a ring in his pocket, and he said that was absurd. At the time he hadn't even thought of marrying Sarah, but here he was, with a ring—his dead mother's own engagement ring—there in his pocket, a modest little circle of white gold, *too* modest . . .

The girl gave him a date. Told him to "mark his calendar."

Was tonight that date?

He doesn't even realize he asked the question out loud.

"Yes. It's tonight, genius." You really should've written it down. I *told* you to write it down. I said, 'Whip out your fancy smartphone and write it the fuck down.' But did you? Mmm. No. You just puked on your shoes." She suddenly pauses, as if in rumination. "Okay, maybe I should have waited till you weren't drunk to give you the news, though at the time I thought it might soften the blow. I'd been watching you for days. I brushed by you on a Monday, didn't tell you until Thursday."

"You're crazy," he says, backpedaling.

"Be that as it may, Andrew, that doesn't change what's coming."

He says it again—"You're *crazy*"—because he can't find any other words, because his brain is suddenly a snarl of sparking, rat-chewed wires, and he knows he's being played. Conned, somehow. He takes a step back, turns—starts hurrying across the basketball court.

She's after him. Like stink on a skunk.

"You're processing this poorly," she yells. "Totally normal, by the way. This was all kind of an experiment for me. I've run it again and again, and it always runs smack into the same dead end every time." She clears her throat. "No pun intended until now. Hey. Slow down. Wait up."

But he keeps hurrying.

"Get away," he says.

"You've got an appointment to keep, huh? Running right toward the reaper's bony hug. Fate, man. Fucking fate! See? I *told* you how it was going to shake out. I gave you all the details—the date, the ring, the ATM machine"—*You no need to say extra machine*—"and yet here you are, not walking but *sprinting* toward the cliff's edge. It's like people *want* to die."

"I'll call the police." He fumbles for his phone. He palms it, turns around while still walking backward and waves the phone at her like it's a weapon. "I'll do it. I'll call 911!"

"Go ahead," she says, stopping. She sucks on the cigarette. "Call them. I'll wait. You call them, you might just save your own life, Andy."

"Andrew. It's Andrew."

"Whatever. Ringy-ringy. 911."

He holds the phone. Hand trembling.

He doesn't call.

He doesn't call because he doesn't have the time. If he calls the police, they might actually show up. Then they'll want to talk to him. Take a statement. But the pawn shop closes at midnight.

And midnight is fast approaching.

Instead, he takes out his house keys. He shoves keys through his fingers and forms a soft, clumsy fist.

He shakes the fist at her.

She laugh-snorts. "What is *that*?"

"I'll hit you. It'll . . . the keys, the keys'll cut you."

"Did you learn that in a movie?"

"In a defense class."

"In a defense class for *who*? I didn't know you were a middle-aged housewife, Andy. You cover it up well."

"Fuck you."

"*There* it is. The anger. The resentment. Nobody likes being told they're going to die. They struggle like a sparrow caught in a man's hand. Flapping and scratching and pecking. You can fix this, Andy. Turn around. Go home. Whatever you're doing out here in pissing distance of midnight, do it some other time."

He kicks stones and slush at her. Like a child. He feels stupid for doing it but there it is; it's already done.

"You're a fucking lunatic!" he shouts at her.

The woman just shakes her head.

"Fine," she says. "That's the experiment, then. I'm calling it. Time of death: fifteen minutes. Go forth, spunky housewife, and meet your maker."

She turns then. Pulls her hoodie back over her head. Flicks her cigarette off into the snow.

The woman recedes. A slow walk away.

She doesn't look back. She's done with him. Good.

He stands there for a little while. Shaking. He tells himself it's just the cold. *Sarah. The ring. The ATM. Midnight. Man up, Andy. Andrew! Andrew. Damnit.* It's like the woman's insanity is contagious. Like she's in his head, a spider spinning a web, catching flies. He lets out a plume of frozen breath.

Then he turns, hastens his step across the last two basketball courts.

Through an alley. Through puddles of dirty ice-mush.

There. Across the street, next to a small alley. Glowing bright, Superman red-and-blue: the ATM. *Almost there,* he thinks, as he darts across the empty street. Above, the sky glows Philadelphia Orange, a blasted burnt umber hue as if a chemical fire burns in the heavens.

Andrew digs out his card with cold-bitten hands, shoves it in the machine. He jumps through all the hoops. Presses all the buttons. Enters his PIN number—and suddenly he realizes it's not a PIN number, it's just a PIN, a Personal Identification Number, and the absurdity of yet another redundancy makes him laugh—

Whew.

Tension flees.

This is okay.

It's all going to be fine.

Except:

The machine won't let him take out more than two hundred dollars. He needs four times that amount. *Damnit!*

He stabs the button. Fine. It spits out two hundred.

Then he crams his card into the slot again.

It beeps. Tells him he's taken out his "allotted transaction amount."

"No no no," he says, hand balling into a fist and pounding on the machine like he's knocking on a door to be let in. "I need more than that! Please, c'mon." But the machine keeps beeping its refusal. The two hundred will have to do. He'll take it. He'll . . . offer it as a deposit to hold the diamond until tomorrow. He'll come back in the morning with more money and then it'll all be fine—

Click.

"Yo, dude, step away from that box."

His blood turns to snowmelt. His bowels to chilled vinegar.

"Come on, come on, turn around, turn around."

Andrew—ten twenty-dollar bills clutched in his left hand— pivots slowly. He can barely breathe. He's going to hyperventilate.

A lanky black kid stands there. Fifteen, sixteen years old. A gun almost too big for his hand hangs leveled at Andrew's chest. The big poofy Eagles jacket makes him look like a parade balloon. His face is half-hidden behind a purple paisley handkerchief.

"I'm gonna take that money now, son," the kid says, starting to reach.

Andrew instinctively pulls the money away—

Wham. The kid clips him across the chin with the side of the gun.

Teeth bite into tongue. He tastes blood. His neck is wet— first warm and wet, then cold.

The kid snatches the money out of Andrew's hand.

The mugger laughs loud, like he's not afraid of anyone hearing him out here. "You do *not* belong in this neighborhood, motherfucker. Shit, *shit*, look at you. Even in this fuck-ass snow your shoes still all shiny. Rich white people shoes are special shoes, I guess."

"My . . . socks are wet."

"Your socks are wet. Listen to this dude with his wet-ass socks." Suddenly the kid yells in his face, eyes wide and white, "I don't give a shit about your wet *fuckin'* socks, I care about what's in your fat *fuckin'* pockets! You got more shit in there, I know you do, rich boy. So open them up and share the wealth. Let's close the *income disparity* in America starting here, tonight, with you and me, motherfucker."

"I . . . Okay, okay," Andrew says, pulling his wallet and handing it over. He can lose that. He can even lose the two hundred. He can't lose the ring. His hand instinctively presses against the flat of his pocket, as if to protect the gold, the diamond, Sarah's love, the whole future.

"Whoa-whoa-whoa, what else you got there, rich boy? Hiding something in that pretty pocket? A present? For me?"

"Hey-hey-hey, no, it's nothing, really—"

Wham. The kid lashes out again. This time Andrew holds his arms up, so the gun cracks him in the side of his hand. He pulls it away, crying out, and when he does, the kid nails him in the temple—

Next thing he knows, the sidewalk is rushing up to meet him—

Red freckles on white snow—

The world is lost in a screaming whine—

The gun in his face, the kid screaming.

He can't even hear what the mugger is saying. He thinks suddenly, *I can reason with this kid, I can make him understand*, and he starts babbling about how he's got a ring in his pocket, an engagement ring, and he needs it or Sarah won't marry him, and his eyes are closed and he's pleading, praying, spit and blood making his words sound sticky—

The gun barrel presses against his head.

The mugger yells, "Gimme that fuckin' ring!"

Andrew thinks, *It's over. That crazy woman was right. I'm a dead man.*

He tilts his head.

Sees the blur of the gun. The length of the kid's arm. The madness in the mugger's eyes.

Then: movement in a whorl of snow.

An avenging angel. A knife-slash of black hair. Ends dyed in blood.

The girl from before, she steps out from the alley.

Her own gun up—

The kid never had a chance—

Bang.

Blood mists from the side of the kid's head.

He drops into the empty street. Blood pumping.

TWO

SCALPER

Little details go off like Pop Rocks. The kid hits the snow, his scalp peeled back like the skin of an unfinished orange, and all Miriam can do is see those tiny details—

Cigarette burns on the back of the kid's hand.

One shoelace on a green-and-white sneaker untied.

One pant leg cuffed. The other unrolled.

The jacket and shirt pull up—she sees two freckles and a mole.

The gun in her hands is small. A little nickel-shiny .38 with a stumpy pig-nose of a barrel. It felt light before. Light like a feather. Now with one bullet gone, it's heavy like a length of chain. Her arm falls to her side.

Andrew looks up at her from between splayed-out fingers.

"I saved you," she says. Her voice sounds a hundred miles away.

"Wh–what?"

"Stand up. I saved your life."

Andrew braces himself against the wall. He tries to stand. His chin is wet with blood. His lips, too. His whole mouth is a slick crimson hole.

He stares at the body. She does, too. Dark blood pumps gently—glug, squirt, glug, like someone's making a cherry snow-cone at a carnival.

"He was just a kid," she says. "Jesus."

"He was going to kill me." Those words spoken past bubbles of blood.

"I think I had that part figured out, Andy."

"Andrew, my name is . . ." But he finishes the sentence with some kind of goat bleat, then drops to his knees and begins fishing out the wad of money from the kid's fist. The cold dead hand is tight on the cash. Andrew has to peel back the fingers like he's peeling an onion.

"Here," she says, holding out a hand.

He gives her his hand, and she thinks, *No, that's not what I meant,* but she helps him stand up anyway. "I mean, give me some of that."

"Some of . . ." But then he looks down at the cash in his hand. Speckled with glistening red. "It's mine."

"Your *life* is yours, thanks to me," she growls. She points at the body. "I did *that*. For *you*. People give money for finding a lost cat. You can damn sure pony up for me saving your punk-ass life."

He scowls. "I need it."

"You cheap sonofabitch. Twenty bucks! Give me *twenty bucks*."

He takes a step back. "This is . . . this is some kind of shakedown. You planned this all along. You even told me. This is some kind of con. Is that guy even dead? Did you know him? You knew him. You crazy—"

The gun is up before she even realizes she's lifting it.

"I did not shake you down," she says through bared, feral teeth. *I just saved the life of a total asshole.* "I knew your death was coming. Fate was a train bearing down on you, Penelope Pitstop. I pulled you off the tracks. Your whole life should be unfolding for you right now—some rich country club wedding, some jam-handed yuppie asshole kids, a big ol' precious privacy fence around a house in the burbs. I *chose* to save you. That life is mine." Her mother's voice springs up like a weed in the loamy dirt of her mind: *Don't do something nice for somebody expecting something nice in return.* Whatever. Fuck her. "Least you can do is spot me cab fare home."

But all he can do is stare at that gun.

Then he calls her "bitch."

She pulls the trigger.

He jumps like a spooked squirrel. The bullet digs a furrow in the brick of the building next to his head.

"Now I don't want the cab fare," she says. "I want a *saving-your-life* fare. I want all the money. All two hundred of it. You give it, you live. You don't, I kill you and I *still* take it, and then I take whatever that ring is in your pocket and I pawn it for good cigarettes and bad whiskey. *Money!* Now."

His hand opens. The money flutters to the ground.

Andrew runs. Slipping, skidding, escaping.

Somewhere, sirens.

"Fuck!" she yells.

She hurries to scoop up the twenties.

She looks into the dead kid's blank-slate eyes one last time. Dead black pupils like a bird's eyes.

Then she bolts.

THREE

INTO THE BLACK

Miriam's back at the apartment. The *water-stain* apartment. The *cockroach* apartment. The *squealing radiator* apartment.

She comes through the door like a black storm, like a funnel cloud sucking up everything it touches. Jace is there. He's still in his coffeehouse barista-bitch apron and he springs up as soon as he sees her, a mop-top hipster gopher at the hole. He chucks aside his video game controller and says, "Dude, I got news. We need to *celebrate* tonight."

All she can do is shove him back onto the couch.

She tells him to go fuck his mother.

Then she shoulders her way into her bedroom.

She stays there for three days.

FOUR

HER HAUNTED HEAD

He shows up as the first light of the morning sun pools under the cusp of the window like hot magma, and she thinks, *It's him.* She's going to pull her head from under the cave of three pillows and there will be the boy in the Eagles jacket, the top of his head flapping loose—his scalp will be the mouth, slapping and yapping, the words gurgling up out of his convertible skull.

He doesn't say anything. But she *feels* him there. A heavy presence in the room. A frequency. Like a TV on mute. Like a whisper-crackle of white noise coming from the corner.

She refuses to look. *I won't, I won't, I won't.*

Eventually, he speaks.

"You did a number on that kid, huh?" Louis's voice asks. Miriam lurches upright. Pillows flumping to the floor. She knows why she looks. Because it's Louis. Not the real Louis. She hasn't seen *him* for over a year. But she's desperate for a friendly face. Even if it's a mask worn by a Trespasser who treads on the forbidden burial ground that is her mind.

This Louis has both his eyes gone. The sockets aren't covered with black electrical tape, though—they're half hidden behind a rolled-up purple handkerchief tied tight around his big Frankenstein Monster head.

"Shut up," she says. "That shitbag was a killer."

"Takes one to know one."

"Shitbag or a killer?"

Not-Louis shrugs, mouth the barest smirk. "Why choose?"

She kicks a pillow toward him. It falls through him, hits the wall.

"You see those cigarette burns?" Not-Louis asks.

"I don't want to talk about this."

"He either did those himself—an act of self-abuse—or someone was abusing him." Not-Louis whistles, a mournful choochoo. "Probably had a hard life. Just a kid. Just a stupid kid who didn't have the presence of mind to know one of his shoelaces was undone. One pant leg unfurled: a fashion statement? A gang thing? Or just a goofy dumb teenager?"

"That goofy dumb teenager had a pistol the size of Colorado."

"And he was going to use it, too."

"He was. That's right."

Not-Louis leans forward. He smiles. His teeth are bright—stinkbugs crawl across the flat white expanse. His tongue, now the flattened head of a rattlesnake with its own forked tongue, lashes the air.

She wants to look away. But she can't. It's all she has.

Call Louis, she thinks. *The real Louis.*

She thinks that every day. Once, twice, many times.

Not-Louis says, "So why this guy? People eat bullets all the time. They get stabbed, burned, strangled, drowned. And yet here you felt the need to step in. Close one door to open another."

"It was an experiment. Just to see." She stiffens. Folds her arms over her chest: the move of a petulant child. For some reason she doesn't want to *seem* like a petulant child, though, so she lets her arms drop and suddenly they feel awkward. Like dead fish staple-gunned to her shoulder-meat, just *flopping* there. She doesn't know what to do with them. "Just one time I want to be able to tell someone how not to die and have them listen."

Not-Louis chuckles. The snake in his mouth hisses.

"That wasn't an experiment," he says. "You knew the drill. You went out there armed."

"Whatever."

"It wasn't an experiment. It was an execution."

"You taught me that. The scales must be balanced, ain't that right? One life saved means one death owed. The killer must be killed."

"You're messing with powerful forces, naughty girl."

She suddenly stands up and yells, "You taught me that, too! You . . . you fucking invisible, unreal, trespassing dickhead! You're always *there*, walking in through the Employees Only door like you own the place. You show up, you whisper these little cryptic ciphers, you let your little thought-bugs crawl into my ears. You *push* me to do these things, and now you're saying, what? That I shouldn't? That I'm messing stuff up?" She gives him two middle fingers thrust up, up, up. She yells, "You *told me* to mess things up! That's my fucking job!"

Suddenly, a pounding on the door.

Jace, through the door: "Are you okay?"

"Piss off, Jace."

"Who are you yelling at?"

"I'm yelling at God! Or your mom! Leave me alone!"

A new voice at the door: Taevon. Their other roommate.

"Girl, it's early. You freakin' out."

"I'll freak out if I want!" she shrieks. Then she stomps over to the door and does a Russian kick dance against it. "Go away! Fuck."

She buries her face in her hands. Trying not to weep. Trying not to tear the door off its hinges. Trying not to fling herself into whatever bleak black expanse she can find.

She hears them mumbling on the other side of the door. Footsteps retreat. *Good. Go.*

When she turns back around, Louis is no longer sitting there.

It's Eleanor Caldecott.

Her stretched, corpse-white face lies marked with striations the color of muddy river water. When she speaks, brackish water slides over her withered lips, splashes against her lap.

"Not everyone deserves to live, girl."

"I made a choice."

"A choice of which we do not approve."

"I'm not your dog. Is that how you see me? Snap and point and let me go to work? I thought *free will* was your thing. Or are you just another version of fate?"

"You have free will. You may choose, even when you choose badly."

Miriam sits on the edge of the bed. "Go away."

"I'm not done speaking," Eleanor hisses.

Miriam screams, "But I'm done with you!"

And, like that, the Trespasser is gone.

FIVE

THREE DAYS WITH THE DEAD

Time runs like blood in snow. Everything is red and melting.

The sun is up. Then it's not. Then it's back. Then ice is hissing against the windowpanes. A mouse chews somewhere in the deep of the wall. A TV comes on. Video games. Maury Povich. Someone yelling. Someone laughing. A knock at the door. A candy bar shoved under it. She eats it greedily, a feral child starving. She sees the mouse in the corner. Eyes glinting, whiskers twitching.

Shoo.

Fuck off.

You're free to go.

The mouse stays until it can get the candy wrapper. It sits on it. Licking chocolate. Then its paws. Then it's gone.

The Trespasser comes. Dead Ben with his head blown apart. Dead gang-banger with his skull popped open. Louis with one eye, no eyes, three eyes. Eleanor Caldecott with a crow's head peeking out of her mouth, squawking, picking tongue-meat. Andrew the yuppie prick with a twenty-dollar bill clutched in the clench of broken teeth. Red Wren, the girl with wings. Harriet, gunsmoke from both nostrils. Ingersoll tumbling down an endless spiral of lighthouse stairs. One-foot Ashley chasing her in a wheelchair.

The Trespasser never speaks.

He-she-it doesn't have to.

Her castigation comes in her own voice:

You shouldn't have killed that kid.

She's killed before. (Uncle Jack's voice intrudes: *Nicely done, killer. But don't tell your mother about this!* Then he laughs, that asshole.) But this time was different. The other times felt earned and owned. Like she'd been drawn into something. Drawn into a grim purpose, into a tug-of-war that wasn't her fight but was hers to lose or win just the same. Hers is the thumb on the scale. Balance by way of imbalance.

But then this. Andrew on the bus. A year's worth of waiting. It *was* just an experiment. Just to see. Is this who she is? Is this what she does? She chose him randomly. She didn't even like him. She liked Louis. Loved him, even. She liked Wren. They deserved life. Andrew deserved—

It didn't matter what he deserved. That's the thing. She wasn't invested in what was owed to him. That kid, the dead kid in the Eagles jacket, who was he? Poor kid. Fucked-up life. Cigarette burns and undone shoelaces. Maybe that two hundred bucks would have changed everything for him. Maybe Andrew would have been his first and only kill. Maybe Andrew was the monster. Maybe he'd become a serial killer. Or run a bank that would one day foreclose on an orphanage. Or maybe he'd just never make anything of himself, maybe the girlfriend would shove that ring right up his ass, maybe he'd skulk off and suck on a tailpipe—

An endless string of possibilities like little crow skulls threaded with barbed wire. There in the sky of her mind, swallows dancing, mockingbirds mocking, the featherless heads of hungry vultures plunging deep into meat but finding no sustenance, the scream of a thunderbird, the shriek of a shrike—

Infinite variables, a ladder made of maybes.

You fucked up.

You chose badly.

Then one day it's over.

SIX

EVICTION NOTICE

She wakes up. Soaked with sweat. Hair plastered to her forehead.

Jace is sitting there.

"You're trespassing," she says.

"What? Oh. Sorry."

Her mouth tastes of nicotine. And lint. And regret.

"How'd you get in here?" she mumbles. She feels around the futon, finds her cigarettes, lights one, closes her eyes. "I locked the door."

"Taevon has a key."

"Ah."

"Taevon also wants to talk to you."

"Mm." She picks sleep from the corner of her eye with a thumbnail. "Lemme guess. He wants to give me fashion tips."

"I think he wants—"

"To kick me out. Yeah, I get it."

"But I have good news—"

"No such thing," she says, lurching upright and into a standing position. "Let's go get this over with."

Out of the bedroom. Into the living room, which is also the foyer and the kitchen and the family room and occasionally someone's bedroom. Taevon sits on the futon couch—when you're half-broke everything comes in "futon," as if "futon" is a lifestyle choice—and next to him sits Cherie, that little Korean fag-hag who clings to him like he's the tree and she's the koala. Miriam rolls her eyes so hard she's afraid they might get lost in the back of her head.

"Miri," Taevon says, calling her that nickname she hates with the garish light and stinking fury of a garbage fire. "This ain't working out, girl."

Cherie purses her lips. "You gotta go, ho."

"I know how you die," Miriam says. "I haven't told you because it's very embarrassing. But I'd be *so* happy to tell you now."

The girl sticks her tongue between the V of her two fingers and waggles it. "Eat me, bitch. You pretend like you're some kind of witch or some shit, but you just want attention."

"Incurable gonorrhea," Miriam chirps. "It's a thing going around. Some high-octane STD that refuses any efforts to treat it. It's going to be awful. It'll feel like you're pissing acid. Your fallopian tubes will swell up like microwaved hot dogs. You know what the worst is, though? Two words: *rectal infection*. Blech. Yucky. Your butthole—"

"Shut up, hooker!"

"—will look like a *blown bike tire*. Really, really sad. What a shame."

It's a lie. Cherie dies from lung cancer when she's in her early seventies. But Miriam read about that supergonorrhea, and gonorrhea sooner sounded better than lung cancer later.

And it makes the little brat mad. Because suddenly she's up off the couch and reaching for Miriam with nails painted like video game characters—Pac-Man takes a particularly vicious swipe; must be his predilection toward ghosts—but Taevon is planting his hand against her chest and shoving her back onto the futon.

"Cherie, shut the fuck up for a minute. You ain't in this con-versation."

Miriam focuses on Taevon. "I saved your life, man."

"Yeah. I know." But the way he says it, she can tell he doesn't believe her. Or is unsure enough for it not to matter.

"He was going to poison you."

"That was a year ago. We let you live here 'cause of it. But you haven't paid rent in what, the last three months?"

"Four."

"You are not helping yourself."

"Yeah, I know."

"And then you be coming all up in here making all kinds of racket and clamor and yelling like you got the devil all up in your coochie."

"The devil is not, for the record, all up in my coochie."

His eyebrows—dyed daffodil gold like his hair against his dark skin—arch like the McDonald's logo. "Well, that's real good to know."

"I'm not good at saying I'm sorry," she says. "It physically pains me. I get a tightness right—" Her hand floats over her midsection. "Right here, like someone is pinching my ovaries with clothespins. But even though it hurts, I'll still say: I'm sorry, Taevon. I'm really sorry. The psychic thing isn't paying as well since winter came, and the last couple days, weeks, months"—*I killed a guy the other night and it turns out I don't feel good about it*—"have been a little weird."

"I'm moving in," Cherie blurts out. Like she's trying to hold in a burp but she can't. It just comes out of her. And she giggles afterward.

Taevon's face freezes into a mortified didn't-I-tell-you-to-shut-the-fuck-up-for-a-minute glare and he pins Cherie to the couch with it.

He turns, starts to say something—

Miriam waves him off.

"It's fine. I'll get my things together. Be out in a few hours."

More like twenty minutes.

She doesn't have a lot of stuff.

Taevon stands, opens his arms. "Can we hug?"

Miriam blinks. "No. No, we cannot."

"Girl, don't be bitter."

"Might as well tell the sun not to shine, Taevon."

ONE YEAR AGO

She's been out all night and now it's morning and all she can do is let the angels of steam rising from her diner coffee wreathe her face, performing their divine task of scaring away this demonic hangover.

So far, they're failing. Fucking angels.

At least Miriam has enough money for breakfast. And maybe lunch. November is witch-tits cold but warmer than it should be, and so last night on South Street she was able to stand there and peddle her wares like a good little working girl. Not *that* kind of working girl.

Shaking her psychic moneymaker.

This is how it works:

Sun starts to dip around five in the afternoon. The tourist crowd thins as the bar crowd and folks going to see a show at the TLA start pouring in. Miriam, she stands there on a street corner—the smells of cheesesteaks, cigarettes, and anger washing over her.

While standing, she holds up a sign: WILL PSYCHIC FOR FOOD.

Ten bucks gets someone a vision.

She tells them how they're going to die.

And she lies about it, most of the time. *Oh, you're going to die in a fiery jet-ski accident. Helicopter crash skiing K-12, dude.*

Eaten by a bear in your living room—I know, right? So crazy! Ebola. Monkey flu. Squirrel pox. You die while base-jumping at the same time you're fucking a Ukrainian supermodel, good for you, high five, up top.

Very rarely does she tell them the truth.

You die alone in bed in thirty years. You burn in a car crash on your way to a job you hate. You choke on a greasy wad of cold cheesesteak.

You die poorly because we all die poorly.

The lie is part of the job.

She gives good story.

They give her ten bucks.

Most people don't want to know how they're going to die.

Most people want to know how they're going to live.

They don't realize how intimately those things are connected.

She tries to sexy herself up—torn T-shirt, knife-slashed jeans, a push-up bra (which for her is like trying to pinch and lift a couple of mosquito bites, but you work with what you have, damnit).

It's hard to be sexy in the wintertime.

Well. Fuck 'em. Today, she gets breakfast from it. And lunch. And maybe tomorrow night she'll be able to afford another motel room instead of crashing under bridges, on park benches, in Hobo King's car. (Hobo King knows all the tricks. "Don't fog up the windows," he says, "because that's how cops know someone's sleeping in there." Hobo King's name is actually Dave and he used to be a cab driver.)

The waitress comes, drops down a plate called the Working Man's Special: sausage, bacon, pancakes, eggs, hash browns, toast. All for seven bucks. Breakfast: the cheapest and easiest way to eat a gut-load of food.

And goddamn if Miriam doesn't love breakfast. She would marry it if she could. Stick a ring on one of the sausage links— a terrible idea, really, because before she knew it, she'd *eat* the sausage link and the ring with it and that probably wouldn't feel great coming out the other end.

Rings. Engagement rings.

She makes a mental note: *Don't forget about that guy from the bus.*

Andrew, that was his name. Still almost a year away. He was kind of a prick. But it's an experiment, she tells herself. Another experiment. She warned him. And in a year she'll see if he heeds her warning.

For now she sits and doesn't eat her food so much as *maul* it. Fingers greasy from sausage. Bacon in her teeth. Syrup on her chin. The waitress comes and gawks for a moment, and Miriam thinks: *I remember you, Susie Q. You're the one who gets breast cancer in ten years, dies in twenty.*

Cancer, cancer, cancer, so often cancer.

Miriam dives back into her food with all the gusto of a starving wolverine. Suddenly, here's the waitress again—

She looks up. Not the waitress.

Three dudes. Boys, practically.

One of them, a shaggy-haired scarecrow in dark hipster glasses. Next to him, a superskinny black guy with hair so blond it looks like pollen gathering on a bee's butt. The third is a pooch-bellied pot-smoker type, hair so ratty with resin you could probably break off a hank and stick it in a bong.

"You really a psychic?" the black one asks.

"We want to know how we die," the hipster scarecrow says.

"Because holy shit," the stoner says. "How awesome."

"I'm off-duty," she says.

"We got money," Black Daffodil says. He elbows Hipster Scarecrow, who in turn elbows Bongwater. They each pull out a ten-dollar bill.

Miriam looks at the money suspiciously. Eyes flitting. "You do know that *psychic* is not code for 'blowjobs in a diner bathroom.'"

Black Daffodil's eyebrows lift so high, she wonders if they'll levitate off his head and fly back to their homeworld. "You ain't my type."

"Skinny heroin-chic type?" she asks.

"Vagina type," he says.

"Ah. You like dong."

"I like it better when you don't call it 'dong.'"

"Fine," she says, snatching up each ten-dollar bill with a thumb-and-forefinger pincer like she's plucking butterflies out of the air. "Let's start with you, Daffodil; chop-chop, put your hand in mine."

She puts her hand out. Tilts the palm up.

The guys all look to one another and she can feel their excitement.

Black Daffodil reaches out—

He sits on a curb outside an Exxon in the middle of the city, traffic on Broad Street, flecks of flurry-speck snow landing in his hair and melting; he's humming a little tune as he plunges his hands in and out of a Funyuns bag. Crunch, crunch, crunch. *Head bobbing along. Doo-doo-doo.*

The other two yahoos come out, Scarecrow and Bongwater. Scarecrow's got a granola bar and Bongwater has five granola bars, some blue-colored Mountain Dew variant, and a gas station hot dog (which is half shoved in his mouth) and he's trying to talk and Scarecrow's laughing and he might be high, too.

They cross the parking lot.

Someone else makes a perpendicular toward them.

Santa Claus. Not the real Santa, if there is such a thing. This is a drunk, dirty Santa. Droopy, stubbly cheeks. A Karl Malden nose bursting with broken blood vessels. Pear-shaped body waddling along in a red Santa coat that's surprisingly clean despite his grimy face. Santa hat askew on his lumpy head.

He's got a six-pack of beer. Bottle in his hand. Open. He takes a pull.

"Yo," he yells, waving, wiping his mouth, looking over his shoulder to see if anybody's looking. One car sits at a far pump, but that's it. "Hey, I got five left in this sixer. Sell yous each one for fie-dollas a pop."

Daffodil yoinks his head up. Purses his lips. "We can buy our own beer, elf. Go on back to your igloo now."

"Horseshit," the guy bellows, sloppy smile on his face. "If yous kids are twenty-one, then I'm the goddamn Easter Bunny."

"I'm in," Bongwater says, veering toward the drunken Santa. Despite the epic snackload in his hands, he's somehow already got a five-spot waving like a little flag. Scarecrow nods, hurries over with a ten, buys one for Daffodil, too.

"Natty Ice," Santa says, taking a pull. "S'good."

"It's shit, but we'll drink it," Bongwater says.

"I gotta go baffroom," Santa says, and it seems for a second like maybe he's just standing there pissing in his pants, but then he jerks like someone just tugged on his ear and he makes a bee-line for the Exxon.

Scarecrow tosses a bottle to Daffodil. They pull out Bongwater's snacks, use the bags to hide the beers, and then they're all eating and drinking and talking shit. Something-something Christmas break. Something-something Professor So-and-So is a real ball-buster. Blah blah Tumblr, Twitter, Batman, Kanye West.

It's Daffodil who gets it first. A line of blood crawls out of his nose. He doesn't notice. Bongwater has to point it out. He wipes it on the bag. A red streak. The other nostril starts bleeding.

He stands.

Something is wrong inside.

Things twist up like a braided rope. Tightening. Fraying.

He burps.

He tastes blood.

The bottle drops from his hand because he can't hold it anymore. It shatters. Ksshhh. His body shakes. Drops. Flops. Eyes *wrenched open, can't close, jaw clenched like high voltage is coursing through him. Heart going so fast it might as well be a drumroll preceding what comes next—cardiac arrest rips through him like a fist through tissue paper.*

—and Miriam yanks her hand away.

"What?" Daffodil asks. She smells the sausage stink on her own fingers. Nausea blooms sick and yellow. She grabs Hipster Scarecrow's hands, then Bongwater's, and it's just as she feared.

Bongwater dies there, too. In the parking lot. Blood. Pain. Seizure. Coma. Heart attack. Boom, boom, boom. Scarecrow bites it later. A week after. Pale, comatose. Tubes and monitors, *beep, beep, beep*—faster then, like a robot orgasm, *beepbeepbeepbeep*, then cyborg peaks, cyborgasm, *beeeeeeeeep*, one long killer cumshot as Scarecrow's body arches up like someone stuck a stun gun between his ass cheeks and—

Dead, dark, done.

Stick a fork in 'em.

Miriam gives them their money back.

They protest.

She tells them to fuck off. They still want to know. She says, "You all die from monkey herpes." When they still won't leave, she threatens them with a butter knife and swipes it in the air in front of them while hissing. That does the trick. They retreat. She shoves her plate aside. The meal is ruined. Their deaths stay with her.

SEVEN

MIRIAM VERSUS THE FRIEND ZONE

"Wait up; there's something I have to tell you," Jace says, trailing after her in his flannel pants and *A-Team* T-shirt.

But she ignores him. "It's cool. Not like I saved your hides or anything. Oh, wait! *Totally did.* Guess your little lives aren't worth as much as I thought. Shoulda let Cracker Factory Santa poison you all anyway. You know he was an escaped mental patient? That he poisoned *seven* other kids besides you? Don't I get a gold star?" She glowers.

"We gave you a place to stay. You were staying under bridges—"

"Yep, like a troll. Thank you for saving me from my troll-like existence for a short time so that I may walk amongst you virtuous mortals, but now comes the time for you to *send me back to my bridge*—"

"That's what I'm trying to say, everything will be okay—"

"Yeah," Miriam says, "it's all going to be peach fuzz and puppy parades from here on out. Me and the other homeless will tickle-fight one another over who gets the last moldy bread-end. Meanwhile, Cherie the awful whorebag cunt-rag bitch-scag fag-hag—hey, so many rhymes!—will be sleeping on my dumpy-ass futon. A futon I actually bought, by the way, but futons are heavy and I have nowhere to go so I guess I'll be leaving it behind. I hope she gets bedbugs in her vagina. And they lay eggs. And she becomes the Mother of Bedbugs—"

As she rants, she tosses items into her backpack. A few pairs of jeans. Handful of white T-shirts. Cigarettes. Bear mace. Tiny minibar bottles of Jameson's. A Santa hat.

"I got you a job!" Jace blurts.

She turns. Makes a poopy face. "Me and jobs don't play well together. My last real job kind of ended with a shooting. And a stabbing, come to think of it."

"I don't mean *that* kind of job—" He fishes in the pockets of his flannel surrender pants, pulls out a folded-up piece of paper: the world's most boring origami. He begins to unfold it. "I ran a Craigslist ad—"

"I definitely do not want whatever this job is. Particularly if it has the word *hand* or *rim* preceding it—"

"No, wait, shut up for a second. A couple months back I put up an ad for your . . . particular talents, the *psychic death* thing, and for a while I mostly just got a bunch of trolls who thought I was a pimp—"

"I don't like where this is going."

"But last week I got this e-mail."

He thrusts the unfolded paper at her. Like a beaming toddler proud of his dirty diaper.

She grabs it. Scowls. Reads.

Her gaze suctions onto a very big number in the middle of the e-mail.

Five thousand dollars.

"Five grand," she says, looking up. "This guy wants to pay me five fucking grand to tell him how he's going to die?"

Jace nods, grinning ear to ear.

"Are you sure he doesn't think this is code for sex?"

"I . . . I called him."

"You called him."

"I thought he might think it was about sex, so."

"And it's not about sex."

"No, he's some rich guy in Florida. A little obsessed with his own . . ." Jace flutters his fingers in the air, a gesture he makes when he's trying to think of a word. "Demise."

"Five grand."

"Yep."

"Rich nutball."

"Yes."

"In Florida."

"Apparently."

"That means I need to get to Florida."

He shrugs. "Well. Yeah."

"Call him." She snaps her fingers. "Set it up."

"Okay," he says. But he just stands there. Staring at her.

"What?"

"What-what?"

"You're looking at me."

"I think it's okay to look at you. You can look at me, too."

"I *am* looking at you looking at me, and at this point I'm starting to wonder what's going on."

He shifts nervously from foot to foot. "I just thought you could say, you know . . . thank you?"

"Oh. Well." Miriam clears her throat, loosens some of that tobacco mucus that nests in her vocal cords. "Thank you, Jace. By the way, I hate that name. *Jace.* Jason—Jason is a good name. Or Jay. I like Jay. It's like a bird. I like birds. Mostly."

"Do you like me?"

"Huh?"

"I like you."

"Oh, sweet Christ on a crumbcake, really?"

"Really what? We've known each other for a year now and we've kind of skirted around each other and flirted—"

"I did not flirt."

"We were flirting," he says, nodding, smirking. "Sometimes people flirt and they don't even know it."

She narrows her eyes. "*Nnnyeah*, I think I'd know."

"You're leaving soon."

"Pretty much now-ish."

He reaches out. Takes her hand. "That bed looks pretty comfortable."

She shoves him backward. Not hard enough to crack his skull against the doorframe, but enough to get the message across.

"Hey," he says, genuinely stung. "Ow."

"Thank your stars and garters I didn't perform dentistry using your asshole as the entry point."

He sighs. "Friend-zoned again. Nice guys finish last."

The temperature in her mental thermometer pops the glass. "What did you just say? Are you seriously pulling that *nice-guy friend-zone* crap? You little turd, how's that supposed to make somebody feel? That my friendship is just a way station to my pussy? Is that what my companionship is worth to you, Jace?"

"It's not like that. I just thought—"

"You thought what? That because you're a nice guy, my panties will just drop because you *deserve* to have my thighs around your ears? Fuck you, dude. Being a nice person is a thing you just do, not a price you pay for poonani. I'm not a tollbooth. A kind word and a favor don't mean I owe you naked fun time."

Now he's mad. Brow stitched. Lip curled. "Oh, like *you're* a nice person? Please."

"I'm not! I'm not nice. And this is not news, dude. I'd rather be a cranky bitch who lets you know what she's thinking than some passive-aggressive dick-weasel who thinks friendship with a girl is secondary to her putting out. You wanted to fuck me? You shoulda just said so. I would've at least respected that, and we wouldn't have to do this boo-hoo woe-is-me pissy-pants guilt-fest."

She throws on her jacket and snatches the e-mail out of his hand and slings the bag over her shoulder. A hard elbow to the gut leaves him bent over and *oof*-ing.

Miriam heads to the door.

He trails after like a bad smell.

Taevon and Cherie watch, goggle-eyed.

"I'm sorry," Jace says, rubbing his stomach.

"You *are* sorry," she says, throwing open the door to the hallway.

"I'm a dick."

"A tiny dick. An insignificant dick. Positively *microbial*."

"Can I call you?"

"Can you . . . No, you can't call me."

"But you have the same phone if I wanted to?"

"I'm going to throw it in a bag and burn it."

"Wait—"

"Bye, everybody."

She grabs her bee-sting breasts at them. A last fuck you.

Then she's out the door, slamming it in Jace's face.

PART TWO

MILE ZERO

"You kill him?" Grosky asks.

Miriam rolls her knuckles on the flat of the table, cracking them. Her mouth the flat line of a heart monitor. "We still talking about that poor kid in Philadelphia?" She taps her thumb on the photo, then flips it over.

Grosky laughs. Vills laughs, too, a half-second too late, like she's taking her cues from the bigger man. "No, no, I mean Santa."

She hesitates. "You're asking me if I killed Santa?"

"That's the best fucking question I've ever asked anybody, but yeah. Did you or did you not kill Santa Claus?"

She pauses. "Girl's gotta have her secrets," she says.

"C'mon. How'd you off the old elf?"

Hands pull Santa into the alley. Before he can scream she's slamming his face into the brick. His nose really blooms now, a rose-petal gusher, and the hat comes off his head and the remaining bottles of Natural Ice drop from his hand and clunk against the ground. She smells the garlic sweat and the booze breath and he tries to swipe at her like a bear knocking a wasp's nest off a tree but he's old and slow and she's young and cranked and the screwdriver plunges between the puffy rows of raincloud cotton that line his Santa's jacket and she sticks it up under his ribcage and into his heart and then she does it a second time and a third for good measure—

"He fell down a flight of steps," she says. "With no help from me."

"Oh, yeah? Guess you think he deserved it, huh?"

"He was going to poison those guys."

"So you say."

"So I jolly well fucking say, yes. I told you, I have the ability—"

"To see how, when, and where people are going to die. Yeah, yeah, we got that, Miss Black, you told us already—"

She interrupts: "No, whoa, get it correct, dude. I didn't say I know *where*. Just the how and the when."

Grosky holds up a pair of surrendering hands. He fakes a look like a child caught sticking peanut-butter-and-jelly sandwiches into the DVD player. Vills continues her fake laugh, a laugh that quickly breaks apart like a cookie under a boot—it tumbles into a raspy smoker's cough.

"I want that cigarette," Miriam snarls.

"I told you—"

"Listen, I know you're going to give it to me one way or the other. So let's hop-skip-and-hasten-the-inevitable over here." Grosky doesn't say anything. She forces a smirk through the mesh wire of her own anger and sadness and says, "Here's what's buzzin', cousin. You either give me a cigarette now or I clamp up and quit talking. I'll hiss. I'll piss myself and kick and scream and bite and gag myself with the cigarette until I puke. I'll bite my lips and cheeks and spit blood—"

The whole time she talks, Grosky just eyes her up. Pink tongue pushing on the inside of his lower lip. He snaps his fingers, and Vills gives him another Bic lighter. Newer, by the look of it. Grosky spins it across the table like a stone skipped across pond water.

She scoops up the lighter. Returns the cigarette to her mouth.

Flame strike, paper crackle, lung pull.

The capillaries in her brain feel like a garden hose suddenly unkinking. Synapses go off like hands twisting a sheet of bubble wrap: *pop pop pop*. Nicotine rush. Like she can feel every individual hair follicle.

"The first cigarette after a while without one is . . ." She beholds the cigarette. A Parliament, by the look of it. "It's a burger thrown to a starving man, a sunny day to a jailbird who spent a year in solitary, an orgasm when nobody's tickled the little man in the boat for oh-so-long—"

"Why'd you kill him?" Grosky quickly says. "Santa. Why him?"

"I told you, I didn't—"

"Let me ask it different-like. Why did you feel the need to save those three boys?"

"I dunno. It felt right."

"Did it feel right to save the yuppie prick from the bus? Andy?"

Andrew, not Andy. Louis, not Lou.

She swallows a hard knot. "No."

"But you did it anyway."

"I got my wires crossed."

Vills moans a perceptible sigh of impatience and starts dragging a chair from the back corner of the shack over to the table, the legs juddering on the floor.

The woman sits. Elbows on table like her arms are a pair of crooked coat hangers. Face in the scoop of her hands.

"Why," Vills says, letting that word drag out, giving the space after it a little oxygen like she's having a hard time conjuring exactly what it is she wants to say, "are you telling us all this? I mean, honey, you're admitting to murder."

"Whoa, I didn't admit to shit," Miriam says. Inhale. Exhale. Cancer cloud. "Who are you? Why am I here?"

The woman's boozy smile tilts further askew: a sinking ship, a broken shelf. "Normally, criminals aren't so quick to confess to the Feds."

"I didn't—" Miriam snorts. "You know what? Never mind. You aren't Feds. Just because you pulled that trick back in the car—looking up the stolen boat, I mean—anybody could've done that. Besides, look at you two. Fat Jersey oaf in a tracksuit. Alcoholic iguana with a smoker's cough. You are the very *picture* of federal investigation. Let me guess. X-Files, right?" She points at Grosky. "You probably ate Mulder. Just gobbled him up like a Christmas turkey. And you"—now an accusing finger at Vills—"are Scully with a bad liver and a starvation diet. Who does that make me? The Cigarette-Smoking Woman?"

Grosky pulls out ID. He flips it. Slides it across.

Thomas Grosky, FBI.

"I've had your people pull the 'show the ID' trick before. And they, like you, were thugs working for a criminal organization."

Vills bristles.

"I dunno *which* organization you're working for—" Miriam says.

"The Federal Bureau of Investigation," Grosky says.

"The BAU," Vills says. "Behavioral Analysis Unit."

Grosky smiles. "We hunt serial killers."

Miriam flinches.

Vills rolls her eyes, offers a clarification: "We *assist* local law enforcement on hunting serial killers. It's far less . . . *rock star* than my partner makes it seem." She pulls the pack of Parliaments, upends a cigarette into the flat of her palm. She grabs the lighter back from Miriam and lights her cigarette. Way she smokes is like she's trying to slurp a thick milkshake through a too-small straw. "Sorry, honey, we're the real deal."

Even in the wet, clinging Florida heat, Miriam feels a chill coil around her spine: a snake around a sapling.

She stubs her cigarette out on the table.

She blows a jet stream of smoke into Grosky's face.

"So, what do you want with me, then? You want to ask about the Mockingbird, that it? It wasn't one killer. Was a whole family of the sick shits. The insane old matriarch, the rapist patriarch, couple of fucked-up boys with one helluva twisted upbringing . . ."

The words die in her mouth. Because Grosky and Vills look at each other like they're sharing a joke between the two of them, a joke with a punch line Miriam doesn't know.

Because she's the punch line.

"We're not here to ask about the Mockingbird," Vills says.

That's when she gets the joke.

"You think *I'm* a serial killer," Miriam says suddenly.

Grosky snaps his fingers. "Give the girl her gold star."

Oh shit.

EIGHT

SHAKE ON IT, DARNELL

"Come on into the office," the salesman says, bundling up against the dry, bitter wind that comes. Invisible hands bounce a McDonald's cup across the car lot. The sales office isn't much to look at. It's about the size of a shoebox with a few windows carved out of it. An elementary-school diorama. "Got a space heater in there. Can fill out all the paperwork and cross the *I*s and tickle the *T*s. You got insurance? If not, I know a guy he can do that *bare minimum* coverage just to get you up on the road and, oh, I'ma need your driver's license to photocopy—provided the damn thing works. Sometimes you gotta kick it and call it names just to get it to turn on. What am I doing, telling you all this out here? It's colder than a Popsicle up a witch's—" He seems to catch himself before he says something inappropriate. "It's cold."

Miriam shivers, pulls her thrift-shop camo jacket tighter around her, rubs her black-gloved hands together like she's hoping they'll start a fire. "Let me stop you there, Darnell. You got five hundred dollars on the sticker price. I'm not going to pay sticker price because I can't pay sticker price. I have two hundred—" She starts counting out the money. "Wait, a hundred and sixty bucks. Sorry. I bought cigarettes, and I'm gonna need gas. Anyway. I'm going to give you eight twenty-dollar bills and you're going to go get me the keys and I'm not going to show you my license or sign any paperwork or do anything in any way that will require more time than it takes for me to drive off this lot in that car."

That car is a 1986 sunfire-red Pontiac Fiero.

Darnell laughs—*huh huh huh.* "You're funny, I like you. You remind me of my wife. She's like a, a, an electrical cord snapping and popping around on the floor. Always making me laugh with her jokes. One time I laughed so hard a piece of buttered corn came shootin' out my nose. It landed right in the gravy boat, which just made me laugh harder—"

"I am not joking. That's my offer."

His laughs slow to a crawl and stop—*huh, huh, huuuuuh.* Like a truck with engine problems, guttering and going still on the side of the road.

"What? You can't be serious."

"Serious as a slap in the face."

"I am not selling you this car off the books for two hundred—"

"Hundred and sixty."

"—bucks and you must be out your damn mind if you think that's what's gonna happen here."

"This car?" she says, taking a finger and drawing a line in the rime of snow and ice on its hood. "Listen, Darnell. I've lived in the apartments just down the block for nearly a year now. And this car has been in this same spot at the back of the lot every time I pass by it. It's a fucking *Fiero*, dude. It's twenty years old. It has 150,000 miles on it, which is *practically* what it takes to get to the moon. I'm going to bet if I open this thing up, it's going to smell like stale Drakkar Noir and chemical pine scent. There is probably a dead rat in the trunk. Maybe a whole nest of dead rats and rat babies." She finishes her drawing. (Spoiler alert: It's a penis.) "You should really be paying me to take this burden of Detroit steel off your hands."

"That never works. The *you should be paying me* thing."

"It's going to work today, my good man."

"Nope."

Then he turns around and shuffles back toward the office.

"Wait!" she calls after. "Damnit, hold on. New offer."

"Five hundred bucks and you fill out some paperwork?"

"One hundred eighty bucks, I fill out *no* paperwork—"

He groans, starts to turn back around.

"—and I tell you how and when you're going to die."

The McDonald's cup rolls between the two of them, ushered forth by the wind. A few wisps of snow blow off the back of a slate-gray Honda.

His voice goes low. "You threatening me?"

"I'm not capable of subtlety. If I were threatening you, you wouldn't have to ask." *And you'd probably already have a barbecue fork sticking out of your neck.* "I have a gift. A curse. A psychic voodoo superpower."

"You're nuts."

"Probably. Doesn't change my offer."

"All right," he says. "Let's hear it."

"I need to touch you."

"I'm married."

"Not your dick. I need to touch . . ." She makes a frustrated growl and bites the middle finger of her glove and pulls it off. "Just gimme your hand."

Darnell the used-car salesman stomps over and thrusts out his hand like he's about to shake on a deal. Her warm, damp hand is small in his icy mitt—

Big hands palms-down on a cold casket, casket the color of lavender, a casket with yellow roses on top, a casket so shiny all the lights of the funeral home are caught in liquid lines, pooling. Darnell is standing there, crying over the domed box of human remains, the box of a body, the box containing his wife, and the tears are stuck in the gray wirebrush beard sticking up out of his cheeks, and he gives in to great, heaving gulps—sobs that

*hit him like a punch to the middle, that fold him over like a bent
chair, that take something out of him, that rob him suddenly of
his breath, of his heartbeat, of everything—*

She lets go of his hand.

She quietly returns the glove to her own.

"Well?" he asks.

And she tells him.

And he laughs.

"You don't believe me," she says.

"I don't know. Maybe I do. It's a good story, at least. And it
got a couple things right. Mitzi does love her yellow roses, and
just this year we picked out a pair of caskets. And damnit if they
weren't on just this side of purple, too." He shrugs. "Plus, it's
good news. This is, what? How far in the future?"

"Thirty-three years yet."

"That's a pretty good run. I'm already closing in on fifty. And I
don't want to hang around when Mitzi's dead. What a miserable
life that would be, you know what I mean?"

"Besides, who'd make you sneeze corn?"

"Damn straight." He hesitates, like he's chewing on it. "Fine.
You got your deal. I hate this little ugly-ass car anyway." He puts
out his hand again. "Gimme the money, I'll get you your keys,
and you can go to wherever it is you're going."

"I'm going to Florida."

"Watch out for alligators, lady."

"And alligator-ladies."

"If you say so."

She gives him the cash.

He goes and gets the keys.

NINE

RED ROCKET, RED ROCKET

The Fiero smells like stale Drakkar Noir and chemical pine scent. Miriam drives to Florida.

YOUNG MIRIAM
LEARNS TO DRIVE

Tires scream on sun-kissed asphalt. The Subaru races across the parking lot, turns sharp, and drifts like it's a pat of butter on a melted frying pan, leaving behind a smear of rubber darker than the blacktop beneath it.

It reaches the end of the asphalt. Jumps it. Wheels in grass spinning, spitting dirt. Turfing the lawn. Then back onto the lot, hard-charging to the far side, toward the curb—it *jumps* the curb. The front tires leap up. Land hard. And they blow out like soap bubbles lanced by a little kid's finger.

Pop! Pop!

The air hisses.

The car sinks.

The engine goes *tink tink tink tink*.

Miriam turns off the car. Then whoops with laughter.

She's not drunk.

Okay, she's been *drinking*, but that doesn't mean *drunk*.

It's just—she's run away from Mother and has been gone for a couple years now and *still* doesn't know how to drive. She's almost nineteen. She's not gonna get a license or anything, but she figures, fuck it. Maybe one day she'll decide to stop walking or hitchhiking and will steal a proper car. Because that's who she is now. The runaway who thinks about stealing cars.

The runaway who sees death. Who chases it and waits for it

to finish its meal. Who chooses what plunder death did not take for itself.

Next to her, Aidan laughs. At first just a little, an uncertain chuckle tickled up from the depths of his belly, but then it's like each chuckle brings a laugh and each laugh brings a whoop and next thing they know the both of them are gasping because laughter has replaced breathing. The sheer hilarity is going to kill them and neither one of them minds.

It doesn't really kill them, of course.

But this *is* Aidan's last day on earth.

She knows it. And he knows it, too.

The laughter finally winds down—a toy whose batteries are empty of juice. And then they're both sitting there. Silent as the gods.

In the distance, the high school sits. Also silent. Saturday doesn't see much going on around these parts, which, she supposes, is why they're here.

Miriam rubs her eyes. Stretches. Runs her hands through her hair—currently pink like strawberry milk. "Damn, I like driving," she finally says.

"Glad to be your teacher," Aidan says. His voice is—it's not small, not exactly. But it's quiet. A librarian's voice, not a teacher's voice. Which is too bad, seeing as how he's a science teacher. And a part-time driving instructor. "Though I think you interpreted these lessons a little bit . . . liberally. Do not try any of this on the actual road."

"Blech," she says, sticking out her tongue. "Whatever, *Dad.*"

He has a fatherlike quality. She has to admit that. He's twenty years her senior. Got kind of a hippie-hipster intellectual vibe about him. Maroon Mister Rogers sweater. Little gold-rimmed glasses. The facial hair is the twist, though: He's got the handle-bar 'stache and chin whiskers of a seasoned Wild West marshal.

He laughs a little, pulls out a joint. It's a fat one, too—thick as his pinky, a little bit crooked. Like a leprechaun's shillelagh. He sparks a Zippo lighter and tries to pass her the weed, but she waves him off.

"Blech again. I don't like all the coughing. Besides, stuff tastes like a skunk's taint."

"You know what a skunk's taint tastes like?" he says, given over to childish giggles.

"Funny," she says. Then she pulls out her cigarettes and grabs her water bottle from the dashboard cup holder—a bottle that does not contain water but cheap-shit vodka. "I already have my two drugs of choice, dude."

"But this"—he gestures with the weed, then exhales a sputtering haze—"rounds all the edges. Bottoms you out. It's slow like honey."

"They're all just variations on a theme, Aidan. All different versions of *stop* and *go*. This is my brake pedal"—she holds up the vodka—"and this is my accelerator." She shakes the cigarette pack at him. "And that's all I ever need."

"Sounds simple."

"I like things simple."

"Your life is anything *but* simple."

She sighs. "You're not wrong. But I'd rather talk about your life."

"What about my life?"

"You're still going to end it."

He pauses. Thinks. Takes another hit—holds it, releases it, coughs, eyes wet. Then he nods. "I am."

"Yeah. Okay." She chews the inside of her cheek. "I won't tell you to do otherwise."

"Thanks. Anybody else would be telling me to live. To love life. To blah blah blah. You know, whatever. You know what Schopenhauer said?"

"I don't even know who Schopenhauer is."

"German philosopher. Atheist. Had two poodles."

"Poodles are weird dogs."

"They barely seem like dogs at all."

"I know, right?"

"Anyway," he says, "to quote him on suicide: 'They tell us that suicide is the greatest piece of cowardice, that suicide is wrong, when it is quite obvious that there is nothing in the world to which every man has a more unassailable title than to his own life and person.'"

"I think I might kill myself someday," she says suddenly. The words just fall out of her. Like rocks out of a sack.

"Why?"

"I don't know. I'm young, but I'm tired. I close my eyes at night and it's just—my dreams are like a boat anchor, man. The things I see. It's like, it's not just the traumatic deaths—the car crashes and fires and stabbings. It's the slow deaths. AIDS and diabetes and kidney failure and liver failure and kid's cancer and rectal cancer and breast cancer and cancer cancer cancer. And did I mention cancer? People just lie there. Disease leaching everything out of them the way I'm sucking on this cigarette. Whittling them down. A stick into splinters. And I can't stop it. I can't stop any of it. I have no idea how to change it for people." She thinks of the little boy and the red balloon, and she almost tells him that story. But something stops her. As if there's someone else out there who will hear it first.

"Suicide is fast. I'm going to use a gun."

"I know."

"Oh, right."

"My first boyfriend used a gun."

"Oh."

"Yeah."

They sit there for a while. Her staring over the wheel. Him staring at the smoldering tip of the joint.

"You can have some of my stuff," he says. "Like I promised. I have a little money. I'll leave it in a bag in the front living room. I'd say you can stay in the house for a while—it's not huge but before Marie left me, we had two dogs in that house and there's a little backyard and . . ." He clears his throat. "But I'm going to be dead in there, and I'd do it somewhere else, but I want it to be there. In that house. In *our* house."

"Thanks."

"You can have the car, too."

"I take the car, they might think I killed you."

"Oh." He nods. "Good point." Then he rolls down the window and flicks the joint outside. "Some kid will find that. Hope he enjoys it. Or sells it for a couple bucks. It's good weed."

"Thanks for the driving lessons, Aidan."

"Thanks for sharing a little of my last day."

Stop and go, she thinks.

It's his time to stop.

Hers has not yet arrived, and so she goes.

TEN

THE SUNSHINE STATE
CAN GO FUCK ITSELF

All the way she's been listening to whatever random radio stations she can get on the dial, and it occurs to her slowly (but surely) that music basically sucks these days. Hollow, soulless pop music, shallower than a gob of jizz drying on a hot sidewalk. Even the country music sounds more like pop music—gone are the singular miseries of *my wife left me, my truck broke down, all I got left is my dog and my shotgun and the blue hills of Kentucky* and now it's sugar-fed Barbies twanging on about ex-boyfriends and drinking Jack-and-Cokes and she's pretty sure Loretta Lynn and Dolly Parton are clawing out of their graves somewhere—though, wait, are the two of them even dead? Shit, she's not sure.

Once in a while she gets a station that plays something worth a damn: Yeah Yeah Yeahs, Nirvana, Cowboy Junkies, Zeppelin, Johnny Cash, Nine Inch Nails, Johnny Cash *covering* Nine Inch Nails. It troubles her that music from the 1980s is now "oldies" music. Hard to picture a bunch of geriatrics thumping their walkers around to "99 Luftballons."

Most of the time the dial just finds static. Whispers of dead air. Crackles of voices lost in the noise.

Sometimes she thinks they're talking to her.

"—*mothers don't love their daughters*—"

"—*dead people*—ksssh—*everywhere*—"

"—fire on route 1—St. Augustine—"

"—wicked polly—"

"—river is rising—"

"—it is what it is—"

Now she's on this hellfire-and-brimstone station. Some preacher hollering on about depravities and Leviticus and the *ho-mo-sek-shul* menace, suggesting that God is so squicked out by two dudes kissing that he's willing to once more drown the world in another hate-flood. Which, to Miriam's mind, suggests that God doth protest *too much*. Maybe that's why he booted Satan out of heaven. Maybe they were blowing each other.

She waits for lightning to strike her in her seat.

It does not.

She cackles.

She finishes off her Red Bull and throws it in the back. It clanks against the other energy drink cans. Those things taste like cough syrup that's been fermenting in the mouth of a dead goat, but shit, they work.

Eventually, her bladder is like a yippy terrier that wants to go out. And the Fiero—which she has named Red Rocket—hungers for gas.

She opens the door of the car at a rickety podunk gas station not far from Daytona Beach, and as soon as she does, the heat hits her. It's like a hug from a hot jogger. Sticky. Heavy heaving bosoms. All-encompassing. A hot blanket of flesh on flesh. Gone is the rush of air-conditioning from the car and already she feels the sweat beading on her brow. Ew, gods, yuck.

This is winter? Thirty seconds in she already feels like a swamp.

Florida: America's hot, moist land-wang.

Everything's bright. She fumbles on the dash for a pair of sunglasses and quickly throws them on. She feels like a vampire dragged out into the sun for the first time. How long will it be before she bursts into flames, burns down like one of her cigarettes? A char-shaped statue of Miriam Black.

She hurries into the gas station—a round-cheeked Cuban dude watches her with some fascination, like he's seeing Nosferatu shy away from the judging rays of the Day God—and darts into the bathroom.

Into the stall. Rusty door closed. Someone has peed on the seat, which always astounds her. Men are basically orangutans in good clothes, so she gets that they ook and flail and get piss everywhere. But women? Shouldn't the ladies be better than this? Why is there pee on the toilet seat? *Hoverers,* she thinks. That's what it is. They hover over the seat like a UFO over a cornfield, trying to avoid the last woman's pee—also a hoverer, in a grim urine-soaked cycle—and then *pssshhh.* Splash. Spray. Lady-whiz everywhere. The cycle continues.

Miriam does the civilized thing—a rarity for her but in bathrooms she apparently reverts and becomes a member of the human species—and wads up toilet paper around her hands to make gloves. She cleans the seat. Scowling and cursing the whole time. Then she sits. And she pees.

In here it's dark and it's cool, at least.

Outside the stall, the bathroom door opens.

Someone else comes in.

Footsteps echoing. Little splashes as they step through water. Then: *clang.*

Something drops. Metal on metal. A loud sound, a jarring sound—it gives Miriam's heart a stun-gun jolt. A scrape. A *splash.*

She peers under the door.

The bent and bitten edge of a red snow shovel drags along the floor. A pair of muddy boots walks it along.

Miriam's sweat goes cold.

No no no, not here, not now.

The footsteps approach. Slapping against the soaked floor.

Miriam feels her pulse in her neck: a rabbit's pulse, thumping against the inside of her skin like a hard finger flicking. Her throat feels tight.

The boots stop just outside the stall.

Snow slides off their tops. *Plop, plop.* Melting on the tile.

Red runnels of blood crawl toward Miriam's feet.

A twinge of something inside her: an infant's fist twisting her guts. Then the woman outside her door drops something:

A purple paisley handkerchief.

The blood runs to it. Soaks through to it.

Fear transforms. A spitting rain into a booming thundercloud. It's anger now, jagged and defiant, a piece of broken glass chewed in the mouth—and Miriam roars, kicks out with her own black boot—

The door swings open. It slams against the other door.

Nobody's there. No woman with a red shovel. No boots. No snow, no blood, no gangbanger's handkerchief.

Miriam sighs. Massages the heels of her hands into her eyes, pressing hard, running them in circles. In the blue-black behind her eyes, fireworks explode and blur and fade—no sound, just silent flashes of light from her pressing hard on her own eyes.

"At least you have both eyes," comes a voice. Louis. Not-Louis.

The Trespasser, more like it.

She opens her eyes. A vulture sits on the lip of the sink in front of the stall. Bowing its featherless match-tip head. Beak clacking as it speaks.

"You're the key," the bird says, "but what's the lock?"

"What?"

"Or are you the lock and someone else is the key?"

Miriam's hands are shaking. "Speak sense, bird."

"Are you going to see Mommy while you're here?"

Miriam flings her keys at the big black scavenger.

The keyring rebounds off the sink, then the mirror, then lands in the well of a different sink. The bird is gone. One black feather remains, stuck to the grimy porcelain with a waxy bead of blood.

Miriam finishes peeing, rescues the keys, then hurries out.

ELEVEN

RINGY-RINGY

Outside in the parking lot Miriam gasses up the Red Rocket with the last of her cash, then parks off to the side, plants her butt on the hood, and smokes.

She lifts her ass off the car and plucks three pieces of paper—small, not quite fortune cookie fortune size, but close—from her back pocket.

Three phone numbers.

One: Louis. She hasn't seen him in more than a year. Hasn't spoken to him, either—she ditched her last phone in the river when she got the hell out of town with old man Albert. Albert, who was supposed to take her south. All the way to Florida if she could manage it. To see her mother.

Which leads her to the next number.

Two: her mother. Back in Pennsylvania, during the Mockingbird murders, she decided—or perhaps *was compelled*—to visit the house where she grew up. Her mother's house, or so she thought. Instead, that fuck-up Uncle Jack was living there. She found out her mother was living in Florida now, doing—what was it? Missionary work? And after all of it was done, after the Caldecotts were dead and Wren was saved, she really thought that she'd go to Florida, see her mother. But she always found a reason to point Albert in a new direction—train museum, amusement park, crayon factory, sex emporium. He knew she was avoiding something. But old Albert was good enough not to go picking scabs.

Albert's dead now. He must be. That's what the visions told her, and they haven't been wrong yet. Dropped dead in the tall, misty woods. Looking at a picture of his wife. And loving her.

Him and Darnell, the car salesman. Men who died with love in their hearts. Is that even a thing she's capable of? What does her heart contain? Vinegar and venom? Grave dirt and formaldehyde? Nicotine and dirty snow?

And she thinks, *These two phone numbers are heavy*. Pregnant with the potential for love, for connection, for *re*connection, even resurrection—but here she worries that these relationships are already dead and buried, and if there's one thing she knows all too well, it's that once you've killed something it stays in the ground where you put it.

Still, she thinks, *Call one of them.*

Call Louis. Just to see how he's doing.

Call her mother. To ask if they can see each other.

But then: that flare of anger. Louis doesn't understand her. Her mother understood her even less. *These are not my people*, she thinks.

She shoves both those numbers back into her pocket.

Then she grabs the third number.

The man from the Craigslist ad.

She calls him. Tells him she's here. In Florida.

He speaks slow. Not stupid-slow, just laid-back-slow. Peach Bellinis and sunbaked lounge-music slow. He asks her where she is. She tells him: Daytona. "Well, damn. Still got about a seven-hour trip till you get here."

She asks him, "Where's 'here'?"

"Big Torch Key."

She hears that gravel-and-grit in his voice, a Springsteen

growl tempered by a Neil Diamond smarm. When he says "Big Torch Key," he sings it as much as he speaks it.

He tells her the address. Gives her directions.

"This isn't about sex," she says. "I'm not a hooker."

"It's all good," he says, though she's not sure that answer means anything at all.

Miriam tells him she'll see him at eight.

He says he's looking forward to it.

Then she hangs up her cheap-shit burner phone and stretches one last time before dropping her sore butt back into the Red Rocket.

The journey continues.

TWELVE

LIKE MOSES IN A RED FIERO

Driving through the Keys feels like threading a needle.

Ahead of her, a ribbon of asphalt: sun-bleached, sand-blasted, salt-brined. In some places, the ocean is ten feet to one side of the road, and ten feet to the other. To her right, Florida Bay, to her left, the Atlantic Ocean, and she's carving a line right between them, a finger tracing the windowpane between two sheets of emerald glass.

Palm trees sway. Flocks of pelicans cross the bruise-dark sky like something prehistoric—a cabal of pterodactyls out of their time. Few beaches. Lots of boats. Old motels with their old motel signs: THE SANDPIPER. THE SUNSET COVE. THE COCONUT COVE. SMUGGLERS COVE. THE LOOKOUT LODGE. THE DROP ANCHOR INN. THE PELICAN. THE PINES. THE CONCH OUT. Big tall signs out of the 1950s. Some gone dark, half-collapsed. Others dirty, half-wrecked, but still lit: red light painting *vacancy, vacancy, vacancy* in the deepening night.

Tiki bars and marinas. Ramshackle stands selling fish tacos and homes hidden behind the palms. Men and women walking in the coming dark with fishing rods and bait buckets. Powder blues. Coral pinks. Green trees. Smeary neon.

It's a kind of dipshit, half-ass, hillbilly paradise—lazy and sunburned and swaying in the wind like the palms on both sides of the road.

This isn't my place, she thinks.

Then again, what place is?

She drives down through Key Largo, through Tavernier, through Islamorada, through Marathon, threading the needle and stitching together tiny islands. It all feels poorly held together by the white bones of various causeways, like all it would take would be one hard wind blown from the puffed cheeks of a drunken god to scatter the islands to the corners of the map.

Speaking of the map: She looks at the one open on the passenger seat next to her, a map nested in the remains of snack food bags and energy drink cans and cigarette packets. Miriam realizes the Keys look like a fingernail bitten most of the way off—but still hanging there at the tip of Florida's broken finger.

A hangnail, she thinks.

It's all one big hangnail.

She feels that way sometimes. Like a hangnail that won't come off.

And suddenly she wonders if the Keys *are* her kind of place.

She keeps driving. Down through the Middle Keys. Over the seven-mile bridge that rises like a hump over the water. Like she's driving over a dead dinosaur's bent back.

She fumbles for a drink in the cup holder—

Something stirs in the passenger seat.

A crow. Too big to be a crow. A raven. Black feathers wild and bristly like the mane of a tarred lion. Ink-dark beak clickity-clacking.

"Almost there," the crow says in Louis's voice. "Killer."

It stoops its head and pecks bits of something spongy and gray off a purple handkerchief beneath its talons. *Peck. Peck. Peck-peck.*

She throws an empty Red Bull can at it.

The can rebounds off the inside of the passenger-side door.

The bird is gone.

And ahead, a sign: BIG TORCH KEY.

THIRTEEN

TORCH KEY

The Fiero drives under power lines. She follows the road that turns off toward the gulf side of Middle Torch Key and winds its way through a salt marsh of scrub and stunted palm. The air-conditioning in the Fiero suddenly grumbles, vibrating like a paint shaker, before giving off a cough and a burning smell.

She curses under her breath. Fiddles with the knobs. Slams the vents with the heel of her hand before finally rolling the windows down.

The humid air crawls in. A few cool breeze streamers come with it.

Bats dip and dart overhead. Shadows blacker than the night, flitting after mosquitoes.

Another bridge from Middle Torch Key to Big Torch Key.

Along the way she passes a shirtless man on a rickety bike. His skin glistens in the yellow of her headlights—red flesh like he's a kielbasa left too long on the grill. He turns toward her, toothless and drunk, and gives a sloppy wave that almost causes him to ditch the bike in a pothole.

She keeps driving.

Big Torch Key.

Nothing out here. She's beginning to think this is some kind of joke. Even in the damp, slithering heat she can feel the skin on the back of her neck and arms prick up, the hairs standing at full attention. Worry tickles at her like a rat licking its paws. Out here it's just road and scrub and mangrove, and it's then she thinks, *This is some kind of game. I drove all the way to Florida to fall prey to some sicko's amusement.*

Of *course* it's a ruse. Five grand? Off of Craigslist? *Shit. Shit!* She thinks, *I have to get the fuck out of here*—fast, too, before she goes too far and drives over a spike-strip and blows her tires and ends up part of some twisted cannibal game out here in the subtropical nowhere—

But then she sees. Ahead, the flickering of actual torchlight.

Glinting off the metal of a driveway gate.

She sees a mailbox—a faded blue dolphin *holding* a mailbox, actually, some kind of roadside statue. Ridiculous and tacky, sure.

But also a sign of life.

She eases the car forward.

The number on the mailbox matches the number on her directions.

She's here.

It's real.

Well. Okay, then.

As if on cue, the gate opens. Mechanized.

It shudders and squeals as it swings wide.

She eases the Fiero into the driveway. White gravel grinds beneath her tires. Ahead, past the half-circle drive, sits a plantation-style house. Bent palms stand on both sides of the house like hands sheltering it. Or perhaps propping it up.

Warm orange light from within. Tiki torches lining the drive, flame licking the air, little vines of white smoke climbing.

The front door opens. A man comes out. Older. Late forties. Early fifties. Hair the color of sand swept down over his ears: long, shaggy, wind-frizzled. His arms are out wide, welcoming. Big smile. White teeth.

He beckons for her to park by the side.

She kills the engine. She gets out, takes the sunglasses off the top of her head, tosses them on the dash.

The man's already on her. Coming toward her fast, arms up and out—

She's already ready for it.

Her wrist flicks and the black four-inch lockback blade from her back pocket opens.

She points it, thrusts it at the open air. *Swish, swish.*

"Whoa, whoa, darling, what the—" He laughs, nervous, taking a couple clumsy steps backward. "I'm not here to hurt you."

"Then maybe don't come up on a girl so fast."

"It's not like that—"

"I don't know what it's like. You invite me out here. Middle of the night. Middle of *nowhere*. Promise me five grand. Then come up on me like a hungry dog sniffing for treats? That's a good way to get shanked, Jimmy Buffett."

He laughs. Still nervous. "Well. I sure don't want to get shanked."

"Then take five more steps backward."

He does.

"What's your name?" she asks.

"Steve."

"Steve what?"

"Steve Max."

"That's two first names."

"I guess it is, yeah."

She keeps the knife pointed at him. A stabby accuser. "My name's Miriam Black."

"Hi, Miriam. I'm glad you came down to meet me."

"Go," she says. "Go inside. I'll follow you."

"Are you going to rob me?" he asks.

"Are you going to rape me and kill me?" she asks him. "Or kill me and rape my dead body?"

"That wasn't my plan."

"And robbing you wasn't mine. Like I said, go. I'll follow."

He smiles. Nervous. Then does as she asks.

Her gaze flits through the scrub and the trees. Looking for shadows. Nothing. Still, something here feels wrong. Paranoia crawls over her like a colony of ants.

With a deep breath, knife in hand, Miriam goes inside.

FOURTEEN

HEMINGWAY'S SPIRIT

The inside of the house is full of dark timber and tan bamboo. Palm fronds. Tiki mugs on shelves. A big-screen TV on the far wall—big enough you could turn it on its back and use the thing as a dining room table for six people. A ceiling fan of thatched wood turns lazily overhead.

Steve precedes her, and once he's inside, it's like he stops worrying about the crazy road-weary chick with the knife in her hand. Like he just lets go of all his cares, letting them float to the heavens on the wings of pretty-pretty butterflies. He saunters over to a one-person bar in the corner, steps behind it, his shirt open, his hand scratching the salty wire-brush hairs growing up out of his bare chest. He's so tan Miriam thinks someone should skin him and use his pelt to make a nice set of luggage.

He reaches down under the bar and she barks—"Hey, hey, *hey*!"—and he quickly jerks back up again, hands up like he's a bank teller about to get robbed. He laughs, nervous.

"Ho now, what's the problem?"

"What's behind the bar?" She waggles the knife at him.

"Rum."

"Rum?"

"I was gonna make us a couple of daiquiris." He pats a stumpy bar-top blender. "Kind of a welcome-to-the-Keys drink. Hemingway's favorite cocktail."

"Hemingway was a diabetic. His favorite drink was a dry martini."

"Oh. No shit? I didn't know that. You read a lot?"

"When I can." *Homeless girls love libraries*, she thinks but does not say.

"I have some vodka and vermouth here."

"That's not a martini."

"Why, sure it is."

"Jesus, dude, I don't want to get into a cocktail pissing match with you, but a martini is gin. Always gin. Putting vodka in a martini is like—"

"Whiskey in a margarita?"

"It's like spitting in my mouth and calling it champagne."

His mouth seems frozen in a rigor mortis smile. "I don't have gin."

"Then I don't want whatever it is you would call a martini."

"Back to daiquiris, then."

"Are you going to poison me?"

He crosses his arms and leans forward on the bar. Ringlets of beach-blond hair frame his face. "Miriam, I understand your apprehension, I do, but this isn't anything . . . weird. I'm cool. We're cool. Here's how we're gonna fix this, okay? Over there on the side table by the patio door, there's a canvas bag, and in that canvas bag is twenty-five hundred bucks. Half of what I said I'd pay you for the vision. You go over there. You take that money. You can leave if you want to. But if you stay, I got a grill out on the patio and a table out on the dock and we can sit out there and eat some shrimp and mahi I got cooking up—little lime, little cilantro, little mango salsa—and then we can get down to business. By which I mean you tell me how I'm going to die and you get the other half of your money and then you can go on your way with a full belly and a fat sack of cash."

"Why?"

"What?"

"Why do you want to know how you're going to die?"

His easygoing smile falls away like dead leaves off an autumn tree. He searches for words. It's like he doesn't even know the answer to that question, which is eventually exactly what he says. "I don't know. I've always been a little obsessed with it. Living life to the . . . well, to the max. It is my last name and all, so I figure I better live up to it." Here an awkward laugh like he knows it's superdouchey and not very funny, but it's out there and now they have to deal with it. "I just want to know how much time I got left. I'm on the wrong side of middle age and you'll see—one day you'll get older and realize that the ride starts to speed up when you think it should be slowing down."

She lets the knife fall to her side and hang there in her hand.

Miriam goes to the white canvas bag. Hooks a finger around a strap. Lifts. Separates. Sees wads of cash piled haphazardly atop one another, held together with little rubber bands.

"You can count it," he says.

"I'm good. It's good."

"You wanna eat?"

She closes the knife and pockets it.

"I could eat," she says, then walks past him out onto the patio.

FIFTEEN

DISEASEBURGER IN PARADISE

Outside: the heady, narcotic smell of shrimp and planked fish on a small charcoal grill. Steve goes on a hunt for plates, doesn't seem to know where he keeps them. He tells her he has a new maid—"Cuban girl, skin like *café con leche*, just pretty as the sunset, but she always rearranges my stuff and it's like a scavenger hunt trying to figure out where."

Miriam sits at the patio table. A dock extends out over the bay water like a red carpet to the deep blue oblivion.

The moon hangs fat in the sky like it might give birth to a litter of baby moons, and maybe some stars, and a swirl of galaxies, too.

Something bites her arm. A mosquito, she assumes, though she can't see it in the torchlight.

She swats at it as Steve puts a plate in front of her. Alongside, a drink. A pink drink. She scowls at it. "Strawberry daiquiri," he says, obviously obsessed with the damn things, and she sniffs at it and pushes it away—too cloying, too strawberry, too pink. She's thinking of just asking for the bottle of rum when something bites her arm again. Twice. Then a third time.

"Ow, sonofab—" *Swat swat swat*. She pulls her hand back and expects to see little greasy skeeter stains, but no such luck.

"No-see-ums."

"No-who-nows?"

"Little gnats. Fast little stinkers. Zip in, take a bite, then they take off again with your blood still in their mouths. Here." He takes a long-neck lighter and lights a citronella candle. The chemical citrus stink fills the air. Whatever appetite she had is suddenly gone—her guts are already cinched up in stubborn knots and she's not sure why.

She pushes the plate away.

"Not hungry?" he asks.

"I'm fine."

He pokes at a shrimp, then pushes his own plate away.

"Pretty night."

"I'm not sleeping with you."

"Didn't say you were. Didn't we already cover—"

"What is this, anyway? Dinner and drinks on a moonlit patio overlooking the water? Maybe this is a real panty-dropper for the girls you hang with, but I don't know you and I'm starting to think it's creepy."

Now he's looking a little irritated. "I just figured you drove a helluva long way and you could use a meal. I had to eat. No reason not to fix two plates. Jeez, you're an edgy broad."

"Maybe it's that you're calling me *broad*."

"It's just a—" He sighs. "It's just an expression, an old word. Damn, I'm sorry I hurt your feelings. You're wound too tight. Like a—a—well, like a thing that's wound too tight."

"Nice metaphor, Hemingway."

"Cripes, you're meaner than my mama."

She scowls. Narrows her eyes. "Yeah. I'm sorry."

"You know, living down here it's like . . . you gotta learn to let things go. Set 'em down on the water and give them to the wind to take out to sea. We're all about the good times here in the Keys. Take some of the money from tonight and do a little snorkeling. Fish off a bridge. Or just lie around not doing a damn thing except reading books and smoking cigarettes."

"I'm not the 'chillax' type of girl."

A wind comes off the water. The torch-fire ripples and whispers.

"What type of girl are you?"

"The type with regrets."

"We all have regrets."

She smirks. "Not like me, dude."

She finally grabs at the daiquiri, figuring, well, if it's poisoned or roofied or he pissed in it then that's just a thing she's going to have to deal with. She bangs it back. It's sweet. *Too* sweet. Berry and sugar and citrus. Underneath all the diabetes, though, waits a swift horse-kick of rum. Boom. It runs through her like a ripple of blue flame across a puddle of gasoline.

Her teeth crush ice. *Crunch crunch crunch.*

She sets the empty glass down.

"You can really put 'em away," he says.

"It's a skill. I'm a champ." She puts her hand down on the table, palm up. "Let's do this. Get it over with. You didn't hire me to drink your booze and threaten you with knives and snark at you like a snarky snark who snarks, so place your hand in mine and let's take a hop in the Grim Reaper's hell-powered stage-coach and see where that bony motherfucker takes us."

He stares down at her hand. "You wanna take bets?"

"Bets on what?"

"On how I die."

"That's morose."

"You seem like the type of girl who likes morose."

"I do." She thinks about it. "Fine. I'll play along. You're, what, fifty?"

"Close. Forty-nine."

"Married?"

"Never once."

"So, no heart attack." She winks. "You eat a lot of seafood?"

He waves his arms, inviting her to behold the majesty of the world around him. "I live out here. Of *course* I eat a lot of seafood."

"And you got a bit of a poochy belly but no worse than most men your age and, frankly, a little bit better."

He chuckles. "That's the sweetest thing you've said all night."

"Can it, Hemingway. Hmm. Let's see. I vote fishing accident. Boat crash. Shark attack. Fishhook to the jugular. Something like that."

"I *do* like fishing."

"Well, there you go." She bites at a thumbnail. "So, what's your bet?"

He pops his lips, drums his fingers. "Cancer."

"How boring."

"I'm playing the odds."

"Smart move. Cancer seems to get us all in the end."

"Fuck cancer," he says, and raises his glass.

"So. Is this a real bet? We putting money on the table?"

He cocks his head. "I think the money on the table is already enough. I don't know that I can do better than five grand. But I like making this a real bet just the same. What do you want if you win?"

"I want to take that bottle of rum behind the bar home with me."

"Deal."

"And you?"

His lips spread into a shark's toothy grin. "I want you to spend the night with me."

"Aaaaand there it is."

"You gotta admit, you're starting to like me."

She *is* starting to like him. A little. Maybe. She doesn't admit it, though. Not yet.

"And you don't think I'm the ugliest duck in the pond."

"You're old," she says.

"I'm not old. I'm *seasoned*."

"A little too salt-and-pepper."

He leans forward. "I still have a little cayenne pepper going on."

"I'm not sure if you're being gross, or sexy, or just plain oblique."

"I don't know what oblique means."

She laughs. "I don't either."

Way the firelight plays off him, way the rum is oiling all her gears, she thinks, *Well, hell, why not?*

"I understand if you don't want to. Probably a bad idea."

"Good news for you, I'm very good at bad ideas. I'm in."

"Shall we shake on it?"

She puts her hand back on the table and he reaches out and—

SIXTEEN

HELLO, MIRIAM

In one year's time, one year to the day—

It's night, and Steve Max is bleeding.

He lies across the patio table of the plantation home, his arms splayed out. His legs, too. They are bound by nylon cord.

His face is swollen from a beating. One eye shut by a rising hillock of puffy, bruised brow-flesh. The other eye wide with a small cut beneath it on the cheek (not a fresh cut, this, but a scar, pale pink against the tan skin). His lips are split. His teeth are broken or gone. His tongue looks like a diseased fish poking its head out of the ruined coral grotto that is his mouth.

The torches all around are dark.

Someone is there with him.

Someone in a dark jacket. Hood pulled tight.

Standing there. Holding two things. First, a small pocket knife. Second, a sheet of white copier paper.

The shadowed figure takes the knife and sticks it in the side of Steve Max's neck—not a deep plunge of the blade, just a quick in-and-out, like he's just trying to tap a barrel. It strikes the jugular. Makes a small hole.

Blood starts to pump like water from a drinking fountain.

Steve Max screams.

The person takes the piece of paper and plants it hard against the beaten man's bare chest.

He pins it there with a hard stab of the knife.

The blade crunches down through breastbone.

This is not a quick in-and-out. The little knife buries to the hilt. It's a death blow. Steve's scream is cut short. His body starts to shudder.

His life starts to fade.

The blade looks familiar. The blade belongs to Miriam Black. It's her knife. The lockback.

As Steve Max starts to die, the shadowed figure takes two gloved fingers—first and middle finger—and dips them in the blood still pumping from the neck.

The wet fingers begin to write on the piece of paper.

HELLO

Dip, dip, dip.

MIRIAM.

Then the index finger alone returns to the pooling blood— now spilling over the edge of the patio table like a sticky red waterfall—and draws one last little comma between the two words. A curious, crimson curl.

HELLO, MIRIAM.

Steve Max belches up a bubble of his own heart's blood.

And then he is dead.

SEVENTEEN

IT'S NIGHT, AND STEVE MAX IS BLEEDING

Miriam comes out of the vision like a meteor punching a hole through the atmosphere—a dark rock in the deep cold that suddenly glows orange, red, white, that catches fire as it falls like a heavenly fist toward Earth.

Her thoughts move a mile a minute, branching, breaking, worming through the maze of Just What The Fuck Is Happening Here—and there Steve Max sits across from her, smiling, eager, *genuinely curious*. Next thing she knows, her body has made its choice with almost no help from her mind: She's up on top of the patio table, feet knocking her plate onto the slate-stone patio (*crash*), and she's like a wild animal—a mother puma cresting a rock to get at the gazelle, or maybe to tell another cat to get the hell out of her territory. The knife flicks. The blade is out.

She leaps.

She knocks Steve Max and his chair over. Lands on his chest like a gargoyle on a ledge.

Miriam takes the knife and lets its punishing tip hover a half-inch above his wide-open eye.

"I do not like being fucked with," she says, snarling.

"Whuh-whuh-whuh—" He can't even say the word.

She can see in his eyes: He doesn't know what's happening.

Of course he doesn't, she thinks, her brain still playing catch-up. *He doesn't know he's going to be ritually slain on his own patio.*

In one year. To the day.

But he knows *something*.

He has to. This isn't just fate. Someone wanted her here. Someone wanted her to *see* that.

"Who hired you?" she seethes.

"What? No—nobody—I don't—"

She takes the knife and slices a quick inch-long cut across the cheek—*not a fresh cut, this, but a scar, pale pink against the tan skin*—and he flinches and cries out and tries to grab at her and pull her off, but again she returns the tip of the knife to just above his eye and she hisses a warning.

"Lie still or I'll take the eye, *Steve*."

His arms flop like dead fish.

His lips purse. Teeth chattering from the fear.

"Someone hired you to mess with me," she says. "Someone asked you to bring me here. They *wanted* me to see how you die."

Her head is doing loop-de-loops. A message written in a murder committed in a year's time. That's dedication. The killer is bound to fate with lash-rope and tight-knot. But how? How would the killer be able to plan so far ahead? Why a message for her?

And using her knife to do the deed?

"I . . ." He takes a deep breath. Tries to calm himself. "I don't know who he is. We only spoke over the ph-phone."

"And what did he say?"

"He . . . he . . . told me to bring you here, to this address. He made it clear that I was not to . . . spook you, because he said you would be easily spooked but that I needed to calm you down and—" Here he needs to calm *himself* down, breathing faster and faster. With her knifeless hand she grabs his chin and holds it firm. "I needed to get you to touch me."

A new thought occurs to her. "This isn't even your house."

"What? N-no. Just a r-rental from VRBO—"

The plates. He didn't know where the plates were.

She's kicking herself now. She should have known this was some kind of trap. Just not the kind she thought.

Whoever's running these head games is even more committed than she realized: renting the house, looping in this dope, but then renting the house again a *year later* so it can be used to murder *the same dope*.

All in order to send her a message.

A little wave from the future. A greeting in wet blood.

Cut with her own knife, or one just like it.

"Who was it?" she asks.

"I dunno, I dunno."

"Who was it?"

His deep Springsteen-Diamond voice goes higher-pitched than she would have figured it could. "I swear I dunno! He, he, he spoke through one of those voice . . . things, voice boxes, changers—"

"Modulators."

"Voice modulator, yeah, yeah."

She sneers. "What were *you* getting out of this?"

"Money. *Money*. He was paying me the s-same thing he was paying you. Five grand."

Ten grand for this ruse. So whoever he is, he's got cash to spare.

Miriam leans down. Gets her face as close to his as possible. The knife is now her partner in this, the tip of her nose parallel with the tip of the blade.

"I could rob him of this plunder," she says. "I could kill you right now. I could steal your death for myself and send *him* a message up through the pipes and tubes of time so a year later he has no message to draw in your blood. And don't mistake me, Steve. I'm a killer and a thief and this is what comes naturally to a girl like me."

She echoes the statement in her own mind: *I'm a killer. I'm a thief. I'll kill you dead, steal your soul, and gank your wallet to spend on cigarettes, which I then use to kill myself.*

But a smaller voice says, *Is that what you really are?*

Is it all a mask?

A magic trick you've performed on yourself?

She suddenly stands up. She backs away from Steve, who sits up and crawls into the chair after setting it upright.

"You were going to sleep with me," she says.

"I . . ." He rubs his face. "Yeah."

"Part of the plan?"

"No. No." He pauses. "He said I could, though. If I wanted."

If I wanted. She makes a frustrated animal sound. "That assumes a lot about me. Don't you think, *Steve*?" His name, dripping with as much septic juice as she can squeeze from it. "Is that even your real name? Steve?"

"It's . . . Peter. Peter Lake."

"Well, Pete. Here's the news: In one year's time, the person who hired you to mess with my head is going to find you. He's going to tie you to *this very patio table* and stick a knife in your neck and then your chest and he's going to write a message to me *in your blood* as you lie dying. And now you're in a peculiar position because there's only one way to stop that from happening: I find who kills you and I kill him first. Them's the laws, *Pete*. That's how the universe works, *Pete*. Fate has fixed us all to its collector's corkboard with sharp little pins, and the only way we wriggle free is by lubricating the pin with someone else's blood."

"I'm sorry. I'll do anything to help you find him, I swear it."

"You're not going to do shit. Because you don't know shit. You're not even a pawn in this game—you're just a bug crawling across the chessboard. So sit back. *Chillax*, bro. Do a little snorkeling. Fish off a bridge. Read a book and smoke a cigarette. Let the adults do the heavy lifting."

She heads back inside. Grabs her keys. Grabs the canvas bag. He follows her inside, staggering like a zombie, like a man who's already dead. She waves her knife at him. "The rest of my money?"

"What?"

"The other half, asshole! I want the other twenty-five hundred."

"Oh. Right." He goes to the bar and comes back up with another bag—this one just a Ziploc gallon freezer bag. Then he fishes for two more just like it and sets them on the bar.

He eases the cap off a bottle of rum. But before he can pull the bottle to his lips she snatches it out of his hands.

"*Mine*," she says.

She snatches up the cash Baggies, too.

"Did he pay you yet?" she asks. It's like he's thinking about what the right answer is, but she helps him decide by giving the minibar a swift kick. "Tell me the truth now, Pete. Or this could get more complicated."

He nods. "Yeah. He paid me."

"Five grand?"

"Uh-huh."

"Good. I *want* it. Go fetch, rover." She watches as he slinks into the living room, opens a chest that looks like a replica of sunken treasure. As he does, she enters the room, kicks over a few couch cushions, tilts a few lamps. Not sure what she's looking for: a bug? A camera? A little man hiding in the couch with a boom mic?

Ste . . . er, Pete, holds up a dirty army duffel.

"Five grand. Well. Four grand. I already spent a grand."

"You're an asshole," she says, but swipes the bag anyway. Then she reaches into the bag and pulls another cluster of money and throws it at him. It thuds against his chest and drops to the ground. "There, that's for you, mop-top. Go nuts. You did your work. Besides, you've only got a year left on your lease so take a drive and enjoy the ride." She sighs and shakes her head. "I can't believe I actually considered sleeping with you."

"I'm sorry."

"Sorry's just a word. Have a nice life."

And then she's back outside. White gravel. Dark night. Into the Fiero and back through the scrub and mangrove. Money in the passenger seat. Rum in her hands. Burned sugar on her lips. Fire in her belly.

Foot on the accelerator. The road beneath the wheels. The night in her teeth and a sign in her eyes: KEY WEST 25.

"So that's when you got the DUI," Grosky says.

Vills jumps in before Miriam can answer. "I read that's one of the most common crimes down here. Drunk driving. Lots of road fatalities."

"Yeah, well," Miriam says, "that's not *exactly* when I got the DUI. By then it was only eight, maybe nine o'clock at night. I didn't get the DUI until—well, I was drunk, but I think it was around four in the morning. Just in case you're taking detailed notes and keeping track of time." She watches Grosky drum his fingers on the metal box. "And we should all be keeping track of the time, I think. With our pretty, pretty watches."

Vills seems to flinch at that. Good. Grosky says, "So, you didn't get busted then. What'd you do next? Go somewhere? Clear your mind?"

"What do you think I did? I went to Key West to get fucked up."

EIGHTEEN

BLACKOUT

Three in the morning and Miriam wakes up in a tangle of sheets grabbing her like river weeds and pulling her down, down, down into dark water, into muddy channels where catfish crawl and corpses hide. She lurches up in bed, gasping, wiping the river murk from her eyes. Murk that's actually sweat. Sweat that stings.

She's naked.

That's new.

Someone moans next to her.

Another woman.

Also naked.

Well.

The sheets bunch up over the woman's hip and leg, showing off a tattoo that starts at the ankle and ends at the curve of the woman's hip and her surprisingly milk-white ass cheek.

"You awake?" the woman moans from beneath the pillow above her head.

Miriam *mmms* in response. And she thinks to add, *And I'm still drunk*, because when she moves her head, it feels like her brain takes a half second to catch up. Same with her eyeballs— she points them places and her comprehension of what's in front of her lags behind like a tired dog.

The woman's hand slides across the sheets like a searching snake and her fingernails—long and green, green like wet fern—dance up Miriam's bony hip and trace languid circles there.

A shiver runs across her skin.

All around, the remnants of a night forgotten: an empty rum bottle, an ashtray so full of cigarettes it looks like a cancerous hedgehog, a bottle of Astroglide, a small red dildo. (Here she hears her own voice saying *red rocket, red rocket*, then laughing.)

An odor in the air. The heady scent of expended lube. The pickled scent of sweat. The sweet-sour tang of worked flesh and sex.

Miriam blinks.

It's been a while.

She got laid and can't even remember it.

Well, shit.

But then the woman turns over—a spiky mess of blond hair, a streak of red lipstick smeared across cherub cheeks, a bared shoulder with ink of a Kraken reaching up and pulling a boat into the foam-capped waves—and suddenly most of it comes back to Miriam in stuttering fits and shuddering starts—

NINETEEN

RUM, SODOMY, AND THE LASH

Driving south-southwest. Down the curved crust of damp bread that is the Lower Keys, through the mangroves, through the dark, watched by black long-necked birds on tall power lines.

Into Key West. Around its edge. Into its heart.

Fast forward: mile zero. End of the line. Money in her pocket, the rest split: some hidden under the seats in the car, some hidden where the spare tire would go in the trunk. Then it's time to park the Fiero—not drunk yet, no sir, no ma'am, but that's on the menu. Key West splays before her, limbs out, mouth open, madness everywhere.

Here: an old man dressed like a pirate, foam parrot on his shoulder, eyes caked with too much mascara and eyeliner. There: a pair of cougars on the prowl, no bras, big tits swinging like soft fruits dangling from a bowed branch, skin like sun-baked deer-hide rugs, the two coming up on a lanky barely legal dude with buck teeth and a lot of gums and a whole lot of drunken slack in his rope and a high likelihood of getting double-teamed by this pair of hungry velociraptors. Across the street: A young guy plays ukulele for money and a pit bull sits next to him with sunglasses strapped to his doggy head. Just ahead: a college-age girl puking in someone's top hat. *Welcome to Key West, bitches*.

Fast forward: She marches through Mallory Square. Men belch fire and a woman juggles and people sell jams and jewelry

95

and other junk from blankets on the ground. Ahead Miriam sees a woman under a fabric sign that says PSYCHIC READINGS I WILL TELL YOU YOUR FUTURE and Miriam walks by a too-tan woman sitting there with her sun-whitened hair underneath a gypsy headwrap and Miriam sticks out her tongue and thrusts up both middle fingers like a pair of *fuck you* antennae—

Fast forward: Miriam finds a rum bar. That's what it says on the sign and that's all they offer and that's fine by her. Two hundred thirty different rums, they say. From fermented dogshit to artisanal spirits tempered in barrels made from extinct trees and dodo bones. She goes to the bar and the guy behind it is an old salt with long ears and a bent nose and a Hawaiian shirt so colorful it looks like a clown exploded on him and he asks her what she wants and she shrugs and barks, "Rum." But he tells her he *knows* that already, what kind of rum? And in what? Daiquiri? Mojito? Hurricane? Painkiller? She thinks *painkiller, I need a painkiller stat,* but then a voice, a female voice, pipes up next to her and says, "Give her the root juice, Dan. Give her the *mama juana.*"

Next thing Miriam knows, Dan is plunking down a shot glass on the bar and pouring something from a jug into it, something brown like Coca-Cola, but turbid, too, like pond water stirred with a stick. She looks at him askance and says, "I'm going to need more than that, my colorful barkeep," and he takes the shot glass and puts down a *pint* glass and fills that up. He laughs. The girl next to her laughs, too. She takes a look at her: chubby-cheeked green-eyed chick with blond hair in floppy spikes, some of them tied off with little pink bows, and the girl is laughing with an open mouth like she knows something Miriam doesn't.

Miriam drinks.

It tastes like—she doesn't even know what. It's got the caramel burn of rum, the sweetness of honey, but it's like licking tree roots, too, like picking up bundles of whatever you find in the woods—thistle and thorn and bark and branch—and distilling it down to whatever the hell is in her glass. It's like birch beer spat from Satan's mouth. She loves it.

She drinks more.

Then she and the woman are laughing together, making small talk that moves fast toward dirty jokes: dicks and sheep and hookers and dwarves and pussies. They're making each other cry, they're cracking up so hard, and Miriam thinks, *I want to know how she dies*, which is a fucking goofy-ass thought that hits her out of far left field, and in her increasingly drunken brain she tries to justify it: *When I like people, I want to know how and when they'll leave me*. But even *that* thought seems off somehow because she doesn't know this woman and has no reason to feel intimate with her—

But then all that doesn't matter, because a couple of douchebros saunter up behind the two of them, hands reaching out and touching the smalls of their backs, gentle, but insistent; Miriam shifts and the bro presses harder, like he owns her. One's got his Oakley sunglasses up over his chiseled head and his breath smells like sour tequila. The other is fatter, his head swollen like a cocktail olive and in this light looks about the same color, and he's showing off crooked white teeth in a lopsided smile—

Douchebros One and Two are trying to buy them drinks, dropping half-slurred come-ons, hitting on the two of them with all the grace and aplomb of orangutans banging their cocks against a telephone pole. And the other woman, the green-eyed spiky-haired blonde, she says something polite, a "No, thanks, we're good here," and it's far nicer than what Miriam would have said, but then the two bros have to go and ruin it for everybody.

The white one with the sunglasses, the one who probably knows all the brands of surfboards and snowboards and flip-flops but can't remember his own mother's birthday, says, "Don't be a bitch. Why you gotta roll your eyes at me?" And then the other

one, the fathead with the darker complexion, is saying something about how the two of them are "probably clam-lappers
anyway," and he says it under his breath but Oakley Boy repeats
it and laughs like a snorting pig.

Miriam's had enough. She blurts, "If you don't go away, I'm
going to retroactively abort the both of you."

And then they're laughing, mocking her. "I'll retroactively
abort you," Oakley Boy says, spitting her words back at her in
a fake bitchy tone, and Fathead adds, "I don't even know what
that means," *huh-huh-huh heh-heh-heh*, and then Miriam spins
around and—*Grrrrk ptoo!*—hawks a loogey right in Oakley Boy's
mouth.

He's suddenly coughing and spitting and trying to backhand
her and knock her off the stool, but she catches his wrist—

*He's old, skin like Bible pages, and he's in a robe the color of a
robin's belly. He's puttering around the downstairs and he's calling someone's name—"Rachel, Rachel,"—but his mind is a block
of Swiss cheese, holes eaten into it by the curse of Alzheimer's,
and then he goes to the cellar steps and calls for Rachel one last
time before his brittle ankle twists and he tumbles down the
cement steps like a sack of footballs. His head hits the floor face-
first. Teeth scatter. He lies there awhile, wheezing and whimpering, pissing his pants, and then he remembers Rachel and him
were never together and Rachel is dead, and then, just like that,
so is he.*

—and then Miriam's other arm darts out, catches his head in
the cradle of her hand, and jams Oakley's skull against Fathead's
skull, and they don't bonk like coconuts so much as they thud
together like two slabs of beef. Fathead trips over his own feet
and goes down, bleating like a sheep. Oakley comes at her but
she knees her stool forward—

It catches him in the balls. He goes down. Howling.

Fast forward: She and the other woman are bolting down

Duval Street past the drunks and pirates and cruise-ship tourists, and the blonde pulls Miriam into an alcove between an art gallery and a Cuban food joint and Miriam starts cursing about those thin-dicked shit-birds, those assholes who think they can saunter into a bar and jam their nickel-sized cocks into whatever coin slot they want just by using a few weak-fuck pick-up lines—

The other woman says, "You have a dirty mouth. I want to taste it."

Then it's her mouth on Miriam's, teeth clicking, skin chafing, two tongues pushing forth and pulling back, a friendly game of *tongue-of-war*. A death vision slides in here, but it's like a kite dipping and swaying in a hard wind and Miriam can't seem to catch it. She chases it like fire chasing smoke, but it evades, always out of reach. Then the woman's hands are on her sides, up and down, fingers past the waistband of Miriam's jeans. Someone nearby sees them, wolf-whistles, and both women thrust up a pair of middle fingers—synchronized vulgarity, a new Olympic sport.

Fast forward: the woman's house, ten blocks away, no clothes—two animals clawing at each other, each trying to make a feast of the other, thighs wrapped around thighs, spin around, tits mashed against shoulder blades, fingers down, up, in, pistoning—

Taste and skin and sweat and lube and something that vibrates and—car outside, Cuban music coming in through open curtains, the whine of a mosquito in the well of the ear, the tiny moan of the woman underneath her, the squeak of the bed frame, the whisper of palms outside—

TWENTY

TOUCH AND GO

"Oh," Miriam says. *"Oh."*

The other woman's hand slides over Miriam's hip—the bones there so pronounced they might as well be the handlebars of a bicycle—and dips down toward her thighs, and Miriam starts to go with it but gasps sharply and plucks the hand from her thigh and sets it on the sheet.

"You want to come back to bed?" the woman asks.

"I want to know your name."

"Didn't I tell you already?" She laughs. "Maybe I didn't. We were pretty drunk."

"I'm still a little drunk."

"Me too." And the hand is back again, the snake up the tree, the vine up the fencepost, and once more Miriam pushes back the shivers and the desire and—less gently this time—plucks the invader's hand off of her. "Okay. Sorry."

"It's not—you don't need to apologize. Obviously we had fun—"

Here the girl's smile transforms into a sharp blade wicked enough to take a man's head from his neck.

"—but I *still* don't know your name."

"Gabby."

"That's a horrible name." That comment darts out of her mouth like a cat seeing an open door—just no catching it and putting it back inside.

The woman—Gabby—sits up. "*Hey.*"

"No, I don't mean . . . I just mean—" And here it goes. "Names are very important; they're how we see people, and no matter who a person is, a funky name will cling to you like an ugly wet dress and nobody will see who you really are, they'll just see the ugly dress. Right? Like what if George Clooney was named Artie Finklenuts. Or if Marie Curie was, I dunno, Grimelda Shatblossom."

"Gabby is not an ugly dress name."

"It's not, it's not, but it sounds like you talk a lot. Gabby. Gab." Her hand forms a little alligator puppet whose chompy mouth opens and closes in a mimicry of talking. "Gab gab gab. Is your full name Gabrielle? See, I like that. That's pretty. You should go with that."

"No," the woman says, her voice suddenly steely, her words bled dry of any of the lust that had been present. "My parents named me Gabby. That is my name. Gabby. Not Gabrielle. Or Gabriella. Or anything else. *Gabby.*"

"They named you after a nickname? Cruel move."

"Go to Hell."

"You're pissed."

"Yes! I'm pissed. We had a good night—*Jesus*, did we have a good night—and now you wake up and you're just being mean."

Miriam scooches to the edge of the bed. Looks for her panties. Spies them on the ground in a little black pile. "I should go."

"I guess you should."

Miriam grabs her panties with her toes like a primate, then begins pulling them up over her hips. "I'm not trying to piss on your parade and call it rain. Before I walked into that rum bar, I was having a strange night. You caught me when I was vulnerable. I'm not good people."

Gabby makes a sound like she just ate a spoonful of salt when she thought she was getting sugar. "Really? You're one of those?"

"One of those what?"

"Those types."

"Those types of *what*?"

"Girls. Women. Who . . . who think they're all damaged and broken and they're anxious or depressed and so they just . . . *inflict* themselves on other people. Ugh! You let them in and everything seems cool but then comes the excuses, the *I'm not worth it*, the *I'm bad for you, Gabby. So sorry, thanks for the quick lay*—" She rolls her head back on her neck and groans. "Stupid! So stupid, Gabby. Jesus."

"I *am* bad for other people. At this point I think it's scientifically proven." She mutters, "I'm sure it's on the Internet somewhere."

Gabby flops back on the bed. From behind her hands she moans, "Another one. I found another one. Why am I always attracted to your type?" She buries her face under the pillow.

Miriam sits back down on the edge of the bed. Gets her jeans halfway up her legs and then just sits there. Staring off at an unfixed point a thousand miles away. Guilt and shame make a bitter cocktail inside her. She finishes pulling on her jeans and she goes over to Gabby and pries the pillow off the other woman's head.

"I'm sorry you think I'm mean."

"Worst kind of apology ever. It puts the blame on me. It says I should really be the one apologizing to you for . . . misinterpreting what was *obviously* a loving gesture."

"Fine. I'm sorry I *was* mean."

"Okay. Great. Awesome. You can go now."

But Miriam hovers. "It's been a while."

"Been a while since what?"

"Since—" She gesticulates over the bed in all its sex-rumpled grandeur. "Since this."

"Since you got some."

"Almost got into it with this dude last year—" *But he turned out to be one of a whole nest of serial killers.* "But that did not work out."

"A dude. Oh. So, I'm your first woman."

"What? Hey. No. You're not the first love-puddle in which I've snorkeled. Though, ah, it's been a few years."

"You're not gay."

"No. I like to think I'm loosey-goosey—"

"You're a straight girl on a gay vacation."

"Jiggling Jesus, don't be so dramatic, it's called being *flexible*—"

"You're just renting out my pussy like it's a vacation home."

"Oh, come on, 'renting out'—"

Wham. It hits her. Vacation home. Rental. Duh. *Duh.* Whoever is messing with her rented that house on Torch Key. Which she already knew. All she has to do is contact the people who rented it out and find out to whom they rented it—easy-peasy titty-squeezy.

"I gotta go," Miriam says.

"And now you run away."

"No, this isn't . . . It's not . . . This isn't *you*, this is something else, this is a problem I maybe just figured out. Someone's messing with me, and I don't like it."

"I know the feeling. So go."

"I'll call you."

"You don't even have my number!"

But Miriam doesn't hear her because she's already out the door, darting toward the Fiero.

NOW

"*That's* when you got pulled over," Grosky says.

Miriam gives a half shrug. "Not exactly. The fucking car died on me ten minutes out of Key West. I paraded around and kick-punched the car a buncha times and then, next thing I know, blue-and-reds. They made me do the alphabet backwards—which, for the record, I cannot do sober—and they said I was too drunk to drive and blah blah blah."

Vills leans in. "What was your plan? What did you think you could accomplish at that hour of the morning?"

"I was going to go back to the Torch Key house. Pound on the door. Wake Peter up if he was still there—if not, break in. People had to have contact information in there somewhere."

"Then what?"

"Call them. Ask them."

"Why would they give out that information to you?"

"I don't know! I can be persuasive. Or violent. It wasn't a superawesome plan, okay? Did you or did you not hear the part where I was drunk?"

Grosky shrugs. "You know, if you hadn't been caught that night, we wouldn't be here right now."

"Then hoorah for fate throwing us together," she says with an eye roll.

"Seriously. You showed up on our radar just as we were looking for you. You take a pretty rough-looking mug-shot. It's funny now, hearing the story, because I said to Vills—Vills, what did I say to you when I saw Miriam's mug shot here?"

Vills says, "He said, 'Looks like she has JBF hair.'"

"'Just Been Fucked' hair," Grosky clarifies.

"Clever," Miriam says.

"I like it. Whatever. Point is, you can think what you want about fate, but it brought us together today. Here in this little shack on the beach. Nobody else around. Very romantic."

"Not an official FBI interrogation room," Miriam notes.

"This one's off the books," Vills says.

"For now," Grosky says.

"So, you two really are Feds?"

They smile, share another of their conspiratorial looks, then nod.

"What do you want with me, then? If I'm a killer, put me away. If I'm a serial killer, throw me in the chair and dissect my brain to find out what's wrong with it. Trust me, I'd love to see the results. Why me? Why here? What's your plan, you two crazy kids?"

Grosky grins big and broad. "We'll get to that, Miriam. Patience."

TWENTY-ONE

JAILBIRD

She thinks it's going to be like it is in all the movies: big jail cell with the gray bars and the food slot, rubbing elbows with thugs and killers who see her as nothing more than sexual breakfast. But the reality is, the bars are really just a black chain-link fence making her feel like she's a German Shepherd in a kennel. And she's only in here with one other human being: a sluggy Cuban sitting half-asleep on the bench, his double-chin pressed down in the chunky vomit shellacking his own chest. At one point she yells at him, "Did you even *chew* your food?" but he barely stirs.

Everything goes by in a flash. They bring her in and ask her questions. Take her fingerprints. Take her photo—for which she puts on her most feral stare, like a rabid raccoon startled from its meal. They take everything she has and tow the car to the impound yard voucher for her personal property.

And here she worries about the money. Because nowhere on the voucher does it list *eight thousand* (er, give or take a hundred) *dollars*. She hid the money around the car. Did they not search it? It's a pretty Podunk police station. Do they give a fuck?

She has to summon all of her willpower to tamp down the screaming shit-fit that threatens to overwhelm her. She wants to ask about the money. But that means they'll find *out* about the money.

Shitfuck.

Instead, she bites her teeth and nods and smiles.

Along the way, she learns how several officers are going to die.

Officer Dorn Chihuly—he of a Tom Selleck 'stache—is going to die on the operating table in twenty years when they try to remove a mass from his liver. Officer Gale Paltrovich, a woman whose body has the shape of a tackle dummy under a bedsheet, is going to choke on a Brussels sprout when she's ninety-two. Officer Carlos Mendez is going to get blindsided by a drunk driver in five years, and suddenly she feels bad and tells him she's sorry, but he doesn't understand and tells her to shut up.

Arraignment came the morning before a judge who looked like he'd been out drinking the night before, a ragged, rumpled old gent. He told her that the charges were drunk driving, *and* driving without a license, *and* driving without insurance. Then it's all done lickety-split and they shuttle her back to her kennel, where now she once again stands next to the barf-caked Cuban.

Now she waits to find out what's next.

There comes a point when Officer Chihuly steps in, tells her it's time for her one phone call if she wants it. He says she won't need to post bail. Because this is her first offense—and a misdemeanor at that—they'll release her on her own recognizance.

But since the Red Rocket's been impounded and she doesn't have a license *or* any money . . .

Then he hands something to her through the chain link.

A couple of crumpled-up pieces of paper.

"These were in your personal effects," he says.

Three phone numbers.

Steve—er, Peter Lake.

Louis.

And Mother.

She smooshes her head against the chain-link. It mashes her nose. She gnaws on it like a beaver. "Thanks," she mumbles, and she expects to be led out to a dirty pay phone that smells like chewing tobacco and misanthropy, but instead he just opens the gate six inches and hands in a portable wireless phone. Jail, it turns out, is *far less* like the movies than she expected.

The cop retreats ten feet, sits on a nearby folding chair. Goddamnit.

She doesn't want to call any of these.

She's definitely not calling Peter. Which leaves her with two.

Calling either of those numbers means blacking out her shame sensors with the heel of a heavy boot—bashing them until they no longer recognize guilt as a speed bump to communication. That's hard for her. Pulling teeth hard. *Pulling out a wolf's teeth while wearing mittens* hard.

If she had the car, she could just ride on out of here. If she had the money, she'd call a cab. *Hello, Rock. Pleased to meet Hard Place.*

She growls.

Louis. Okay. If she calls Louis, she's going to have to tell him—what, exactly? *Hey, big fella. Been a while! Remember how I abandoned you and haven't called or written? I've really made some forward progress. Did I mention that I'm calling from jail?*

And as for Mother . . .

Same conversation really. Except she's been gone much, much longer. Been gone years. So much heinous fuckery to report on. So much disappointment. So much anger and resentment and abandonment. That relationship is a howling ghost in the void, so distant and strange it's barely even real anymore.

Call Louis.

Or call her mother.

She winces. Like she's trying to pass a kidney stone.

Fine. *Fine.*

She makes her choice.

She dials the phone.

PART THREE

VILLAGE BY THE SEA

INTERLUDE
NOW

"I wanna ask you some things," Grosky says, pulling out a Luna bar and unwrapping it with all the grace of a baboon ripping apart an orange.

"It's your dime," Miriam growls.

"Some things about your . . . gift."

"It isn't a gift."

"Okay. Unpack that a little."

"It isn't fun. It sucks. The end."

Vills smirks, and it's the smirk someone wears when they're trying to humor you but really they think you're an asshole in ugly shoes. "That was a real good story, Miss Black."

Grosky pulls off a little bit of the granola bar—something with chocolate chips in it, though Miriam catches a whiff of mint, too—and then he chucks it to her like he's feeding an animal at the zoo.

He begins to eat the rest.

She takes it, sniffs it, pops it in her mouth. "Luna bars are for chicks, you know," she says.

"What?" he says. "No, they're not."

"They are. They totally are. They're marketed to women. They probably have like . . . estrogen in them or something. They put fluoride in the water, and estrogen in the Luna bars. Look at the wrapper."

111

He pulls out the wrapper, peels it back. Starts to say, "I don't know what you're—" But then he stops. "Ah. Oh. Yeah, look at that. *Love the way your legs look*. Black text, pink circle. Huh." He shrugs, eats the rest of it.

"Your man-boobs are going to grow lush and full of milk," she says.

"You love to make out like I'm this fat piece of shit," Grosky says. "But I swear to you, I'm healthy. My wife thinks I'm a handsome guy. I'm strong. I'm tough."

"So tough you can eat Luna bars unironically."

"Oh, please, take a look at *you*," Grosky says, giving her a flip little gesture with his hand. "Too skinny. Too severe. You're all corners. Anybody who hugs you must come away bleeding."

"You have no idea."

"I don't, but maybe you'll tell me. Because despite your efforts to fritter away my time by having me answer your insults, I still got questions. About your *gift*."

"Fine, fuck, whatever."

He leans in. Close enough where she could grab him if she wanted. She could lurch up, claw his eyes out—of course, she'd be doing this with fingernails bitten down to the soft tips.

"You ever use the gift to . . . you know, predict the future?"

"You mean win the lottery and stuff."

"There you go. Or bet on a sports game before it happens."

"I'm never that lucky. I never see lottery numbers. Or sports scores. Maybe one day I will but, so far, nope."

"Still, you must've seen some pretty wild shit in the future. I mean, you see someone who's gonna take the permanent dirt nap in fifty years, you've probably gotten glimpses of . . . what, of flying cars and robots and, I dunno, some real *Star Trek* stuff."

"Not really. I've seen cars. They're still cars like you and I know them. They still drive on roads. Clothes are still clothes, and the styles just ape the looks from decades past. Mostly, I see hospital rooms. And hospital rooms are the same dreary, nause-ating places in the future that they are now. I don't know much about the future. I only know how people die."

"Okay, okay," he says. "That's a shame. I guess I'm at least happy we're still around in fifty years. Global warming doesn't kill us."

It kills some of us, she thinks but does not say.

"Another thing I don't understand. So, you find out some-one's gonna die, and you decide you want to stop it, then the only way is to get your hands bloody. Kill the killer."

She nods. "That's right."

"That's fucked up. You ever try . . . not doing it that way?"

"I don't follow."

"I mean, you ever try to intervene *without* killing anybody?"

"For years. Dozens of times. Maybe a hundred."

"And it never worked out."

"No, it did not." She doesn't like where he's going with this. Doesn't like him poking. She's tired of all this. She thinks to ask him what time it is again, because the time, *it matters*, but he keeps talking. Keeps pushing.

"Can't you just change the circumstances so the killing becomes impossible? Joey Titsonthebottom is gonna kill Mary-Sue Black-and-Blue, and he's gonna do it with a Beretta 9mm and so you take the Beretta 9mm and throw it in a furnace."

"Fate rewires itself to get the job done. There, Joey Tits goes and gets an identical weapon. Or he rescues that one from the furnace—a furnace with fires that went out soon as I tossed it in there because, you know, that's how fate wants it. I want to save Mary-Sue, Joey's gotta go."

"What if you broke his hands? Shattered 'em with a pipe."

"He'd find a way. He'd push past the pain."

"What if you . . . cut his hands off?"

She rolls her eyes. "Then he'd probably die and Mary-Sue would still get to go to the prom or become an astronaut or whatever it was her life had in store for her. And if he didn't die, he'd probably find a way to shoot her with his mouth, or his feet, or with a pair of fucking robot hands. Fate fights back, Agent Grosky. It twists like a snake in your grip, and the only thing you can do is cut its head off *before* it bites you. I've tried shit like this. You want an example? Fine. Here's an example—"

She tells him about Delilah Cooper.

"This is a couple years after I left home. I meet this girl. Teenager. Only a year younger than me at this point, and she's the perfect example of *has her whole life ahead of her*. About to graduate high school. About to go to Yale in the fall to study environmental law. Has one of those nice-guy boyfriends. Has a family that loves her and cherishes her and isn't actually a pack of serial rapists keeping women chained up in their basement. Her whole life is this little gift basket of raw potential. And I meet her and I hate her because already at that point I'd seen what the world was like, and I thought, *Here's a girl who's gonna get thrown into the metaphorical wood chipper soon as real life gets a look at her*—you know, she'll go to school, get hooked on Oxy, start dating one of her professors, and after she flunks out, her parents will disown her and then one day, she'll be *just like me*.

"So I wanted to see where she ended up. Like, in a gutter somewhere, track marks up her arm? In the trunk of someone's car? Or maybe just a sad end to a sad life in some gray fuzzy cubicle. So I reach out and touch her forearm a little—like I'm trying to console her on the life I've imagined for her—and then it hits me. She's dead *later that day*. She gets in her little sporty black Toyota whatever, she drives too fast, starts texting her nice little boyfriend, clips a guardrail, careens to the other side of the road, flips *that* guardrail, and boom. The car rolls down the embankment. Hits one tree. She's still alive, but then the car catches fire and she can't get out, she's trapped—smoke and heat and the buckle won't unbuckle and the fire, if you'll believe it, starts coming in through the air vents—like little fingers of flame tickling the air, melting the dashboard. She burns alive in the car. And it's horrible." She hears her own voice crack. *Keep it together, Miriam.* "Struggling and screaming. Hair burns. Skin burns. Eyeballs pop."

Grosky looks pale in the cheeks now.

Vills looks unfazed.

"So I think, I can stop this. I can change this so easy. She dies in her car, and we're sitting outside a froyo shop and right outside *is her car*, and I think, this couldn't be simpler. Remove the instrument of her demise and the demise cannot occur. So, she goes to the bathroom and *I* go outside to the car, and I take my knife and I squat down and I slash the tires. Or I try to at first—puncturing tires is harder than it looks, but I manage to hit the sidewall and they start hissing air. Then someone sees what I'm doing and my next and only move is to run like a rabbit. So I run."

"You're gonna tell me the girl still dies," Grosky says.

"Hey, spoilers, asshole. But yes. Yeah. In a few hours I walk by the spot where she was supposed to go off the road and lo and behold, cops, ambulances, a charred body pulled from a blackened Toyota."

"She got the tires fixed," he says. "Fix-A-Flat."

"Actually, no. But that probably would've worked. Took me a while to piece it together but what happened was, she calls her twin sister. *Identical* twin sister. And you know what that identical twin sister drives?"

"An identical car."

"Right as a rimjob, Agent Grosky. The sister—Lila—brings the car, then decides she's going to stay and have a frozen yogurt with some cute boy, and so Delilah takes her *sister's* car. And then . . . same scenario. Texting. Crashing. Burning alive."

Grosky breathes hard, nostrils flaring. Like he's picturing all of it. "I see why that might mess you up a little."

"The thing is, I don't know if it was supposed to be that way all along or if . . . fate stepped in and made a few crucial readjustments. Maybe I was always a part of it. Maybe what she was texting was a message to her sweet boyfriend about the crazy bitch who slashed her tires. Maybe I made it happen. That's the other trick, Agent Grosky. When I show up like that, I'm the pivot point. The fulcrum. It's like I'm meant to be there even when I don't want to be. Like I'm some kind of fucked-up version of Johnny Appleseed, traipsing across the country either causing people's deaths or stopping them—"

"And you can only stop them by causing other deaths."

"Yeah."

"You got quite the mission laid out for you," he says.

"I guess."

"You ever wonder . . ."

"Wonder what?"

"If it's real?"

"If my gift—" *Shit.* "My *curse* is real."

"Uh-huh."

"Shut up. I know it is."

Grosky shrugs. "Because maybe you're making it all up. Maybe your brain's just inventing things to patch up the holes in your mental wall. Trauma eats away at us, Miriam. PTSD for some people is like always being on the edge of the knife. But for others, it's like that knife keeps cutting apart all the things that keep us grounded in reality. And when we lose parts of ourselves, we fill in the gaps with things that seem sane and real but are so far off the books that . . . well, you start to have conversations like this one with a guy like me."

"It's all real," she says. Her hands ball into fists. *But what if he's right?* She banishes that thought to the wasteland.

"You know who might say that kind of thing?" Vills suddenly asks.

"You frizzy-haired twat," Miriam says, "don't you even say it."

"A serial killer. A serial killer who has invented a complex supernatural justification so she may continue killing and salving the guilt over the act. A serial killer who has come to believe that she is a preternatural agent caught in a cosmic battle between fate and free will and that only she can turn the tides away and loosen the sinister grip of destiny."

"That's very poetic," Miriam seethes. "And once upon a time, I really worried that maybe it was all in my head. But you'll see. The *both* of you will see. By the end of all this, when it all shakes out, you won't doubt me anymore."

"Sounds like a threat," Vills says.

"Maybe it is."

"All right, all right," Grosky barks, knocking on the table. "Let's move this along. So, Miriam. You had your one phone call to make. I gotta know: Who'd you call?"

TWENTY-TWO

RECOGNIZANCE

Late afternoon. Hot. Like being squeezed in a sweaty fist. Miriam stands outside the Monroe County detention center just northeast of Key West. It's the sunniest jail building she could imagine: bone white, banded with seafoam. The water's not far off, and the sound of the sea lapping at earth reaches her ears. A pelican snoozes on a nearby post, shovel beak pressed into damp feathered breast.

The late-day sun glints off a coming vehicle.

A turquoise Chevy Malibu circles the lot a few times like a dizzy shark, then loops around one last time and pulls up next to her.

Evelyn Black gets out of the car.

Her mother.

Jesus.

That woman has always been a dark little sparrow on stumpy legs—a human gallstone, a bitter apple seed, a black cancer shadow on a CT scan. And she's still that woman with her black hair (now shot through with streaks of gray) and bangs that look like someone cut them with a camping hatchet, with her dark sunglasses, with her pursed lips like she just dry-swallowed an aspirin and is trying to work it down her throat.

But she's also cloaked in the garb of Florida: beachy peach T-shirt with a palm tree on it, khaki shorts, a pair of flip-flops.

Flip-flops.

It's like watching the Devil paint his toenails pink.

The two of them stand there, an ocean of unsaid things separating them. Miriam grinds her teeth. Her mother starts to say something but then the words blacken and die, grapes to raisins.

Finally, Miriam says, "Hi, Mom."

Her mother nods. "Hello, Miriam." Her gaze drifts toward the detention building before she tilts her head toward the car. "Door's unlocked."

"Great."

"Good."

"Great."

TWENTY-THREE

ARE WE THERE YET?

The choice went like this:

Miriam heard Gabby's voice in her head—*they inflict them-selves on other people*—and she thought, *Yep, that's about right.* She's a curse. A weapon. A punishment. The ol' albatross around the neck. And so she asks herself: Who does she want to punish more? Who should catch the bite of the whip, the cut of the knife?

Louis, well . . . she's tired of hurting him. Last time she saw him, he was ready to give up and give in, ready to become a killer in service to her twisted worldview. But that isn't him. He isn't a killer. He's killed for her once already. And if she knows Louis, that death will cling to him like a hungry ghost. Always eating away at him.

She's done her damage to that poor bastard. She's chipped her name into his granite, and any more than that might bring his whole foundation crumbling down. Thinking about him makes her soul sink and soar, and it fills the hole between her heart and her stomach with equal parts *panic worms* and *love petals*, and the reality is, she cares too much about him to hurt him any more. (Even though right now her most burning urge is to pick up a phone and call him so she can cry and tell him all of this.)

Ah. But her mother.

Cruel, conservative Mother. Mother with her Bible. Mother

with her box of matches and her lighter fluid and the ring of stones where she burned any of the books and comics and CDs Miriam had snuck into the house. Mother with her prayer. With her judgment. With her guilt.

Always with the guilt.

And so the choice became easy then.

Mother had done damage to Miriam.

So maybe it was time Miriam did some damage in return.

Now she sits in the passenger seat of the Malibu, flitting a sneaky gaze toward this woman who purports to be her mother but who may in fact be an alien creature nesting in her mother's stolen skin.

Because things are *not* adding up.

The peach shirt. The khaki shorts. The flip-flops.

That's part of it.

Her mother is fastidious. Or was. Growing up, if Miriam tracked mud in the house, she'd be on her knees for hours, scrubbing stains while Mother looked on, sniffing dismissively and shaking her head, and when Miriam finally thought the stain was gone, her mother would descend upon the ghost of those footprints and continue her white-knuckled exorcism of filth.

Every piece of dirt, every dust mote, was an enemy combatant. She was like a mother monkey picking lice. Pick, pick, pick.

The car, though . . .

It's a mess.

An old coffee cup in the cup holder. Some mail piling up in the back seat—circulars and coupons and penny-pincher papers. A layer of fuzzy dust gathering in the space where the windshield meets the dash.

And then there's the ashtray.

It sits, pulled halfway out.

It's filled with the stubs of cigarettes.

She thinks, *This is someone else's car.*

It has to be. She can smell the smoke in the upholstery. It makes *her* want to smoke. But instead she just stares. At this imposter. This mystery woman clothed in her mother's flesh.

They're quiet. Both warily watch the other. Miriam watching when she thinks her mother isn't looking and her mother looking when she must think Miriam isn't watching. But they both see. They both know.

Finally—

"Do you need me to drop you somewhere?" Mother asks.

She blinks. "I need my car out of the impound, but impound's already closed for the day." *The car's broken anyway, but I could sure use that money.* "So. Ah. Eh, no. No."

"I can take you to my house."

"Okay. Yeah. Fine." Miriam clears her throat. "Where, ah, is your house again?"

"Delray Beach. It's a drive."

"A long drive?"

"Long enough. Four hours."

"Oh." Not like she has anywhere else to be. "Okay."

Another seven-mile span of silence.

"So, what have you been up to?" Mother asks. A slow-pitch softball of a question, a question to an acquaintance you haven't seen in six months, not a daughter who ran away from home almost a decade before.

Oh, you know. The usual. Seeing how people are going to die. Stealing from them. Or saving them by killing other people. I was a drifter and a thief. Now I'm a psychic assassin battling fate and—I'm sorry, am I boring you? It's so mundane, I know. But hey, it's a job and I'm pretty good at it, so you can finally be proud of me, Mommy Dearest.

Instead she says, "Traveling."

(Like asking John Wayne Gacy, "What have you been up to?" and he says, "Entertaining children.")

"Oh. That's nice."

"It's all right. And, uh, how about you?"

"I moved to Florida."

"I can see that."

"Yes, of course." Her pinched lips form a small, puckered smile that fades as fast as it arrived. "I did some work with Habitat for Humanity, but mostly I just . . . I just retired here. It's nice."

"It's hot."

"It's Florida."

"It's *winter*."

"Are you wearing sunscreen?"

"What? No. Like I feel like covering myself in glop and smelling like a piña colada all day? Ew."

"You should. You're fair-skinned. You'll burn."

"Ugh."

"And get some bug spray. A lot of mosquitoes down here and they've started to carry dengue fever—"

"Bug spray smells even worse than tanning lotion. It's like stripper perfume, except it also kills flying insects."

"Your hair is short."

"It is. It was long last year."

"Oh. And it's got some . . . color."

"That's because . . ." Miriam throws up her hands. "Because, I dunno, I fuckin' like color."

Miriam drops that f-bomb just to see her mother flinch—*two for flinching, you cranky prude*. But she doesn't flinch or wince or make any face at all. She just stares placidly ahead and finally says:

"You're different."

"I'm not. I'm the same girl I always was, just now on the outside for everyone to see." Her mother gives her a look. Not angry. Just sad.

"What are you doing in Florida?" her mother suddenly asks. Under her breath she adds, "Besides getting drunk and arrested."

Ah. Ah! *There it is*. There's the judgment. The gavel banging. The executioner's ax falling hard. Ha-ha! "I'm here for work, *Mother*."

I'm here because someone wants to send me a message. And I don't yet know what that message is.

"You don't look dressed for work."

"You don't look like my mother. Though you're damn sure starting to *sound* like her."

"We're both different, then. Fine."

"Fine."

"Fine."

And they drive the next three-and-a-half hours in silence.

THE FATHERLESS GIRL

"I want to go see his grave," Miriam says.

Her mother looks up from the kitchen table, where the woman is—as she is once a month—hunkering down and figuring out how she's going to pay the stack of bills gathering in front of her.

Mother says nothing; she just gives a quizzical, irritated stare.

"Some of the other girls at school make fun of me," Miriam says, as if in explanation.

"I can't imagine why."

"Because I don't have a father."

"I don't understand how you'd make fun of someone for not having a father, Miriam. Put it out of your mind."

And she goes back to her bills.

But Miriam persists.

"They say I'm an orphan girl. Or that Daddy left me because I was too ugly. Or that you don't even know who he is. Or that you're a lesbian—"

Here her mother perks up, this time with her brows knitted together. "Don't say that word to me. The Lord does not abide that lifestyle. Nor does he abide us acknowledging it." Mother sets the pen down. Crosses her arms. Her mood darkening to a black watercolor smear. "Children will find a way to make fun of you for anything and everything. Your name. Your clothes. The way you speak. The way you chew. It just means they feel weak and they're trying to make themselves feel better by passing that weakness along to you. As I said, put it out of your mind."

Miriam thinks, *That's easier said than done.*

This should be the end of the conversation.

Miriam is twelve years old. She knows how this goes. Her mother is already angry with her for the interruption.

She shouldn't push.

But in a rare moment of rebellion—

She pushes.

"I still want to see his grave," she says.

"Well, you can't," Mother says. Short. Clipped. Final.

But Miriam pushes again.

"You say he died from cancer."

"Yes. Bowel cancer. It was unpleasant."

"I should be able to see his grave, then. Why don't we go and put flowers on it? On what day did he die? We don't pray for him. I don't even know his name—"

Mother stands, uncoiling like a spring. "Leave it alone. He died. We were saddled with medical bills. He didn't take care of himself. Death comes for those who refuse the responsibilities given to them, Miriam."

"You're angry at him. You're angry at him for dying."

Her mother thrusts a short, persecuting finger in her face.

"Say one more word, daughter, and you will go to bed without dinner. I will lock you in your room. I will eat alone. You will pray for temperance to stay that tongue, and I will pray that God sees fit to grant it."

Miriam's mouth hangs open. Tears gather in the corners of her eyes. Should she say anything at all? Even an acknowledgment? A "yes, Mother"? A "God bless"?

All she does is nod.

Her mother nods in return.

Then the woman goes back to her bills. And Miriam goes upstairs to cry. A familiar routine.

TWENTY-FOUR

NO SLEEP FOR SINNERS

Miriam reclines on a bed with pineapple bedsheets and feels her blood throbbing in her ears, her skin hot and alive like everything is heat rash and poison ivy and biting invisible flies. All she can do is lie there and stare up into the vortex of a spinning bamboo ceiling fan and think about her mother and how angry that woman makes her.

It occurs to her suddenly that she didn't inflict herself on her mother so much as she inflicted her mother on herself.

Oops.

They didn't say squat for the rest of the trip. Miriam slept a little. Dreamed of dark waters. Dreamed of the river trying to drown her. Wren's face down there in the gloom. Caught in the mummified grip of Eleanor Caldecott. Eleanor's fish-nibbled lips opening up, a gassy flurry of bubbles speaking words lost to the water but still found inside Miriam's head as a haunting echo: *Fate has a path. You step in. You change lives by ending lives. Poisoned girls. Damaged girls. Ruined girls. Girls who will themselves become ruiners.* She screams through the stirred water, *Good things, truly good things, don't come without sacrifice!*

Then Miriam awoke and they were there at a little house in the middle of Delray Beach, a little beige two-bedroom sheltered by drooping, wet, grief-struck palms. Evening had fallen.

A couple of geriatric mummies walked an arthritic, trembling poodle nearby.

They went inside, everything in the house cast in a kind of Kmart version of British Colonial décor. The dark woods and the tan walls, the faux bamboo, the woven baskets for TV remotes and other sundries, the thatch mats instead of plush carpets. All of it with a faintly chintzy sheen, like a cheap-ass version of the rental place occupied by "Steve Max."

The house wasn't a mess, exactly.

But it wasn't clean, either.

The ceiling fans were dusty. The stovetop pocked with stains. Dishes sat in the sink.

And then: the dog.

A little moppy-boppy Yorkshire terrier who slid around on the wood floors like an unmoored bumper car, little claws scrabbling to find purchase—the dog circled her, yapping and growling and rolling around like he wasn't sure if he hated Miriam or loved Miriam. Then he ran off and peed in the corner and humped a couch pillow.

Good times.

Mother said nothing except "Your room is in here," and then she showed Miriam the way to the second bedroom.

Which is where she now reclines.

She turns and rolls over to try to get comfortable—

And stifles a scream.

Louis lies next to her.

His one ruined eye lies open like a hole dug in the ground. Rich, loamy earth falls from the socket. Shiny beetles wrestle in the dirt. He smiles. "Home sweet home."

"You scared the hell out of me."

"You seemed bored. Thought you could use some company."

"Please eat a sack of lightly toasted dicks."

He smiles. His teeth are yellow like nicotine-stained wallpaper.

"You have work to do."

Prickled flesh rises on the backs of her arms, her hands, her neck.

"I haven't heard you say that in a while." *Not since girls started dying at the Caldecott School.*

"This is important. Someone wants to hurt you."

"I bet you know who it is."

His one good eye winks.

"Tell me and spare me the drama. I'll go. I'll handle it."

"What fun would that be?"

"I decide what's work for me and what isn't. You're not my boss. You're not my father."

Louis sits up. More soil slides out of his eye socket, this time carrying segmented mealworms that ride the tide of earth and land on the pineapple sheets. "Maybe I am your father. You really don't know. He's dead, or so you've been told. Maybe I'm his ghost, come back to my baby girl to help instruct her in these troubled times."

"Maybe you are. Maybe I don't care."

"You should care," he says. "Because if you don't handle this soon, everything you know and love will be torn apart. You know what you need to do. Find out who was renting that house."

Her mother has a computer. Miriam saw it in the back corner of the living room on a little desk caddy-corner to the TV stand. The devil only knows if it's hooked up to the Internet—she has a very hard time imagining her mother using the Internet. Then again, nothing about this place resonates with that woman. It's like being in someone else's house.

Miriam's about to say something, but then—

Cigarette smoke.

The ghost of it.

Fresh smoke. Not old.

Drifting in from the cracked window.

A *neighbor*, she thinks, but then she hears her mother out

back, talking to the dog, whose name is apparently Rupert. "Go on, go get your cookie. Rupert. Cookie. *Rupert*. Cookie!"

Then the sound of lips on cigarette. Sucking. Exhaling.

Her mother is smoking.

"I have to see this," Miriam says. Her fingers ache to have a cigarette between them, too.

"Time is falling off the clock," the Trespasser says in Louis's voice. But when she turns to see him he's Ben, her high school boyfriend, the one who took her virginity, the one who put a baby in her, a baby that did not survive thanks to his wretched mother and her red snow shovel. And here Ben does as he did back then: He has a shotgun tilted toward his head, mouth open, barrel digging into the roof of his mouth—

A twitch of the finger—

Miriam's cry is lost in the sound of the blast—

CHOOM.

She squeezes her eyes shut—

And when she opens them again, the Trespasser has gone.

TWENTY-FIVE

SHARING IS CARING

"This is one for the record books," Miriam says, coming out through the patio door and stepping onto a small verandah. Mother sits on a small bench, a long cigarette in her small fingers. Rupert the Yorkie starts yapping.

"I don't know what you mean," Evelyn Black says, sucking on the cigarette like she's a mosquito hungry for blood. She blows a jet of smoke out toward the small eighth-of-an-acre yard with the tall privacy fence and the climbing pink flowers.

"I'm talking about you. Smoking a cigarette."

"I used to smoke before you were born."

"You're shitting me."

"Don't use that kind of language. Please."

"It doesn't sound the same if I say, *You're pooping me.*"

"So don't say it at all."

"I'm just saying," Miriam says, hovering next to the bench, "I have a very hard time picturing you smoking back then. Or ever. I have a hard time picturing it even though you're sitting *right there*, smoking like you can't get the cancer in you fast enough."

It's then she thinks, *Touch her. Find out how she's going to die.* Part of her aches to know. A kind of revenge. But it terrifies her, too. She's afraid to see what waits in the darkness, afraid to reach into the hole and see what poisonous thing lies in wait.

She hates this woman, or so she tells herself—but there's a real difference between thinking it and acting on it.

She hears the Trespasser's voice in the back of her mind—

She's your mommy. Poor widdle Miriam doesn't want to know how her mean old momsy-womsy meets the grave.

"I don't have cancer," her mother snaps.

"Give me one."

"What?"

"A cigarette." Miriam snaps her fingers. "C'mon."

"I'm not giving my daughter a cigarette. Especially a daughter who doesn't know how to say the word 'please.'" Inhale. Exhale. "I raised you better than that, young lady."

Did you really?

"Fine. *Please* give me a cigarette."

"No." That word, said so bitchily. Like it gives her pleasure.

"I will smoke my own, then," Miriam says, plucking the crumpled pack from her back pocket. "But just know that you're contravening Smoker's Code established in the late 1800s by Sir Smokey von Smokington and his wife, Esmerelda Cancerface, who *decreed* that smokers smoking together shall *share their cigarettes* like good little tobacco monkeys."

Miriam sparks her lighter. Lights the cigarette. Pleasure blooms in the back of her brain—a surge that shoulders past all the fear and frustration she's feeling in the bend of her belly.

"You're very crass and very strange," Mother says. "You're not the daughter I raised."

"And you're not the mother who raised me."

"You're rude."

"Crass, strange, rude. You know what else I am? Gone. This was a mistake. Obviously. Enjoy your cigarette."

She turns and throws open the patio door.

"Wait," her mother says.

She waits.

A pause. Then: "I'm sorry."

"Now I know you really are an alien."

"Don't be mean. Please." Miriam hears no anger hiding in those words. They're soft and sad. An honest plea.

All Miriam can say is "Okay."

"Will you sit with me?"

"Yeah." She feels smacked around. She doesn't know why. She doesn't like this woman. She doesn't even *know* this woman. Miriam tells herself she stays just because she's curious. As if she's reading a book and wants to find out how it all turns out.

She goes. She sits. They smoke.

The dog jumps up in Mother's lap. It licks a liver spot on the woman's arm as if it tastes like ice cream. *Slurp slurp slurp.* It's kind of gross and Miriam wants to say something, but in a rare moment of restraint, mentally duct-tapes her mouth shut.

Her mother finally speaks. "You've been gone a long time."

"I know."

"That boy . . ."

"Ben."

"I don't know what happened between you two—"

"You do too know. He—" She almost says *fucked me up against a tree* but is able to catch those words before they go flying out of her mouth. "We had sex, and I got pregnant."

"But he killed himself."

"He . . . did."

"I don't understand why."

"Because . . . because because because," and suddenly she growls and bites the knuckle on her thumb and thinks, *I don't want to sit here and talk about this.* It's much easier to be snarky and mean and stab her mother with sharp pointy words, but this is *real talk* and she's never done it with her mother, not ever, not that she can remember. But here it comes, the gusher, the geyser, the can't-stop-it-if-she-wanted-to. "Because he was a fucked-up kid who had a fucked-up family and because I was horrible to him and because we were both teenagers with crazy hormones and immature brains and romantic ideas about life and death and all the things that fall between them—" And now she's trying to stuff emotional gauze in the sucking chest wound she's feeling right now but oh no, the blood keeps coming. "It was my fault, I was a jerk, and that word doesn't even cover it. I wasn't a jerk, I was a monster, a monster in a way that only a spurned, bitter teenage girl can be, and next thing I know, he's dead and I'm pregnant. And then . . ." But the words die in her mouth because if she says more she'll cry and she can't cry in front of this woman. So instead she smokes. And stares. And trembles. "You know what happened then."

"I wanted to kill her," Evelyn says. "I wanted to kill that horrible woman."

Whoa.

Miriam sits up straight. "I . . . I didn't know you felt that way."

"I thought about it, you know." Mother stares up in the shuddering palm leaves above their heads. "I thought I would go over there and . . . beat her the way she beat you. I had a shovel in the shed out back I used for gardening. I'd take it to her house. I'd knock on the door. Then I'd beat her to death. Because she took something from you and that took something from me, too."

"Jesus," Miriam says, and then realizes that above all else, Mother will be stung by blasphemy, and she quickly mutters an apology, but her mother seems to have not heard. Evelyn Black just sits, the cigarette between the V of her fingers burning down. The ash growing long, like a witch's bent finger. "What, ah, happened to Ben's mother after I left?"

"She went to jail. They took your testimony in the hospital."

"I remember. Sort of." She also remembers the morphine.

"They let her out not long ago. Overcrowded prisons."

"Oh."

"I hope she takes a lesson from her son. I hope they still have that shotgun, and I hope she's willing to take her own life just as she took the life of the child inside you."

Miriam almost cries out at a small uterine twinge inside her—like a corkscrew poking through skin and twisting. She doesn't even know what to say to that. Hearing something like that come from her mother's lips . . .

"It is what it is," Mother says suddenly. "Onward and upward. Hold on one second. We need something."

She goes inside.

Miriam sits, heart pounding, gut churning. Lips dry. She hears the distant cry of a child somewhere, several houses over, and it damn near kills her.

Evelyn Black returns with two glasses.

And a bottle of crème de menthe.

The woman's drink of choice.

That's what Miriam stole from her mother that night when she went out into the woods and met Ben. They drank it. They coupled, clumsy and unaware, mouths tasting of too-sweet mint.

Her mother can't remember that. It would be too cruel. A vicious commemoration. When handed a glass, Miriam takes it and stares into it as Mother pours a few fingers of the liqueur—a draught of leprechaun blood, dark and impossibly green. Her mother clinks a glass against hers and Miriam takes a sip. Her mouth puckers at the too-sweet mint, and nausea flops around inside of her like a clubbed fish on the deck of a boat, but she keeps drinking it because she doesn't know when she'll ever get the chance to drink with her mother again.

And then her mother touches her.

Hand on her sleeve. Not skin. Just touching fabric.

Miriam wants for the fingers to dip—maybe by accident, or maybe Evelyn will reach for her daughter's hand as a matronly gesture. Then the death vision will come fast as lightning and Miriam will ride it to whatever sad end the woman meets—

But then Mother withdraws her hand.

"We look forward," her mother says. "We *move* forward. Eight years isn't that long. A blink of an eye. You have your whole future ahead of you. You can . . . meet a good man. You can . . . still have a child—"

"Mother—"

"Because I want grandchildren—"

"*Mom.*"

Her mother looks at her.

"They told me I can't have children."

Her mother stares. "What do you mean? That's not . . . I don't understand. They told me there was damage, but, but . . ."

"They told you. They *had* to have told you. Were you just not listening?"

"That was a hard time, Miriam, a very hard time—"

Miriam's teeth bite down on the rim of the glass. She really doesn't want to talk about this. She wants to throw up. Her tongue wets her lips and she holds the cigarette and glass between both hands, palms clasped around these two vices as if in prayer. "It died inside of me." *And with it, something else gained life.* "When they pulled it out there were . . . problems. Infection. I . . . I don't know, it was a long time ago. I came out of a fugue and the doctor was there and he held my hand and told me, he said I'd never have kids. The scarring . . . it was . . ." She unclasps her hands and holds them up as if in defense. "I'm not having children. Okay?"

"There's always adoption—"

"I don't . . . I can't."

"You have options."

"And I don't want them!" Miriam says. "I don't *want* children. At no point do I think I'd be a good mother. I'd be a fucking *horrible* mother. My luck, I'd have a daughter and I'd ruin that kid like a dress on prom night. She'd hate me. I'd hate her. The cycle continues."

"If only you hadn't . . ." Mother lets a sigh swallow the words, and she picks the dog back up and puts Rupert in her lap.

"If only what? Say it."

"If only you hadn't . . . been the way you were. To the boy."

"To Ben."

Her mother makes a small nod.

Miriam stands. "Goddamnit. *Goddamnit goddamnit shit.*" She takes the glass of crème de menthe and tosses it and the ice onto the lawn, then chucks the glass after it.

"Miriam!" Her mother looks on, horrified.

"I should've known we'd get here."

"You can't just . . . act like this."

"You blame me. You blame me for *all* of it."

"If you had been *nicer* to him—"

"Oh, that's some perfectly polished horseshit, isn't it? How *convenient* that you don't see yourself in this—you with a fucking bag over your head. Let me rip off that bag and tell you what I see: I see a shitty mother who kept me feeling bad about myself for the better part of my life."

Evelyn stands, eyes wet and shining, shaking a finger. "I did my best with you, Miriam, I tried to teach you values—"

"Values. Values! *Values?* Oh fuck you. You had me pray to a god that didn't seem to give a damn about any of us. You wouldn't tell me anything about my father. You burned up anything that gave me any pleasure at all. And you act all shocked that the first chance I got I'd run into the woods and fuck some dude and get knocked up. What values did you think you were teaching me? Because I learned ignorance. And anger. And self-hatred. And anger on top of anger! Don't act surprised that I have this *cyanide cocktail* in my heart. Like they say on that old dumb-ass drug commercial: *I learned it by watching you.*"

She flicks her cigarette into a nearby birdbath. *Sssss*.

Then she turns to leave.

Her mother stands. "Miriam, don't you walk away—"

"Let's just agree that I disappoint you and you disappoint me. Okay? And you want to know why I'm glad I can't have kids? Because I'm afraid I'd turn into *you* and my kid would turn into *me*. Good night."

The castle razed, the earth salted, she storms back inside.

A tempest shattering its teacup.

"You made her cry?" Grosky asks.

"I made her cry," Miriam says, batting the ashtray back and forth like a hockey puck between two goalies. She closes her eyes and tries to shut everything out. All the noise. All the memories. She tries to forget how this story ends but how can she? An impossible quest with too many monsters.

"I made my mother cry once," Grosky says. He's up and walking around now. Miriam has to admit: He has a lightness to his step, like he's less a fleshy boulder and more a roly-poly balloon. Like his bones are hollow. *Like he could move fast if he wanted to.* "I was seventeen years old and I thought I was tough shit and I called her the c-word. I don't even remember why. She wouldn't let me go out with the guys or some shit. So I called her that word. She slapped me across the face so hard I thought I'd have a hand-print at graduation, at my wedding, at my funeral even. Then after she slapped me she just broke down at the kitchen table. Sobbing."

"That's a heartwarming story. Isn't that a Norman Rockwell painting? *Chunky Son Calls Slap-Happy Mama a Cunt?* The 1950s were a more innocent time."

Grosky doesn't laugh this time. He just levels those pinch-skin eyes at her. Vills jumps in.

"So what'd you do?" the woman with the ink-scribble hair says to Miriam. "You made her cry, then what?"

Miriam says, "I went in, laid on the bed, and waited. Mother... stayed outside for what seemed like forever, crying. And not regular crying, but the gulping, hard-to-catch-your-breath, drowning-in-a-puddle-of-your-own-sorrow kind of crying. I thought about going back out there, but I'd kinda made my exit and why ruin the theater of it? I was still mad. So I waited her out. She went inside. Eventually found her way to bed. That's when I found my way to her computer."

"To find out who was renting out that house," Vills says.

Miriam nods.

"And?"

"It took me a little while to find the ad—but you don't find a lot of rental places on Torch Key. Eventually I found it and gave the people a call. Nice guy. Gay, maybe. I made up some hasty horseshit about how my boyfriend Peter Lake and I were filming a porno there—I said, *all very tasteful, mostly anal*, which I thought was funny. He did not, which was the point. He gets mad and I explain, yeah, ooh, I'm mad, too, because the director skipped town and he owes us a check—and I said, we should both call him, but I only have his cell and he's not answering that, so, hey, could you spare a porn star a moment of kindness and give me his other phone number? And he gave it to me."

"You like to lie," Grosky says.

"That's not true, actually. The truth is usually way more interesting."

"But you lie a lot."

"The truth is a hammer, but a lie is a screwdriver. A more elegant tool. Sometimes you just want to pick a lock, not break a window. Even though breaking a window is always more fun."

Vills pulls out another cigarette, lights it, hands it to Miriam. Then lights her own and plants her elbow on the table, leaning on her hand. "So, you called the number."

"I called the number."

"And?"

"It was a club. In South Beach. Nightclub called Atake."

Vills tenses up. There it is. "Atake."

"Uh-huh."

"So what did you do then?"

"What do you think I did? I went to Miami."

"And who did you meet at Atake?"

"C'mon, Catherine. I think you know."

Now Vills really tightens up—chin off her hand, elbow off the table—and for a half a second her eyes are hot pins trying to stick Miriam to the wall. But then Grosky tilts his head down to get his own look, and Vills fake-laughs it away. "No, I don't, and that's why I'm asking."

"*That* is where I met Tap-Tap."

PART FOUR

305 TILL I DIE

TWENTY-SIX

DAUGHTER OF THE YEAR

She steals her mother's car.

No way around it. While her mother's asleep Miriam sneaks into the kitchen and over to a pelican-shaped pegboard by the front door where the keys hang, and she snatches the Malibu's keys.

Rupert barks at her. *Roww roww roww yap yap yap.*

She takes a mop bucket from a nearby closet and sticks it over the dog. The mop bucket moves around like a Roomba. The dog's barks echo within, then eventually the dog quits and just sits under his dome.

Miriam leaves.

She stops, though. On the front stoop. That surprises her. She wills her feet to go, urging them forward like she's trying to make an old person drive faster. But her stubborn feet just stand where they are, and it's like they're nailed to the walkway with iron spikes of pure guilt.

Mother will be crushed. You're running away again.

I'll be back, she tells herself.

Bullshit.

I'll at least drop off her car.

How sweet. What a nice daughter you are.

Oh, don't get sarcastic with me.

You're the one arguing with yourself, princess.

She growls and goes back inside.

She takes five hundred bucks from her stash and drops it on the breakfast nook table. Then she leaves a note:

> *Renting your car for a few days.*
> *Here's some cash to cover it.*
> *See you on the other side.*
> *—m.*

Miriam hurries off before she feels any other emotion besides the burning itching pee-pee-dance desire to get as far away from this place as humanly fucking possible.

TWENTY-SEVEN

THE GOOD NEWS GOSPEL

Night. The sky a dark sea. Highways looping to other highways—arterial knots. Streetlights smear.

Miriam's tired as she heads toward Miami Beach. She stops at a gas station along the way, fuels up with some kind of cheap-shit teeth-rotting cappuccino that sprays out of the machine like foamy diarrhea.

It keeps her awake. It does its job. But it leaves her feeling like she's running along a serrated blade—like she's sawing herself in half with every step taken, every mile driven, like she's about to spill everything that's inside of her onto the seat of her mother's Malibu.

She passes by a fruit stand. Derelict. Half-collapsed on the side of the highway. She sees a crooked sandwich-board sign and she's certain that it reads HELLO, MIRIAM in drippy red paint, but when she blinks, all it says is ORANGES AND BANANAS.

"You believe in God?"

She jolts, startled. Almost swerves into the passing lane. A primer-colored pickup truck blasts its horn and zips past.

The dead thug kid sits in the passenger seat.

Stringy brains connect his shattered skull and matted hair to the back of the seat. He twirls a long black feather between his fingers like a rock star with a drumstick. When he shifts, his puffy winter jacket goes *vviiip vviiip*.

"Go away. I don't want the conversation."

"Maybe you *need* the conversation, though. Maybe it's time to ask yourself about God. The universe. The Devil. All that."

Wicked Polly . . . May the Devil take you without care.

"I don't worry about that stuff."

"You oughta. Maybe that stuff is worrying about you."

The highway circles down toward Miami. Over bridges. Ahead she sees what first seem like massive white buildings but then she realizes: They're cruise ships. Epic white whales parking themselves at the dock, one after the next, like skyscrapers turned on their sides.

"I don't give a shit about God," she says, "and here is where you flip it and say that *maybe God gives a shit about me*, but I really don't think He does and I'm not really even sure He exists. So." She shrugs. And goes to turn on the radio. A blast of samba music fills the car—*chaka boom chaka boom whistle whistle horns—*

But the thug kid turns it back off.

"Maybe you're on the side of the angels," he says. With the end of that feather he picks something red, raw, and meaty from between his teeth and flicks it against the window. *Spat.* "Maybe God gave us free will and you're on His side. Or maybe you're the rebel, yo. Maybe you're the Devil on our shoulder. Messing up God's great-ass plan."

"This metaphysical talk is gonna make me meta-fist-i-cal you in the mouth."

"Lemme put it a different way." He sucks air between his teeth. "Are you life? On the side of the living? Or are you death? A rogue reaper saving those who were supposed to die and killing those who were meant to live?"

"Yawn."

"I know this shit bothers you."

"How do you know that?"

"Because it bothers me."

"So you're admitting you're me."

"Maybe. Or maybe I'm admitting that I'm inside you. Or that you're me. Or that we share brains—especially since you blew mine out, *boom*."

"If you keep talking I'm going to steer this car toward a light pole and shear it in half and leave you in a mechanical heap by the side of the road."

He leans over toward her. She smells his breath. It smells of roadkill ripening in a wet ditch. He taps the end of the feather on the dashboard, *click click click*. "I'm just warning you, Miriam Black. Forces have been aligning against you for a while. You've been fucking with this Jenga tower for too long, and it ain't long before it all comes clickety-clackety falling down."

She scowls. "What forces? What the hell are you—"

A lemon-yellow Maserati cuts her off in traffic, honking its horn as it speeds away. She turns back to the passenger seat.

The Trespasser is gone.

TWENTY-EIGHT

DEATH ON THE DANCE FLOOR

This is Atake.

The bass is like a Tyrannosaur stomping through the chambers of her heart: The *doom doom doom* making her blood jump with every hit, up through her feet, vibrating through her bones, her teeth like a teacup rattling against its saucer—ceramic buzzing against ceramic.

It's hot. Wet. The throng of bodies moving in tandem forms a single beast made of flesh and sweat and lust. Girls in bikinis. In lingerie. Dudes in stylishly torn vented tank tops or no shirts at all. Women on raised platforms, pretend-fucking black glossy mannequins—Miriam thinks, this is probably their *job*, getting paid a hundred a night to come in here and sex up fake men so the real men below get stiff, get hungry, spend money on real drinks for real women with fake tits, and the cycle continues.

Fingers of light dance above their heads—this way, then that, then both ways. Steam rises from dancing skin, trapped in the beams.

Miriam moves along the edges. Less of a wallflower and more of a barracuda stalking the shadows of the reef.

She hates this place. She hates the music. She hates the people dancing *to* the music. Some buff dude in a hot pink Cuban fedora with his guayabera shirt open down to the tops of his pubes comes up and starts knocking his khaki-clad cock against her like a woodpecker looking for grubs in a tree—grinding on her so hard she's surprised she doesn't see sparks. Miriam throws a hard elbow backward—

Four years from now he's in a nightclub bathroom, every-thing black and white and silver and the mirror is cracked but he doesn't care because he's drunk and high and buzzing like an electrical current. Outside the music matches the vibration in his veins, the thumping in his chest—this guy just wants to keep the party going so he kneels by the sink and pops open a bindle of cakey white powder and shakes out a generous but zigzaggy rail of coke. He shoves the tip of a drinking straw up his nose and he dives into the powder; the high hits him like a shuddering wave of high-voltage awareness, but then it keeps going, keeps amping and ramping and suddenly it's like everything in his body is closed in a vice. His eyes roll, nose bleeds, mouth foams, over-dosed and overdone—

—and the guy in the pink fedora *oofs* and doubles over. He says something, yells it even, but the words are gobbled up by the hammering bass.

No time to get into a fight with some *cabrón*. She's trying to find answers, not fistfights, and she's not sure she'd win against that muscle-brain anyway, so she takes a sharp left into the throbbing throng of flesh.

She does it without thinking.

It's a mistake.

Bodies. Skin. All around her.

The first vision hits her—

She's with her three friends and they're older now by a few years and they're crossing at the corner by this old Art Deco–style café with the horizontal lines like the melting sun and the rounded lemon-yellow corners and they're laughing and they have hella shopping bags and those little pillow-puffs between their toes like they just got pedicures. Then the girl's flip-flop gets caught on the curb—it rips and she tumbles forward, her nose mashing flat against the street just as a pink fifties Cadillac vrooms up, tire on her head, popping it like a hairy pimple—

Miriam staggers—

Twenty-three years from now, guy standing in an empty house with polished floors, the ceiling fan on above his head. Only piece of furniture in the room is a chair, and the guy's got a big rope in the crook of his arm. He goes over, turns the fan off, already starts to feel the sweat crawling down the tip of his crooked goblin-dick of a nose and with the toes of his bare foot he pushes the chair beneath the fan (the legs of the chair make a comically loud groan on the polished wood) and he unfurls the noose end of the rope and that goes around his neck. The rest of the rope he winds around the base of the fan. Then he pins a note to his T-shirt that says I LOVE YOU, JENNY *and beneath it* FUCK YOU, JENNY *and before he can even knock the chair out the damn thing breaks beneath him CRACK and suddenly it's grrrk kkkk thhhhsssss beet-red eyes bulge tongue out head bulging purple like a well-fed tick black nowhere the notes fall from his chest and slip down through a heating register and he paws at the air trying to get them back but he's seeing stars seeing nothing—*

Miriam cries out, but her voice is lost. Backpedal, turn. More skin—*doom doom doom—*

—he won't remember anything because of the anesthesia, but the doctor nicks an artery, blood sprays, they can't clamp it, a red mist ends it all—

Sweat drips in her eyes. She pulls her arms in, *no more, please, no more,* but she's in the thick of it, a prison of skin, emerald lights and a sudden mist of water from pipes above, *pssshhh.* Someone shoves her—

—a piece of bagel caught in the throat—

Someone grabs her hand—

—the sharp stick of a hornet's sting—a big fucker, too—big as a thumb, big enough to carry ordnance to bomb a Smurf village. Then comes the swelling, the head-woozy, the thick-feeling, the throat-closing. Anaphylactic shock shakes the guy like a baby, and the seizure—

Miriam shuts her eyes like that matters. She opens them and spies a bar through spears of light rising through the mist but then the crowd closes in on her again—

—the truck hits her car doing 120 mph—

Holds her breath, starts moving through the jostling bodies—

*—*POP POP POP *gunshots in the night, hands grab the purse, footsteps recede, dead before she hits the ground—*

She wants to throw up. The sound of rustling wings. A glimpse of a big black bird flying overhead through the strobing lights—

—the fireworks go off in her hand one after the other and she burns alive in fires that go from red to green, the whistling shrieking in her ears as everyone screams, oh what an Independence Day this is—

*—he touches the wire coming out of the drywall and *BZZT *full-tilt boogie—*

—the house fire cooks him like a microwaved hot dog—

—she drowns in her own lung fluids—

—he chokes on his own puke—

—the little plane hits the ground and practically evaporates—

—heart attack—

—dog attack—

—blood—

—no—

She extracts herself from the dance floor like a splinter. She feels drunk, and not in the good way. Her guts queasy and greasy like they're slipping around on a blood-slick floor.

The bar. Behind spires of red light. Hovering in the mist.

It would be an oasis, but it's pressed with throngs of people, another wall of flesh. Each touches a doorway into yet another demise: another gateway to Hell. She can't do that again. She feels like a raw nerve in a cracked tooth.

Instead, she circumnavigates all the way to the far end of the bar. Where nobody stands. It's the bartender's blind spot, but whatever. Right now she doesn't even want a drink so much as she just wants a place to stop, to think, to breathe. *To live,* a little voice says.

This is worthless. A place cram-packed with cock-rockers and clam-jammers lost to the reverie of sex, sound, booze, skin. It's then she smells herself: She stinks of beer. Someone must have spilled it on her out there. Awesome. She entertains a moment when she sets the place on fire and quietly locks the doors behind her. *Firestarter*-style. Or maybe she could go all Carrie on them. Two books she remembers her mother burning way back then and it's only now she grasps the irony there.

Whatever. Nothing to be learned here tonight. She'll come back tomorrow. When she can actually ask a question or three.

She's about to turn and flatten herself against the far wall and skulk out of here like a darting skink, but then the bartender—a mocha-skinned square-jaw in a too-tight deep-vee—says, "Oye, whatchoo drinking, girl?"

She hates when people call her girl.

But she likes when people give her drinks.

What to do, what to do.

She holds up a finger. "Shot of vodka. Tito's."

He spins, pivots, she sees the glint of light on the vodka bottle. He turns back around and next thing she knows there's a highball glass sitting there with a lime on the edge and bubbles, and he says, "Vodka tonic," before hurrying down to the other end of the bar.

She didn't order a vodka tonic—you add tonic, you might as

well add water, and if you add water you might as well throw the drink on the ground. Still, she sees the bubbles tickling the side of the glass and she thinks it might be good to settle her stomach.

So she grabs it. Toasts the air.

Slams it back.

The bubbles burn the back of her throat.

She drops the glass back onto the bar, *kathunk*.

Then she gets the fuck out of there.

Outside, the air is still hot, but there's a breeze and it presses her soaking wet shirt to her chest and she suddenly feels woefully out of place. Everything here is glitzy, glammy, neon-smeared. She sees women with fake, round kickball-tits shoved into short-short dresses that show off the bottoms of their bottoms. Muscle-head dudes who could snap her in half like a candy cane. Then the gay guys—guys who radiate fabulosity, stomping around on big tall heels, swishing around in mesh shirts and sunglasses shaped like hearts, coochie-cooing the air with werewolf finger-nails. Miriam doesn't belong here. (*Doesn't belong anywhere.*) She's a black buzzard in the land of pretty, pretty peacocks. A dirty fingerprint on a colorful dress.

She thinks, *I'll need a hotel for the night*, and she figures she'll cut back to the car through the alley behind the club. Already she's feeling the vodka tonic, which surprises her—but maybe it shouldn't. She's tired as hell. Hasn't eaten a damn thing all day. Her body is a romper room for whatever booze she sticks in it.

She staggers into the alley. Fishes in her pocket for a cigarette, but her fingers don't seem to want to pull out the pack. They finally manage and the pack drops into a puddle, *sploosh*, and she tries to curse, but it just comes out a mushy utterance—the emphasis of vulgarity but without the specificity.

Miriam looks up.

And it hits her.

She's been here before.

Which is entirely impossible. Because she's never been to Miami.

And yet—

The alley is awash in long shadows and the fringe glow of neon from the mouth of the alley, metal steps leading to the door to the back, the dull thump of music behind it, mirrored shades, curved blade—

Oh, God.

She has been here.

In a vision.

Ingersoll—

She tries to turn, but her knee gives out. Her head feels like cotton soaked in paint, goopy and thick, all the colors starting to run together.

I've been drugged.

Suddenly, a gloved hand closes over her mouth. She tries to scream, but her cry is muffled. A boot kicks her leg out from under her and she falls—

Another gloved hand over her eyes.

Someone's got her ankles.

Her body, lifted up.

The sound of duct tape ripping off the roll.

Someone laughs.

Then they begin to move her.

TWENTY-NINE

MISTER MIDNIGHT AND THE GHOST OF HAIRLESS FUCKER

Words reach her like murmurs through water:

"... this is the bitch? I don't believe it ..."

"... cut her now? I could get the saw ..."

"... want her to *see*, want her to be *awake* ..."

The kick-thump of booming bass somewhere beneath her.

"... how'd this little squirrel steal our drugs?"

"... she looks like a drowned rat ..."

"... hey-hey, hand me that pipe ..."

Click, hiss. Fire. Smoke. Acrid.

"Do it."

Tape is ripped off her eyes.

Then her mouth.

It takes a little skin with it. Blood trickles over her raw flesh.

Light bleeds in at the edges, washes over everything.

She's on her back. Hands belted together. One leg is tucked in and under her. The other leg's extended out, her boot held in the grip of a man she doesn't recognize: a pouty Ecuadorian with gold teeth and a pale tongue sliding over the metal.

She's flanked by two other men.

And she recognizes them both.

Both look familiar, she knows that much. It takes her a second. Her brain's a heap of meat mush and thinking takes effort, like trying to blow a raisin through a drinking straw. The one is a scabby, crater-cheeked tweaker with a tangle of unwashed hair. The other is a big motherfucker. Black like motor oil. Got a little red vest with gold buttons hanging over his ox-yoke shoulders. Bare, sweat-slicked chest sticking out. Shiny chains nesting in afro-puffs of chest hair.

That's when it hits her.

They're from the vision. Ingersoll's death. Hairless fucker. The one who came after her with his killers, Harriet and Frankie. The drug lord who cut off Ashley's foot. The one who took Louis's eye.

The first man she killed.

When she first met Ingersoll she got the measure of him, saw a vision of his demise. Ingersoll came walking out of a club, down a set of metal steps, and then two men emerged and attacked him. Mister Midnight—the big black sonofabitch—at the front with a curved head-lopper blade. And behind Ingersoll, the tweaker—Daddy Long-Legs—with a little pistol.

Ingersoll took them both out. Bit into Mister Midnight like he was an apple. Cleaved the tweaker's head in half just as the addict shot Ingersoll right between the eyes, *bang*.

That's what *would have* happened.

But then Miriam intervened—the rock that breaks the river, the road nobody was supposed to travel. Fate-breaker. Resurrectionist.

She starts laughing at the same time she's almost crying because what a *fantastic fucking irony* this is. She took out Ingersoll and saved the lives of these two men and now the same two men have her strapped to a table, ready to do whatever it is they want to her.

Fate has swung back around and hit her right in the face.

The ghost of Hairless Fucker must be pleased as a fuzzless peach.

"I don't know who you are—" Miriam starts to say, her voice

fast and throaty, but Mister Midnight presses a tree-trunk finger to his lips.

"Shhh," he says. "You are Miriam Black, yes?"

She hears that Haitian patois in his voice.

She winces and nods. "And you are?"

"They call me Tap-Tap."

"That's a dumb name."

He raises a hand and brings it down toward her face—and just before the palm connects he slows it down and gives her two little pats. "Tap, tap. Hah. See what I did there? That's not why they call me that, though. No. Back in Haiti I drive a *camion-nette*, a bus, a taxi-bus, big colorful one. Blue skull on the front. Flowers painted on the side. Lots of people hanging off it. Good way to make a little money as I deliver drugs to those who can afford them."

"That's a very nice story," she says, trying to hide her fear behind the bluster. "I look forward to the Lifetime movie."

"You think you so funny. Can I tell you another story?"

Christ, is everybody a storyteller?

He begins before she offers permission. "My mother, back in Haiti, used to come out every morning onto a very small balcony. Small enough just for her. Too small for me, even now. She would stand there with a cup of coffee and *pain haïtien* and she would dunk the bread into the black coffee. It was a small moment of pleasure, you see? My mother, she was a . . . how you say it? Consort. Consort for a rich man. A drug lord. Haitian-American man name of Dumont Detant. Man I work for when I become a teenager, driving—ah! You guess it. The tap-tap.

"So, she would go there every morning, eat bread, drink coffee. She would do this before he woke up and wanted what-ever it was he wanted from her—her pussy, her mouth, to hit her, to make her clean the floors or make the bed. This moment, very important to her, very *precious*. But one day a gull show up. A gull—a bird. Big, gray thing. Patchy feathers, almost like it's got a sickness." He pronounces it *seek-knees*. "The gull show up and swoop down and steal her bread."

He puts his massive hands on Miriam's shoulders. Gently presses down—a casual reminder that he doesn't have to expend much effort to hold her to this spot.

"This go on again and again. Gull show up. Steal her bread. She try to hide. Try to shield the bread. The bird waits till she brings it out to dip it—still gets the bread! Few times bird doesn't get the bread, bird *shits in her coffee*. Worst of all, the gull now has friends. Other gulls come, think my mother is weak. Think the sight of her means a free meal.

"Now, you say the same thing I say, I say, *Maman*, go inside! Eat the bread inside and *then* go to the balcony. But my mother, she say no. She has this one thing, and she wants to keep it. So what does she do?

"One day she set the coffee on the ground and take the warm bread and break it. Fan the smell upward with her hand. She keep the bread held low. Down by her waist. The bird show up to steal his bread with his ugly rat-bird friends and she *snatch* him out of the air!" He makes a fast swoop of his hand and a fist. "And now she got him. And in front of the other gulls, she break the bird like she break the bread. She snap its wings one after the next. Then she take its feet in her fist and she gives a twist—they pop right off the bird, her hand wet with its blood. Last thing she do? As the bird is squirming, going *flop flop flop*, she take its head to the balcony edge. She place the beak on the iron railing. Then she slam her hand down on it like she trying to open a bottle of Prestige beer. The beak? Shattered."

"You seem to think—"

"Ah ah ah." He silences her. "That is how you teach a lesson to those who steal from you, Miss Black. It show them a lesson.

And it show the other thieves what will happen to them if they try. The gull in her hand did not die. Not then. She did not kill it. The bird, he roll around on the balcony until soon he push his way through the iron bars and fall to the ground below. *Then* he died. Mister Gull kill himself. Kill himself from the shame of what had been done to him."

"I didn't steal anything from you—"

"You stole our drugs."

"I didn't—I didn't! The thing with the meth wasn't me—"

"Hey, Jay-Jay," Tap-Tap says to the one she thinks of as Daddy Long-Legs. The white trash tweaker. "She says meth? Why we talk about meth?"

Jay-Jay just laughs a nervous laugh.

Miriam tries to say something else but—

Tap-Tap grabs her face with his hand and squeezes so hard she thinks her jaw might pop out of its socket. "Meth? This is not meth you stole! You stole cocaine. You kill *three* of my men. You destroy my submersible!"

What. The.

Her mind starts doing panicked acrobatics even as Tap-Tap gives a nod and an impatient gesture at the man standing by her leg, a man she almost forgot about. Goldie suddenly pulls from beneath the table a rusty hacksaw. Miriam squirms, starts to cry out as the man leans hard on her leg and—

Two weeks from now leaning over the front of a bone-white Cadillac, a Ruger Mini-14 resting on the hood, taking shots fast as his finger can pull the trigger, pop-pop-pop, and someone, a big someone, hides behind a dune and offers return fire from a boxy pistol. Goldie's finger pulls one last time and this time the gun just goes click and he makes this face of confusion like he thought maybe he had infinite magical video-game bullets and then just as he starts fumbling for more ammo the man behind the dunes fires again and a round catches Goldie right

*between the teeth. Gold veneers flip out of his mouth in a pin-
wheel of blood as his brains eject—*

—Goldie rests the teeth of the saw against the top of her leg.
The promise of pain bites into her shin bone.

Cutting off legs.

That was Ingersoll's trick.

"My old boss," Tap-Tap says, "he like to cut off body parts.
Just like *Maman* break apart that gull. Mister Ingersoll would say,
nature red in tooth and claw. Then he cut some poor madda-
fucka's leg or arm or even his *dick* off. I be honest with you, I let
that practice go. Almost like I forgot how much fun it can be!
But then we get this tip. This man call me and say, *'Oye, Tap-
Tap, bro, I know who took your coke. I know who fucked up your
submarine and kill those three Columbian boys.'* And he tell me
your name and where you'll be and when you'll walk into my
club, and then he say, you know what he say? He say, *'With her
you gotta do it old-school, Tap-Tap. You cut her leg off. Teach
her a lesson about what it means to go messing with things she
should not be messing with.'"*

It's then her brain stops with the acrobatics.

Because oh, shit.

All the tumblers of this lock fall into place and the door suddenly opens and she figures out just who it is who's doing this
to her.

It's Ashley Gaynes.

He's a liar. A con man. Last time they met, that suave, cocky
prick drew her in and next thing she knew he was telling her
about a suitcase full of meth he stole. Stole from a man named
Ingersoll and his two killers, Harriet and Frankie. An act that
lost him his leg to Ingersoll's hacksaw in the back of an SUV. She
knew he wasn't dead. But she thought he was ruined, beaten,
that she'd never see him again.

This is revenge.

Stealing drugs.

Blaming it on her.

Having *her* leg cut off in parallel.

. . . messing with things she should not be messing with . . .

She suddenly stammers, "Somebody's fucking with you, Tap-Tap, playing you for a fool—"

But he obviously doesn't like that answer and he gives a hard nod to the man at her feet and she tries to pull her leg out—

The man yanks the saw back.

The teeth chew into her leg. Bite into her shin bone.

Just one pull. Then he stops.

She screams. Blood pools beneath her. Soaks down to her sock.

The plea falls out of her, words strung together with nary a nanosecond between them. *"I know who did it I know who did Jesus shit Christ fuck I know who did it."*

Tap-Tap sticks out his lower jaw like he's a boar showing off his tusks. Then he gives a slight shake of the head to Goldie at her feet and suddenly the pressure from the saw teeth in the wound is gone.

She can't help it. She gasps. The retreat from immediate pain is a surprising kind of—not pleasure, exactly, but *relief.*

Tap-Tap gets his face close to hers.

She smells garlic and cigar smoke.

"You—you—you—" she stammers, admonishing herself to *get it together, you stuttering idiot, you're bigger than this, better, tougher, don't give him the satisfaction of scaring you,* but it's hard not being scared when someone's about to take your leg as a trophy. "You don't really think I could pull off hijacking your submarine and stealing your drugs." *Play off his chauvinism.* "I'm just a little girl. I barely eat. I got bird bones and broken wings. I'm not even a gull. I'm just a dark little sparrow."

"Then *who*?"

"His name's Ashley. Ashley Gaynes. He's stolen from your . . . people before. Ingersoll cut off *his* leg. He's trying to give me to you so he can get away clean. And he wants to punish me. He wants me to hurt the same way that Hairless F—" *Whoa, do you ever watch your mouth?* "The same way Ingersoll hurt him. I . . . I can confirm it, you just, you just call a man who works for you, his name's Frankie. Gallo, I think. Frankie Gallo."

FRANKIE

Running through snow ain't really running at all, Frankie thinks as he charges through pine trees stuck up through the white expanse like black spear tips. It's more like jogging. Jogging with cement on the bottom of your boots and shit inside of 'em.

His feet punch through the crust of snow. Already his legs are on fire from pistoning through the frozen wasteland up here in the goddamn Rocky Mountains, chasing after Dicky Morningdove, a half-Choctaw squirrel-fucker who stole a bunch of government bonds from Wayne Prevette, the man currently employing Frankie to protect his illegal logging operation.

Frankie thinks, *Jesus fuck, how far I've fallen.*

He misses the good old days. Horrible as they were.

He misses Harriet. Horrible as she was.

Ingersoll, well, that creepy human mannequin could go fuck a duck. Cutting people up. Saving their bones so he could try—and fail—to see the future. Freaky fuck deserved what he got.

Still. Working for Ingersoll was better than working out here. In the middle of God's Frozen Nowhere. Chasing Dicky Morningdove: that loser with his lazy eye and his love of pills and those stacks of 1970s biker magazines showing off those 1970s women with their 1970s bushes. Frankie saw a stack of those old magazines while trying to figure out where Dicky got off to, and to him every chick inside those pages looked like she had a

Diana Ross afro (or worse, a Donald Trump toupee) between her legs.

Ahead, Dicky is churning through the snow, big bow-kneed legs pumping like he's a lizard running across a hot parking lot.

Frankie thinks, *Just shoot him*.

He's got a pistol. A Walther, slung under his arm.

But if he shoots, he might kill the little bastard. And then they'll never find Wayne's money.

Instead, Frankie feels at his hip. Got a hatchet hanging there. Up until now he didn't know what the hell he'd ever do with a hatchet—Wayne just said, "You come up here, you work for me, you carry a hatchet, Gallo. Ain't no *what* or *who* or *why* about it." Now, though, Frankie's thinking maybe Wayne had a point. Because here he is grabbing the hatchet off its loop and cocking his arm back—

He gives it a hard throw.

It whirls through open space. The faint whistle of cold air cut. And the wooden handle clocks Dicky in the back of the skull. *Thwack*.

It's a clumsy hit. Wildly imperfect. Just the same, it causes Dicky to stumble—and one leg cuts in front of the other like a rude shopper, and next thing Frankie knows, Dicky's pitching face-forward into the snow.

Of course, he meant to hit the sonofabitch with the hatchet's *blade*, but he guesses that's why they say *the end justifies the means*.

Frankie stomps over as Dicky scrabbles to stand.

Panting, he plants his boot on Dicky's left shoulder, draws his gun, and fires a shot through Morningdove's left hand.

White snow, painted red.

The gunshot echoes up the mountain and down.

A murder of crows takes off from nearby pines.

Dicky gulps air and sobs.

Frankie sniffs, pulls back his hood, runs his hands through his greasy hair. "I hate you, Morningdove. I don't wanna be doing this. Jesus. You stole, what, two grand from Prevette? Worth it? Worth the loss of your hand? Tell you something, Dicky, that other hand is lookin' mighty good, too. I took your left this time, but next time I'll shoot the hand you use—"

"I'm a lefty!" Dicky howls.

Frankie rolls his eyes. "Fuck, whatever. Just tell me where you stashed the cash and I won't hafta—"

His cell rings.

One thing he can say being up here in the mountains. Great cell reception. Shitty radio. But clear signal on his phone.

He looks at the display.

Miami.

Huh.

He answers it. "I'm fuckin' busy. I don't work for you anymore. This better be good."

"I got someone here says she knows you." He recognizes the twangy voice. Tap-Tap's man. His second. What the fuck's that tweaker's name? Jay-Jay. Stands for John-Jacob or something.

"Like I said, get to it. Fuckin' busy."

"Her name is Miriam."

Frankie stiffens. Panic pulls his puppet strings. "What?"

"Yeah, yeah, Miriam Black. Says you can vouch for her."

Vouch? "What's she sayin'?"

"She's saying—well, some drama around here about some coke went missing, a whole lotta coke, and she's saying it's not her, she got set up, saying you can tell us what's what. She steal drugs before from Ingersoll? Said she's being screwed by some other girl named Ashley—"

"Ashley ain't a girl. It's a guy," Frankie says.

"So you know what she's talking about?"

And here Frankie thinks, *It's decision time.*

Miriam's the one who put a bullet through Ingersoll's head, and by his mileage that's a-okay. That fuckin' guy was a monster. Happy to see him go.

But Harriet.

She killed Harriet, too.

Shot her through a bathroom door.

Harriet was a monster, just like Ingersoll. She worshipped the boss. Woulda cut her own feet open and walked across a swimming pool full of lemon juice for Ingersoll. She wanted to *be* him. And yet, she and Frankie worked together. Not just as partners, but like two strange-shaped puzzle pieces that look nothing alike but somehow *fit* perfectly, one next to the other, on every job.

He misses Harriet.

Here, Dicky at his feet thinks he sees a chance and starts to roll over and try to get his feet under him.

Frankie sighs and puts a bullet right in Dicky's ass. The man howls and screams and thrashes around, blood squirting out of his butt cheek like he's one of them water wiggle toys from way back when. Some of it splashes on Frankie's jeans, and the screams only get louder and louder—

Frankie presses the phone to his chest and puts another round through the back of Dicky's head. The half-Choctaw thief slumps forward into a pile of his own brains.

Well, shit. Now he's going to have a hard time finding Wayne's money. But, then again, fuck Wayne Prevette.

Frankie raises the phone.

"I know her," he says, and he's honestly about to tell Jay-Jay to do whatever he wants to her because she's a Sunday paper full of bad news, but then he remembers that last time he saw her. There at the base of that lighthouse. Ingersoll upstairs, about to cut out the trucker's eyeballs. Miriam showed up. Put a gun to his head. Told him he's gonna be a grandfather someday. Asked him if he liked this life. He said no. And then, like that, she let him go.

Suddenly he says to Jay-Jay, "She's not the one. Isn't her sticking it to you. She's right. If that Ashley asshole is still alive—we cut off his foot—then it's him. She didn't take your drugs."

Then he hangs up.

He looks down at the body in the snow. Steam rising from blood and brains. He says to the corpse, "I really do need to get out of this life."

And then he pockets the gun, grabs his hatchet, and heads back down the mountain.

THIRTY

A LOW, LOW OFFER

Jay-Jay hangs up the phone and gives a shrug and a nod.

Tap-Tap makes a look like he's disappointed, a kid whose parents won't take him to the circus, and next thing Miriam knows he's unbelting her hands and Goldie is letting go of her leg.

The big Haitian picks her up and sets her down on the floor.

Her leg almost kicks out from under her. The cut across the shin isn't a life-ender, but it's bleeding like a throat-slit pig. Pain radiates out from the wound: ripples of bone-scraped misery. The bass from the club below doesn't help; she can feel every glitchy dubstep *wah-wah-wah-boom* in the wound like a fisting heartbeat.

Tap-Tap tosses her a rag from a cobwebby pool table across the room.

"Clean yourself," he says. "You bleed too much."

She bites back any snark that threatens the sting of its lash, and takes the dusty rag and presses it against her leg.

Then Tap-Tap strides over. Bowling ball fists on his broad hips. "This is how it work now. You get to keep your leg. You get to keep your *life*. But that is not a gift. It is a deal I'm making. A . . . how you say? A *bargain*. You will bring me this man with the girl's name—the one who stole them. If you do not bring him to me, I will come back to you and I will take more than your leg. I will cut your tits. I will stuff you full of snakes and worms. I will turn your head into a candle. Because I have been dishonored. Because the universe likes to be balanced."

She swallows a hard knot. "Lemme guess. A voodoo thing?"

"Bah." He waves her off. "Ingersoll believed in ghosts and pigeon guts. I don't truck with that shit. But I believe in vengeance. I believe that if you take from me I will take ten times from you. Debts will be paid and this debt is now on you, Miss Black."

He offers her a hand.

What else is she going to do?

She shakes it.

He grinds her knuckles together like he's trying to make bone flour.

No death vision finds her. Not for him. Not for Daddy Long-Legs over there—Jay-Jay. She's already seen how both were going to die, and she saved them from that fate.

Now she just has to save herself.

And that means finding Ashley Gaynes.

THIRTY-ONE

GULL HEART

Miriam tries not to panic as she drives, but her emotions are like that poor gull: wings broken, legs twisted from the body, beak snapped. Flopping around and pumping blood.

Before her is the world: the highway, the night, the lights above the rain-slick streets of Miami, and all of it seems hopelessly infinite—earth and road and ocean and sky in every goddamn direction, long shadows stretching across countless miles—and Ashley Gaynes could be hiding in any bolt-hole or doorway along the way. Finding him will be like looking for a clean heroin needle in a pit full of dirty ones.

She has no idea what direction to point the car.

She finds her foot tamping down on the accelerator.

Her speed ticks upward: 55, 65, 75 . . .

She's pissed. Him. *Him.* Ashley. That asshole. They screwed and she *got* screwed. Getting tangled up with him was like getting snared in a ring of thorns. Hard to get out of, and when you do, you bleed.

Now he's gravitating toward her once more.

He's the one who kills that asshole at the Torch Key house.

He's the one screwing with her.

He knew she'd be at that club. How? *How?*

Was he watching her?

He had to be.

Was he watching her down in the Keys, too?

Could be, rabbit, could be. And that tracks, doesn't it? If he's here messing around with Tap-Tap's drug biz, he's doing it locally. They didn't send a cocaine submarine to Canada. It would have been here. Somewhere along the coast.

Maybe even down in the Keys.

That means he's here. In Florida.

Right now.

Good. That helps. It doesn't fix the problem, doesn't deliver him in a bolt of lightning into her passenger seat, but it narrows down her choices from the Entire Known World And Maybe The Moon to Somewhere In Florida. He's here somewhere. Laughing at her.

75 . . . 85 . . . 95 . . .

He wants to punish her.

She gets that now. He blames her. Doesn't he? He thought they had something. Last time they were together, he said, *You love me.* She told him he was dreaming. He said she wanted him. *Needed* him. And then Hairless Fucker and his two thugs showed up and that was that. They took them. Cut his foot off. Probably would have cut more off, too, but Miriam lashed out, started kicking—Ashley tumbled out the door, leaving his foot behind.

She probably *saved his life.*

But that's not how he sees it, is it?

He thinks she took something from him.

And now he wants to return the favor.

How far would he go?

She tops the car out at 100.

Oh, God.

Miriam suddenly knows where to point the car.

THIRTY-TWO

A TALE OF TWO MIRIAMS

It's early. Sun's not even up yet. Miriam comes in the door and finds her mother sitting at the breakfast nook, hands steepled, the note Miriam left sitting in the corral of her arms.

Evelyn Black starts to protest, thrusts her finger up in the air and starts to say something about betrayal and lies, something about running away from your debts and obligations, but Miriam can barely hear the words—it's like she's one of the kids in a Peanuts cartoon listening to an adult talk, *wah wah wah waaah wah.*

She storms over to her mother.

Her mother stands, frustrated, that finger still waggling, a castigating inchworm wriggling—

Miriam reaches out.

She captures the finger and the hand in her own and—

The ocean moves beneath them. The boat bobs in the surf. Mangroves line a nearby island, the trees standing in water like spiders on tippy-toes, like they don't want to get their feet wet.

Mother sits bound to a folding chair and to the deck railing behind it. Her nose is busted, streaming twin swallowtails of blood. Her lips are stretched around a tennis ball duct-taped into her mouth—the skin cracking, splitting, bleeding.

Evelyn Black watches her daughter behind a cabin porthole window. Fear courses through her like it's a living thing.

Poor Miriam pounds on the glass. Her hands are bloody, leaving greasy ketchup streaks behind. The window is unfazed, unbroken.

Ashley walks forward with an unsteady gait.

His knee dead-ends into a black rubber support cup from which protrudes a narrow flagpole of metal. The metal disappears into a dirty gray sneaker. The fake metal leg utters small squeaks and hisses as he walks.

He goes up to the porthole windows where Miriam on the other side screams and punches the glass. He waggles his fingers as if to wave at her.

"A tale of two Miriams," he says. He points to the bloodied handprints. "This is for you, the Miriam who's here." Then he sweeps his arms across the sky. "And this is for you, the Miriam who's touching her mother and seeing her death. You came for a show, so I sure don't want to disappoint!"

He stoops his head. Whispering. Murmuring words unheard. As if conferring with an invisible conspirator.

He laughs. Then he pulls a hunting knife from his belt.

"You know what they did?" he asks suddenly. Each word is laced with vibration—shot through with black veins of fear and giddiness. "They went to my mother. I don't know if you knew that. That's how they found us. They went to her and I'd sent a postcard to her and that was how they knew where to start looking. You know what they did to my mother? They shot her. Then they flipped one of the burners on the stove. Then turned up the nozzle on her oxygen tank." He claps his hands. "Whoosh. My mother was a hoarder. Lot of junk in that house. Tinder for the biggest campfire the town of Maker's Bell ever did see."

He takes the knife, sticks the point up under Evelyn's chin. Evelyn tries to scream around the tennis ball. She thrashes. It's no use.

"I'm going to take your mother from you, and you're thinking, *but why? And I'm saying to you, it's because of a thing you already know. Don't you? An eye for an eye. A tooth for a tooth. Your mother for my mother. And I hear your screams from behind that window and I know we've already had this conversation but we're going to have it again for the benefit of"*—once more he addresses the sky with the knife before returning it to the pricked skin beneath Mother's chin—*"and I want you to know that I blame you for my mother dying. I put a lot of faith in you. It was because of you that I was even in the Ass-Crack of Nowhere, North Carolina. With all the Waffle Houses and rebel flags and fixin's and y'alls. I went to you because I thought you were the one for me. A partner. A real partner. And you fucked me, then you fucked me over, and they fucked me up. My mother died and what did I get out of it? You fawning over that bull-headed trucker. Me losing my leg and getting dumped on the road. And you left me!"*

Miriam inside the cabin screams. Her shrieks are dulled by the glass.

She begins to bring her elbow against it.

Slowly, it cracks. Kkkkk. Ksssshhh. Like the ice of a frozen lake beneath someone crossing it. A ribbon of hope twists inside Evelyn: She's doing it. Miriam's breaking free.

Ashley shouts, "But now I have my own gift, you dumb cunt. Now I have a machine gun too, ho ho ho. And now I'm going to take what's owed to me."

Tears spill down over Evelyn's broken nose, down over the wrinkled tape, around the margins of the tennis ball. Please, Miriam, please.

Miriam's elbow crashes through the porthole, her arm studded with glistening, blood-slick glass.

Ashley laughs. And pounces.

He stitches the hunting knife in and out of Mother's chest. He stabs her so hard it sounds like he's punching her. The hilt of the knife and the base of his fist pound against her chest, whump whump whump. *Again and again. Mother's body spasms, the pain is cold and bright—*

Then Ashley stops—

Gets under the chair—

Grabs both front chair legs—

And lifts her up over the edge of the boat and into the water.

The water is dark. It grabs Evelyn, pulls her down. Cold water shoots up her nose. Streamers of blood drift into the blue, diffusing. Above her the boat floats like a white whale clouded in red—

Miriam, I'm sorry—

Evelyn Black dies in the water.

THIRTY-THREE

THE TIDE IS RISING

No no no no—

Miriam jukes left, lurches toward the sink.

She dry heaves. Strings of spit that taste like Red Bull and salt water. Copper blood and vodka burn and the grit of sand.

"Miriam!" Mother chirps in alarm. She comes over to her daughter's side and it's like there's a barrier gone between them. The woman now touches Miriam's arm, rubs her back, takes a washcloth, wets it over Miriam's shoulder, and presses it to the back of Miriam's neck. "It's okay. Okay. Shh. If you're drunk, it'll pass. Every hangover goes back out to sea eventually—" And here Miriam waits for the judgment to come, a drop of poison in a glass of refreshing water. But then Mother says, "I used to have mornings like this. It's okay."

Jesus, Mom, who are you?

Eventually Miriam sits down. She feels clammy. Queasy. Like she's out there on that boat rocking back and forth. Watching her mother die.

It strikes her then: Even as she was watching her mother die, someone else was watching her. Ashley. Talking to her like he knew she'd be here with her mother, here to touch her. Is he here now? Is he following her? She lurches up out of the chair, almost knocking it over.

"Miriam, it's okay, sit back down—"

"Have you seen anyone?" Miriam asks. "Anyone suspicious? Particularly someone with a fake leg. Talking to you. Watching you. New neighbor. Weird guy on the sidewalk. Anyone?"

"No, no, what is this about?"

Miriam growls, charges through the house in denial of her nausea and heads out onto the street. Everything is quiet. The air so humid you could gargle it. Little bungalow houses darkened by fat-bellied palm trees. Down the block an old coot in a pink V-neck and noisy Hawaiian shorts pulls weeds from a flowerbed around his mailbox—and Miriam storms over, her mother trailing behind. The silver-haired retiree looks up, startled.

"You," Miriam barks. "You see anyone around here?"

"What? Who are you?" His eyes dart toward Miriam's mother. "Evelyn, is that you? Who is this? What's happening?"

"Ernie, this is my daughter, Miriam."

"Oh, hello, Miriam." He offers a hand clad in gardening gloves.

She bats his hand away. "Don't *hello, Miriam* me, you old shriv. I need to know if you've seen anybody strange around here. Anybody at all. One-legged guy? Maybe smells like cat piss, looks like he's on meth? Got a pair of binoculars, probably."

"No, I—I swear."

"Don't lie to me, dude. God's watching. And with your advancing age you're a lot closer to Him than I am. God doesn't like liars. You don't want to get to Heaven and he's all ready to fuck your ass straight to Hell—"

Suddenly, her mother is tugging on her arm. "Oh, Miriam, let's go."

She hesitates. But then she sees the pleading look in her mother's eyes. *Since when do I care about what my mother wants?*

That answer comes easy: *Since you saw that she's going to die in three days.* Three days. Murdered by Ashley Gaynes.

Ernie says good-bye as she allows Evelyn to draw her back

to the house. Once inside the foyer, Miriam thinks, *Okay, Mom, I'm going to tell you something now*, and she's about to tell her mother what happened after Ben Hodge's own mother beat her down with a snow shovel in the school bathroom, about to tell her the truth about her curse, her power. She thinks, *Maybe I need to give it a godly spin*, like tell the woman that this is something God gave *to* her or took *from* her or, or, or—

It's then she realizes.

She looks around the kitchen.

Looks beyond it, to the living room.

To her own mother's neck.

No pictures of Jesus on the walls.

No cross on a gold chain.

No prayers muttered. No entreaties to Christ to save her, save her daughter, save the world. Not a single religious utterance.

"You lost God," Miriam says suddenly.

"What?"

"You don't . . . you don't go to church anymore."

"How'd you—" But then she nods. "It's true. I suppose you're looking around and seeing something missing. I didn't think you'd notice, honestly. But it's true. I don't . . . I don't believe in that anymore."

"Why?"

"I lost my child. I lost my grandchild. God did nothing to stop it. Which left me to believe He was either horribly cruel or simply not present at all. Believing in his cruelty was too painful. It was more comforting to instead suspect it was all just a fantasy."

"The Bible shows a very cruel God, Mother."

"Yes," her mother says, short and clipped. "But it never felt pointed at me. I couldn't handle it. I'm not Job. I cannot abide the stress test of faith on trial."

"I'm sorry."

"It's not your fault."

"You think it is."

Here, Mother is silent.

"I have something I have to do," Miriam says. *I have three days to save your life. I have three days to find Ashley Gaynes and sink his body below the surf.* "I need your car again."

"Miriam, my car is—"

"This is important. This is everything. If you want to make up for lost years, then I need this."

Mother pulls away. Bristles. "How do I know you won't run away again? Steal my car and leave me high and dry."

"Because I came back. Tonight. I'll come back again."

"I suppose I can have Helen next door take me places."

"Thank you."

"Will you at least eat a sandwich first? You look . . . rough."

Miriam breathes. Feels the nausea wash back out to sea, pushed there by this small kindness offered by a mother she hasn't seen in a long time.

"I'll have a sandwich, yeah. Thanks, Mom."

Evelyn gets out the bread.

PART FIVE

LOS MARTIRES

"That's a nice necklace," Miriam says, halting the story. She levels her gaze at Catherine Vills and the gold chain around the woman's neck, a neck thin and fluted like the stem of a champagne glass.

Vills scowls, her woozy grin becoming a bridge to disdain. "You can't even see it." All that's there is a whisper of gold disappearing beneath the high collar of her blouse. "It's nothing special."

"You sound defensive."

"I'm not defensive."

"When you say it like that—*I'm not defensive*—you just sound doubly defensive. Like, when a guy loudly protests how he doesn't gobble donkey cock, you can be pretty sure that guy *totally* gobbles donkey cock any chance he can get. Can I see the necklace?"

Vills hesitates. Now Grosky is watching them with increased interest—one brow arched. His curiosity is a fish on the line: hooked right through the cheek. Finally, Vills draws the necklace out with a spidery finger.

The diamonds glitter. They almost look like a halo—an angel born in the counter case at Saks Fifth Avenue.

Grosky whistles.

"That watch is nice, too," Miriam says. "It's a Movado, right?"

Vills tucks her wrist away under the table, which only makes it look like she's hiding the evidence.

Miriam says, "I had a watch, too, once. A really spiffy calculator watch. I didn't do much mathematizing on it, but you could spell *BOOBS* on it if I turned my wrist upside down. I really loved that watch. I once sat across from a guy—just like we're sitting across from each other right now—and he . . . gave it to me."

"You kill him?" Vills asks.

Miriam sneers. "I did not." *But he is dead.*

Grosky interrupts: "Focus up. I want to get back to it, not talk jewelry with a bunch of hissing cats. I don't get it, Miriam."

"Don't get what?"

"You just bailed on her. Your mother. You learn she's gonna suck seawater through stab wounds in—*one two three*—days and all you do is bail on her. Why didn't you stick around? Check the house for bugs or hidden cameras? This prick was spying on you. So he had to be nearby."

Every inch of her goes taut like a strangler's rope. "He wasn't. I had a hunch." She sniffs and stares. "I wanted to be the hunter, not the hunted. So that meant leaving my mother to find him."

"Maybe things would've been different had you stayed."

She flinches. "Maybe they would've. I'm fond of bad decisions."

Everything feels off-kilter. Like she's trading power to these people and getting nothing back. Offense, not defense. *Hunter, not hunted.* So before the fat fuck or the bony bitch can say anything else, she steers the conversation right back where she wants it. Looking right at Vills, she says: "So, shiny watch, pretty necklace. Where you getting the bling, Miss Thing?"

"We're talking about you, not me," Vills says.

But Grosky's lip twitches again. *There's that fishhook again . . .*

"I'm not saying," Miriam says, "*but I'm just saying*. You don't look like the type who can afford that kind of shiny. You got a new love in your life, hmm?"

Vills hesitates.

Grosky must detect Vills's reticence, and he's clearly not the type to let voids go unfilled. "You got a man, Vills?"

She nods. "I do."

She's lying. Miriam knows this.

That will come out in time.

"Good for you, Vills," Grosky says, clapping her on the back like she's a fellow player who just scored a touchdown for the team. "I always said you needed to get a man and get laid." He gets a playful look on his face. "Oh, wait. It *is* a man, isn't it? You going scissoring like Miriam here? That's okay, I don't judge. I think they should be able to get married. And I always wondered if maybe you had a thing for the bearded taco."

"For the record," Miriam says, "I'm a supremely vulgar human being and even I think *bearded taco* is a disgusting term. My vagina is a beautiful flower, thank you very much, not a pube-shellacked burrito. Uck."

Grosky just shrugs.

Vills says, "I don't want to talk about this anymore."

The agent shifts in her seat, looking uncomfortable.

Which is exactly what Miriam wants from her.

Discomfort.

THIRTY-FOUR

VACANCY

Three days.

In three days, Miriam will watch as Ashley Gaynes returns to her life and stabs her mother to death on a boat.

She can't let that happen.

She can't even let it *get* to that point.

When she saved Louis, it was by a hair's breadth—a half second between Louis getting dead and Louis staying alive. That's too small a window. She can't crawl between seconds like that again.

Which means finding Ashley before any of this happens.

Three days to find him. Three days to *kill* him.

He's somewhere in the Keys. He *has* to be. It adds up. In the vision, he's out on a boat. The vision didn't show her much, but it looked like what she saw when she was down in the Keys: the crystal blue-green waters. The swampy mangrove. He would have been watching her there, too. At Torch Key. Maybe even in Key West.

Plus, the whole mystique of the Keys—it's mile zero. It's *the end of the road*. She appreciates the poetry and he would, too. Or he'd at least expect *her* to appreciate it, and since this seems to be about her . . .

The hot breath of the day comes in through the car window and she takes it all in: the stench of sea wind, the stink of fish, the smell of sun and salt and sand. Again threading the needle through palms and inlets, past marinas and dinky motels.

She sees one such dive motel: THE CONCH OUT INN.

The big weathered sign sticks up above the black palms like the flag on a mailbox, except this flag is shaped like a conch shell, most of the color blasted out of it except for a few zebra striations of bright coral.

Beneath the sign is another sign: VACANCY.

That's all she needs.

She whips the Malibu into the lot.

Time to get a room.

THIRTY-FIVE

THE SPIRIT OF THE THING

Miriam gets the key from the proprietor—Jerry Wu, a chubby-cheeked Chinese guy with a New York accent. Jerry says he bought the place a couple years back and is trying to fix it up. Right now it's a mish-mash slap-dash cram-together affair: not a motel so much as a bunch of buildings and trailers (and even a small Quonset hut) connected by a walkway made of mismatched stone pavers. A walkway winds between palm trees that shed bark the way a leper sheds skin.

The key in her hand is on a massive boat anchor keychain—made of pewter or something. It makes her hand smell funny. Heavy enough, too, that she could probably use it to gag a shark.

The anchor says FLORIDA KEYS.

Keys, keys, everywhere, keys. *It's keys all the way down.*

Keys with locks she hasn't found yet.

The room is toward the back. Not far from the water and the boat loading ramp, not far from a fallen hedge of prehistoric bougainvillea where she can see into the neighboring lot—a trailer park.

(It occurs to her that she can't seem to get away from trailer parks. She gravitates toward them like flies toward garbage.)

As she goes to unlock her door, someone whistles to her.

She turns. Through the hedge of little purple flowers she sees an old dude sitting on a ratty fabric deck chair. He's got the muscle tone of a crumpled jerkoff tissue. Skin like you'd find on fried chicken: sun-crisped and wrinkly. Long Fu Manchu beard. Bald on top, but long hair, too—gray streamers, wispy as dandelion seed.

"Fuckin' taxes, man," the guy says.

She pauses, key hovering before the lock. "What?"

"It's like they fuckin' tax you comin' in and goin' out," he says, waggling a finger at her. He's got the cadence of a burnout. Got that marijuana wheeze, that LSD stare. "We're rebels down here, girl. Conch Republic. Look it up, look it up. April 23, 1982, they set up some border patrol shit up at the top of the Keys, searching cars for drugs and Cubans and whatever and we were like, *Hell, no, we won't go slow*, and next thing you know we seceded from the United Suppressions of America and formed a micro-nation of pirates and scallywags and free-born deviants. The Mayor declared our independence and claimed himself prime minister. Then he declared war on the Untied Subjugators of Anarchy."

Miriam turns. Hands on hips. "How long that last?"

"Like, five minutes. He broke a loaf of bread over some Navy dude's head and then surrendered, demanding a billion dollars in aid and reparations."

"I bet that worked out well."

He shrugs. "It's all in the spirit of the thing, man."

"Thanks for sharing."

"You look new here is all."

"I don't live here."

"You better put on some sunblock, man. Looks like you're starting to burn up."

"Yeah, yeah, yeah." *Sure thing, Tommy Chong.*

She unlocks the door and walks in.

Closes it behind her.

Thumbs the deadbolt shut.

And about pisses her pants when she sees Ashley Gaynes sitting on the bed.

THIRTY-SIX

THE FOX

He's grinning like a fox in a pile of bloody chicken feathers.

Miriam acts before thinking. She sees a glass lamp full of seashells on a nearby dresser, palms it, flings it at Ashley's head.

He claps his hands—

The lamp shatters against the wood paneling—

A cheesy flea market painting of a lighthouse rattles on the wall and drops to the floor, the frame popping out of joint—

He's gone.

Gone off the bed. Like he never existed.

A little bruise-purple seashell rolls up and taps her boot.

Suddenly: someone knocking at the door. She whirls—

There's the Fu Manchu burnout peering in the window. "Hey," he yells through the door. "You okay in there?"

She quickly yanks the blinds shut over the window.

"Fine," she yells. "Just . . . doing some karate to break in the room."

She wheels, tosses her backpack on the bed—

And there's Ashley again. Sitting on the other side of the room. Next to the window unit air conditioner. Running the sharp end of a black feather up and down the AC grating—*t-t-t-t-t-tink, t-t-t-t-t-tink*.

"You gonna drink that," he says, "or is it just foreplay?"

Miriam clucks her tongue. "Cute. First thing you—*he*—said to me when we met. Very cute. Trespasser motherfucker."

The Trespasser does a good job mirroring the Ashley from her vision. Dark eyes, flashing like new quarters. His hair is no longer pushed up over his head in some ill-gotten fauxhawk; it now hangs down around his ears. Messy. Tar-and-feather black. Still got that wicked boomerang smile, though. He produces a hunting knife out of nowhere. Twirls it.

"You're too pretty to leave for dead," he says.

"Quit with the script," she says. "I've read that book already."

"Howzabout this," he says. "Time is always your enemy. Have you noticed that? It's chasing you, and you're chasing it. A dog and her tail."

She sits on the edge of the bed. "That's life, isn't it?"

"A game you lose?"

She *mmms*. "Like pinball. Get as many points as you want, you always lose the ball in the end."

"Three days," Ashley says. He whistles low and slow. "Not a lot of time to do the work that needs doing."

"I've had worse and done better."

"Not when your own mother's life is on the line."

Suddenly, the knife he's holding is no longer a knife.

It's a string. And it dead-ends at the base of a red Mylar balloon. The balloon dips and bobs in the breeze coming off the AC unit.

Blood drips from the bottom of the balloon. Runs down the length of string to Ashley's hand.

She sees now that he's wearing a Santa hat. A roguish lean to it on his scalp. He winks, kisses the air.

Someone knocks on the door.

The balloon *pops*.

Ashley—the Trespasser—is gone.

Miriam lets out a breath she didn't realize she was holding and flings open the door.

"I told you, you old stoner—"

But it's not the old stoner.

It's Jerry Wu. The proprietor.

"Eh, hey, Miss Black," he says. "I forgot to mention earlier—" And here he's trying to get a look past Miriam at the broken lamp on the ground, but she's tilting and leaning and putting her body in the way. "I do a fish fry here every night. Free fish, catch of the day sorta thing."

"Yeah, yeah, great, whatever. Thanks, Jer."

"I'm about to head out. I offer all the guests the chance to go out with me. You do much fishin'?"

It's weird hearing a *Noo Yawk* accent coming from this little Asian dude in Florida. She supposes that's racist, but these are the thoughts.

"Do I look like a fisherman? Fisherwoman? Fisher . . . person?"

"No worries. Not for everybody. Five o'clock, free fish. See ya later."

He turns around, and when he moves she sees it—a big-ass bird standing nearby on the stump of a cut-down palm. Long neck. Black feathers. Lean, crooked beak the color of bright butter. And those eyes. Like someone hammered emeralds into the bird's head.

The bird stretches out its wings like it's the Batman about to pounce.

Jerry walks up to the bird and grabs it by the neck.

To Miriam's surprise, the bird doesn't seem to mind.

As Jerry cradles the thing like it's his buddy, she asks, "What the fuck is that thing? It's like some kind of Satanic duck."

"She's a cormorant," he says with a chuckle. "Her name's Corie."

"Corie the cormorant."

"Right, Corie the cormorant."

"And you do what with Corie the cormorant? Is this a sex thing?"

He laughs, and not in a nervous this-girl-is-freaking-me-out way. "No, I don't bang the bird. She helps me fish."

"Still don't get it."

"You wanna come see? I'll show you. Last chance."

She thinks, *I don't have time for this*.

She has seventy-two hours. Less, now.

But that bird. Those eyes. It's like the damn thing is watching her.

Over a year ago, when she was facing death at the hands of the Mockingbird, she was able to do something she'd never done before. Without meaning to, she was able to enter the mind of a nearby crow—not just as a passenger but as its puppet master.

It saved her life.

She hasn't been able to do it since.

She's stood around trying to psychically *urge* pigeons, doves, blackbirds, crows, sparrows, robins—every stupid bird hopping around on this stupid earth—and none of them seemed to give a good goddamn.

They mostly just flew away. Some took shits.

Still. A little practice time with a bird in close proximity. A pet bird. A *trained* bird. And she can ask Jerry questions about the Keys. Better than sitting around, flicking her clit.

Besides, I happen to like last chances.

"You know a lot about the Keys?" she asks him.

"I know some things."

"Then I'm in," she says. "Let's go fishing."

THIRTY-SEVEN

THE FISHER QUEEN

Miriam thought, *Oh, we'll just stand on shore and cast lines and something-something bobber-bait-chum-rod-and-reel,* but oh, no. They're out on a boat not far from shore. Miriam didn't expect to be in a boat. She doesn't like boats. Doesn't like water. Especially since almost drowning in the Susquehanna. Just thinking about it gives her the shivers, even in the heat.

This is not a big boat. Two-seater. So they're right there on the surface, water slapping against the side, and Miriam's brain does strange things and she thinks that the slapping sound reminds her of the sounds made during sex—skin on skin, thighs against thighs—and now she's thinking about Gabby and that's more than a little awkward because Jerry's staring at her like he knows she's thinking impure thoughts.

The bird is looking at her, too.

It oinks like a pig at her.

"It just oinked at me," Miriam says. The boat rocking back and forth. Her stomach going the other way.

"She," Jerry corrects.

"*She* just oinked at me."

"Yeah," he says. "They kinda grunt?"

She presses her fingers to her temples and tries to tell the bird to do something, anything. Jump. Fly. Nod. Poop. All it does is oink. She's not sure why she has her fingers to her temples other than she saw it in a movie once and it just *feels* right.

Jerry's looking at her again.

"You put some suntan lotion on, right?"

"What? Yeah. Sure." She mentally commands the bird to open its mouth and get her a cigarette. The bird clacks its beak together but does nothing more. Almost like it's mocking her. "It's—*she's*—mocking me."

"She's not mocking you."

"I think she's totally mocking me."

Jerry laughs again, starts looping a rope around the bird's neck.

"What are you doing?" Miriam asks.

"This is my fishing line."

"This is goofy."

"I know, but it's pretty cool, right? My family are fishermen on the River Li. Or were, anyway. A lot of them used cormorants to fish. Way it works is—" He finishes looping the rope and then he positions the bird so it's facing the water. "The bird goes down in the water—" He gives the bird a gentle shove and the bird squawks and dives, disappearing beneath the waters. "And then catches me some fish."

"And she doesn't eat them? Because if I were that bird, I'd just eat the fish."

"She tries to eat the big ones but the rope around her neck prevents her from swallowin' those suckers. She can eat the little ones, but that's okay—I don't want the little ones. Meanwhile, the big ones stick in her throat. You'll see."

"So you're choking a bird underwater for fish."

"She eats, too. And she likes it."

"That's what every man says."

And here she sees she's reached Jerry's discomfort point. It happens eventually. Rare is the other human who doesn't mind being dragged over the deepening lines of impropriety while talking to Miriam Black.

With her, every conversation is a land mine.

Eventually: *boom.*

One of the few people who could hack it was Ashley Gaynes.

How fucked up is *that?*

Jerry shifts nervously now.

"You're not from around here," Jerry says.

"Neither are you," she says.

"Yeah, but I live here now. You, you're just passing through." He says *through* as *true.* "Who are you?"

She thinks for a moment to use the truth to break a window, see how he handles all that broken glass and ugly reality, but this calls for the touch of the screwdriver because a lie will be more useful. "I'm a bounty hunter."

"Like on the TV?"

"Uh-huh. Looking for a, uh, perp." *Is that the word? Perp?* "A perp hiding out here in the Keys somewhere."

"The Keys seem small, but they're pretty big."

"No kidding. Where would a—" But before she can finish the question the bird emerges from the water with a splash. Throat bulging like a snake that ate a fat-ass rabbit. Jerry helps the bird stand on the edge of the boat and he reaches into the creature's mouth like he's rooting around in a trash can for something he accidentally threw away—

And he pulls out two fish.

Plop. Plop.

The smell of seawater and the life that comes with it crawls up her nose. Corie the cormorant squawk-oinks.

Then it gives Miriam a look.

She's sure of it. It turns that freaky turquoise eye right toward her. The skin around it is puckered and leathery, kinda what she imagines a dinosaur's asshole looks like. It blinks, but it doesn't blink—*something* slides over its eye, something cloudy and opaque that darkens the eye but does not hide it.

Jerry must see the look on Miriam's face. He says, "Nictitating membrane. She slides that over her eye so when she dives she can see underwater. It's like a reptile thing."

"But she's a bird."

"The dinosaurs never went extinct. They just became birds."

That explains it. "So they're all operating on a reptile brain."

"More advanced than a reptile's. But at the core, yeah—it's still that prehistoric kill-screw-sleep-eat thing."

Miriam thinks, *That sounds familiar.*

Maybe that's why she likes birds and they like her.

Though the way this one's giving her the shit-eye, she's not sure.

Suddenly the bird splashes back into the water.

"Sorry," Jerry says. "You were saying?"

"Oh, ah. Yeah. I was gonna ask where you think a . . . perp might hide out down here."

He thrusts his tongue into the pocket of his cheek like he's thinking. "Well, lots of places. Thing about these islands is, there's a whole lot of 'em. Like, close to two thousand of them. Some of them are practically no bigger than this boat. But it's not just the ones the roads connect—it's like, all these little outliers." He points to little dark pockets of palm and earth out on the horizon. "Now, most of those islands are down by Key West. Lots of places to hide down there. That's why the Keys are known for some . . . less savory actions, you know what I mean?" *Knowwhaddamean?* "Smuggling pot. Smuggling coke. Making meth. Smuggling Cuban immigrants out of the Keys. Bringing bodies down to hide *in* the Keys."

The enormity of the situation is a tsunami crashing down on her shores. Three days to find a ghost. Three days to fail.

"You ever hear about submarines carrying drugs?"

"Oh yeah, sure. Sometimes they come up from Cuba or Columbia. Narco-subs, they call 'em. They used to use fast boats, then switched to these little subs that couldn't go deep. But they go pretty deep now. Radar slides off 'em like water off Corie's back."

"Do those go through the Keys?"

"Sure they do. Usually down through those little islands I was talking about. You lookin' for someone into the drug thing?"

"Yeah. They could be anywhere."

"Too bad you're not psychic," Jerry says, laughing.

And she starts to laugh with him, but it's a fake, forced laugh. *Oh ha ha ha ho ho ho you silly cad I am a psychic except I'm the wrong type of psychic and I can't just—*

The world plunges into the water.

It's like her mind is wrenched out of her body. Dragged down, down, into the deep. Down through a flurry of bubbles. Through a tangle of weeds. Her throat feels full. Something moves in her esophagus. Something *struggling*. She can't breathe. Can't turn around to go up. She's sinking like a stone.

Please stop please help.

Below her, a great abyss lit by spears of light—the shine of fish swimming, catching the sun, in and out of brain-shaped bulges of coral. She's pointed toward it like an arrow falling through open sea.

I'm the bird.

Holy shit, I'm the bird.

But then, down in the coral—

She sees a body. Fish-eaten. Waterlogged. The gray meat of the skin sloughing off, swaying like seaweed.

She knows the body.

She knows that face.

It's Eleanor Caldecott.

The woman's jaw creaks open. More bubbles unmoor, drift-ing to the surface. A green eel hides in the well of her throat—

Impossible. She's dead. She died in the river, not in the sea . . .

But then the woman speaks—rotten jaw opening and closing—and Miriam hears the voice in her mind, words like bubbles rupturing:

YOU ARE NOT ALONE
WE ARE FIXED BY TRAGEDY
DARKNESS AND CLAMOR

Then, a childish voice, the voice of Wren there in the deep, sliding around bubbles like a curling worm: IT TAKES ONE TO KNOW ONE . . .

And then the world shifts, spinning on its axis. Light behind is now above, the liquid jewels of sun on the water's surface.

Everything shimmers—

Miriam gasps, her body jerking like it's been hit by a King Kong fist. She gags. Chokes. Spits over the side of the boat just as the cormorant launches up out of the bay, throat clogged anew with fish.

Jerry stares. "Hey, you all right?"

He reaches out for her arm—

She tries to pull away. *No no no no—*

Seven days from now, Jerry swings a gaff hook at Ashley Gaynes in the parking lot of the Conch Out Inn, and Ashley deftly sidesteps it. Jerry throws everything he has at him—puts all his energy into swinging that hook—but even on a fake leg Ashley isn't fazed. He moves, almost casually, like he's just trying to get out of the sun—and with every small and calculated movement the hook cuts through the air, swish, swish, swish.

Ashley's like a cat playing with its prey.

Finally there comes a point when he looks bored and rolls his eyes, and Jerry tries one more time to swing with the hook and Ashley just leans back, lets the hook grab open air only an inch in front of his nose—

Then he pulls a .357 revolver out from a hip holster like he's a Wild West shooter, and he puts a round in Jerry's gut. The hook clatters.

Ashley grabs Jerry by the throat. Holds him close. Whispers in his ear. "Where was she staying? She had a bag. Full of money. I want it back." Jerry tries to spit on him. Ashley punches Wu in the throat. Jerry wheezes.

Ashley turns his head to the sky.

He's speaking to her again.

"You like the show, Miriam? Everyone you touch, I kill. You're a poison pill, a toxic cloud, you're the human equivalent to—"

Suddenly, a black shadow above his head. The cormorant lands on the back of his shoulders, beating him with its wings, stabbing at him with its beak—a clumsy, inelegant attack—and Ashley screams like a woman, lets go of Jerry, backpedals with the gun up—

The bird keeps coming—

Bang, bang, bang—

The cormorant drops to the ground, squirting blood.

Jerry clutches his middle, staggers forward and falls to his knees and paws on the ground for the hook—

And finds the .357 pressed against his temple.

His life disappears in a flash of powder and furious thunder.

Miriam bats his hand away and recoils to the far end of the boat, which is not very fucking far but right now she doesn't want to be touched, doesn't want to look at this poor bastard whose life is now hitched to hers just because she chose his motel, doesn't want to look at the bird and its freaky gemstone eye, doesn't want to look anywhere but in her own lap.

She fidgets with a cigarette.

Fumbles with her lighter.

Drops it. Growls.

The vision lingers, like how if you recorded over one VHS tape, you might still see the ghost of the old recording still haunting the screen.

In the vision, Ashley shows up at the motel. Kills Jerry. Kills the bird. But seven days—? That happens *after* her mother. He's doing cleanup. He just wanted the money. The money she took from "Steve Max"?

Jerry stares. The cormorant looks up at other birds—pelicans—flying overhead. A millstone grinds in Miriam's head. It feels like it's pulverizing her to dust. But then something clicks—

. . . too bad you're not psychic . . .

. . . you are not alone . . .

She knows that others exist like her. People with powers that don't add up, that don't fit into any boxes. She met a storefront psychic—Miss Nancy—who told her she was the hand of death. Then Eleanor Caldecott had her own strange power: the ability to see the consequences of a person's life, chained together in a single vision.

That's how she'll find Ashley.

She needs to find a goddamn psychic.

Another psychic, at least. *A real one,* she thinks with no small irony. Someone with an ability that does something worth a damn.

"I need to go back to shore," she says.

"Yeah, you got it," Jerry answers. Then he fires up the motor. Never taking his eyes off her. Like he's afraid she might bite.

If only he knew what it meant to be caught in her gravity.

THIRTY-EIGHT

PSYCHICS AT SUNDOWN

The drive back down to Key West feels like she's being chased: hounded by a massive wolf, pursued by a hungry shark, stalked by a beast of death whose shape transforms but whose teeth are ever-sharp.

The Malibu passes the Torch Keys and she thinks of that poor Parrothead fucker, sliced up on a patio table as a message for her.

She thinks of her mother, stabbed to death on a boat.

Of Jerry Wu, shot to death in his own parking lot.

She keeps her lead foot from falling. Just barely. Can't have a cop stop her. Not now. Has to keep clean and clear. It's the only way. Her base urges—those *reptilian* urges—want out of their bottle but if she wants to save lives she's going to have to stopper them up and bury it in the sand.

Just before she hits the Land of Mile Zero, she stops off at the impound yard a mile north of the jail. The guy lets her in and she navigates an uneven, mostly empty lot until she finds the Fiero parked toward the back. She pops the door, doesn't even bother with the ignition yet—

Most important thing is the money.

She looks in the back, under the seat.

Nothing. No money.

Cold fury cuts through the sweat. No money was on her

"voucher." They didn't list any bag of cash. Which means one of those cops took it.

Her first impulse is to get back in the Malibu and drive it through the jail wall and up every ass of every cop in the joint until one of them starts spilling money like a hammer-struck slot machine.

But that won't get her anywhere.

Except, you know, *thrown in jail* again.

Calm. Breathe. Cigarette. Yes.

She pops the trunk. With a trembling hand she flips up the flap to expose where the spare tire would usually go—

And there sits a bag. Full of money.

They found the first bag, not the second.

Which means she still has five grand.

She laughs around her cigarette, then on a lark tries to start the Fiero. The engine sounds like an old woman gasping before she dies. That answers that question, then. Miriam throws the keys as far as she can and heads back to the Malibu, and takes the Malibu into Key West.

Key West is packed. People all over the streets. Same mix of miscreants and deviants: the rich white Jimmy Buffet fans, the sailboat hipsters, the freakshow pirates. Tourists and locals and aliens.

Miriam parks the car and makes a hard charge toward Mallory Square and, in particular, the sign she saw the last time she was here: PSYCHIC READINGS I WILL TELL YOU YOUR FUTURE. The whole square is in some kind of sunset celebration. People gathered to watch the blob of orange sherbet melt into the creamsicle ocean—drinking and singing and watching all the little shows and buying all the kitschy tchotchkes (*Say that ten times fast*, she thinks) they can find. Mimes with trained cats, pirates juggling rum bottles, freaks breathing fire and lifting barbells with chains hooked to nipples stretched like taffy—

The psychic's not here.

She orbits, wanders, can't find her.

Damnit. *Damnit.*

Ah. Wait. There. There! She's at the far end. Near the pier. Just setting up. Wrapping her platinum-blond head in the gypsy scarf. The woman sees Miriam coming and says, "Hey, doll. Not open yet. Sorry."

"Don't care. Take my money."

"Eager, are we?"

"Time is ticking."

"Time is always ticking, isn't it?"

"Dispense with the banter. Take my cash." She waves two twenties—twice as much as the woman charges, per her signage. "Read my . . . aura or my cards or sniff my pheromones or whatever it is you do. I need help."

The woman shrugs as if it's not worth fighting. Then sits down cross-legged. She whips a tie-dyed cloth off a crystal ball and opens up a carved wooden box to reveal a deck of Tarot cards.

The Death card leers up. Ragged woodcut skull behind an ink-black cloak. Scythe reaping wheat that looks like people.

It's a good start.

"My name is Miss Gina. I can look into the ball," the woman says. "Or I can read your cards or your palm. Your call, doll."

"I'd rather you not touch me. Unless it's necessary."

"It's . . . not, no."

"Then whatever. Don't care. Chop-chop. I got a bug up my butt here, lady. I'm hankering for a hunk of psychic karate."

She flings the two twenties at the woman.

The bleach-blonde psychic scoops up the money with the aplomb of a practiced stripper. Then gets out the Tarot cards. She pulls out a small satchel, and Miriam smells the heady stink of something herbal. "This is a purification satchel in which I've placed sage and angelica and anise—"

"Mmm*nope*," Miriam says, waving her arms in a way that might suggest *the bridge is out, turn back around.* "Move past all that stuff. Get to the juicy-juice, please." *Lives are on the line, bimbo.*

The woman looks suddenly nervous. She clears her throat and begins to shuffle the Tarot cards. Then she hands the deck to Miriam. "Cut it, doll."

Beyond the edge of Mallory Square, the sun has melted into a gloppy napalm line pooling at the horizon.

Miriam bisects the deck, slaps it back together.

The woman takes it. Begins to spread out the cards. "This is called the Celtic Cross—"

"No Occult 101 please, just . . . read, interpret."

The woman flips the first card.

"The Seven of Staves," she says.

The image on the card is of a man with a pageboy haircut standing on a hill and holding a staff that looks like the knobby cock of a cave monster. He's trapped in a prison of similarly shaped knob-cocked staves.

"What's that mean?"

"It means you're facing great difficulties on all sides of you—"

"Everybody's facing great difficulties. That's called *hey, look, reality.* We're all besieged by assholes and inadequacies. Next card."

Flip.

On the card: A naked nymph gazes up at a six-pointed star in the night sky above a meadow. Sheep graze nearby.

"The Star," the woman says with wonder, as if Miriam just won the metaphysical lottery. "Hope and faith are your allies in life's difficulties, and you'll find that clutching optimism to your bosom as this woman does with the light of the star—"

"No, no, no, none of that sounds right. Here." Miriam reaches across and begins flipping each card herself. Three of Cups. The

Lovers. Four of Swords. Something called a Hierophant, which sounds but does not look like a type of elephant. After each flip, Miss Gina tries to explain what the card is, but she doesn't get in more than a few words before Miriam is flipping the next. Finally, at the end, Miriam flips over the Hanged Man. "There!"

"There?"

"What's that card?"

On the card another page-boy asshole is hung upside down by his heel. Dangling from a tree. "That's the Hanged Man. He means you'll need to look at your problems from another angle—"

"*You* are my other angle. You." A carpenter's nail of anger hammers through Miriam's heart. She swipes her hand across the blanket and knocks all the cards out of their cross configuration. "Goddamnit! You're not a real psychic, are you?"

Tourists look over, alarmed.

"What? Of course I am." She laughs nervously, like this is a joke, a show for the marks all around. "I have been blessed by the—"

"Cut the hokey horseshit, Gina. You're just looking at cards and interpreting them with the most milquetoast, mediocre interpretation. And you'd do the same by looking into that gaudy crystal ball or by looking at the lines running across my palms. Am I right?"

"I think you ought to leave."

"I think you ought to give me my forty bucks back."

"Fine." The woman crumples up each twenty and throws the little capitalist boulders back at Miriam. "Take them and go."

Miriam stands up. Sticks her index finger out like she's trying to dissect her with the power of her pointing. "You just wasted my time. I need a *real* psychic. You get it? I need someone who can help me find something, and time is breaking apart in my hand like a chip of once-wet sand. Thanks for nothing."

She moves to storm off.

"Wait!" Miss Gina yells after her.

Miriam keeps walking. But the woman catches up, steps in front of her, hands up. A little white business card sits slotted between Gina's index and middle finger. She levers it toward Miriam.

"You need to find something, Sugar is your gal."

"My *gal*?"

"She's the real deal. She's not a . . ." Gina gestures with her eyes toward the whole of Mallory Square, to all the freaks and performers and tourists. A gesture as if to say, *Not a fake like me.* "Take the card."

Miriam takes it.

On it is handwritten one thing: *MM 47.5.*

"I don't understand," Miriam says.

"Mile marker forty-seven and a half," Gina says.

"Mile marker. Key West is at mile zero, right?"

"Got it."

"Thanks, Gina. You're not as awful a person as I thought."

Gina shrugs. "You're Sugar's problem now, bitch."

THIRTY-NINE

NEW OLD FLAME

Purpose has its leash and collar on her. It drags Miriam forward through the streets of Key West toward the car. Through the drunks and the pot-smoke haze and the clouds of sunblock and Axe body spray. She's trying desperately not to touch any of them, not because she can't handle the visions (or so she tells herself) but because they're a distraction from the task at hand.

And then:

Gabby crosses the street in front of her.

Miriam thinks to hide, thinks to dart into the crowd but it's too late. Gabby's not crossing the street all casual-like. She too is a woman with a mission, and hers is to cross paths with Miriam.

She's got the tips of her blond hair dip-dyed pink, and Miriam thinks, *A girl after my own heart. Can't settle on a single hair color.* But then that momentary ember of affection is cast away in the wind of Gabby's anger.

"You're here," Gabby says.

Miriam tries to juke past her but sees the crowd has closed ahead of her, sealing shut like the wall in that Edgar Allen Poe story. *The Cask of . . .* something-or-other.

"I'm here" is all Miriam can think to say.

"And you weren't going to call."

"I kinda thought we'd reached the culmination of our time

together." She clears her throat. "Also, I forgot to actually get your number."

"You can't just do that to a person. I like you. Liked. Whatever."

"Listen, we're both adults and adults do this sort of shit all the time. They . . . they crash into each other and they rub their genitals in and around one another and then they move on—"

"No, adults do the *adult* thing and take responsibility for when they have somebody else's heart in their hands."

Miriam winces. Still looking for an exit. "Bad news: I'm not a particularly good adult."

Gabby grabs her hands—Miriam flinches, a knee-jerk reaction whenever somebody touches her and she doesn't expect it. But then she remembers: Whatever death is in store for Gabby is lost to Miriam, sucked under the raging rapids of a rum-drunk.

"Come home with me," Gabby says.

Miriam smells the alcohol coming off her.

"You're drunk," she says.

"And you're not," Gabby answers. "So get drunk with me."

"Gabby—"

Gabby runs her hands up Miriam's arms. She gets close. Miriam smells not just alcohol on the woman's breath but wine— red wine, lush and assertive, wine that darkens her lips, wine that stains her teeth. "I could make you feel good again. We had a pretty good thing going. I like you. You like me even though you won't admit it. We do fun things naked." Her knee presses up against Miriam's thighs, trying to tease them apart.

It starts to work. A deep heat spreads.

Miriam's got that little twist inside of her—like a knot cinching tighter, like a whip pulled taut between two strong hands. And she thinks, *I want this.* Her id is like a monkey in a box, hooting and howling and desperate for egress and she wants nothing more but to let this crazy love-monkey out so it can run rampant once more—

But she instead grabs Gabby's wrists—gently—and pushes her back.

Gabby scowls.

"I can't," Miriam says. "Not now. I have something I have to do—"

"Shit," Gabby says, looking and sounding deflated.

"Listen, this is a big moment for me. Any other time, I'd have just given in. Okay? I have the self-control of a lamprey. I smell blood and I need a taste. But I . . . I have something important to do. I'll come back. I'll call you. Maybe we can do dinner. Like a real date." Even as she says these words, she fears they sound like lies. She fears they *are* lies.

"Sure," Gabby says in a way that suggests she knows they're lies, too. She runs her hand along the side of Miriam's head, flipping a crow's tail of hair over the top of the ear. She gives Miriam a light peck on the cheek. Then she presses something into Miriam's hand. "My phone number. Since you *forgot* it last time. Just in case you really are serious."

Miriam says nothing. She pockets the number.

Gabby staggers across the street.

Miriam wants to call her back. Or follow after.

It's time to get the fuck out of here.

FORTY

GIMME SOME SUGAR

Mile marker forty-seven and a half.

All that's there is a burned-out . . . well, it's not a storefront. Not exactly. It's like a concrete hut cast over a little shop—a shop like a place you might go to buy bait or ice cream or corn dogs.

The glass is smeared with soot. Half-shattered but still clinging to the frame. The concrete too is smudged with licks of old fire.

Above it all is a sign that says: PSYCHIC.

It's crooked. A bird nest sits at the top. Spiders weave webs between the protruding letters.

It's empty. Like it's been bombed out.

Miriam's itchy, edgy, tense, like she's dancing on the point of a sword, like with every plié or pirouette it's driving the blade deeper—and now she's here at a fire-gutted stop-off on the Overseas Highway. Alone. Entirely alone and no better than she was before.

She thinks: *Go back. Find Gabby.*

Then: *Or call Louis. Tell him everything. He'll come.*
He'll save you.

A meaner, cockier voice inside her counters with:

You don't need saving. You're the one who saves people, remember? Then, a question: *What am I, a fucking superhero?*

The world shudders at that thought.

Time to curtail all the internal dialogue.

"Hello?" she yells.

Her voice echoes under the curve of the concrete.

A little lizard darts out in front of her. Scurrying along like the ground is lava and even a moment's rest will cook him up good.

No-see-ums bite into her arms. Mosquitoes hover, too, waiting their turn. All of them looking for blood.

It's then she feels hot. Stung all over. Like her skin is tight, *too* tight, pulled taut over her muscle and bone.

Her arms are lobster red.

She feels her neck—

"Ow, shit."

Sunburned. She has a sunburn.

She mocks everyone: "Oh, Miriam, you should really wear sunblock." Then she mocks herself in turn: "Nah, I'm a certified badass indestructible bitch. The sun tries to burn me, I'll kick him in his fiery balls. I don't need no stinking sunblock." She sighs. "I'm so stupid. Stupid for this. Stupid for being here. Stupid for ever leaving my mother."

She buries her hands in her face. Even that hurts.

"The sun is brutal," says a voice behind her.

Miriam wheels, reaching for her knife—

A woman stands holding an electric lantern. She's tall and wispy, *hovering* there in a white sundress cinched at the waist with a yellow scarf. Smooth skin and long hair the hue of wet sand. Dark freckles on her cheeks. Pale eyes like someone drained them of their color.

"Hi, Miriam," the woman says.

"You Sugar?" Miriam asks.

"I am."

"How'd you know I'd be here? Gina tell you?"

"Is that who sent you here?" She *mmms*. "No. She didn't tell me."

"You're saying you just *knew*."

Sugar winks. "I am and I did."

"Because you're psychic."

"I am."

"So you know what it is I want?"

Sugar walks—drifts, almost, like she walks so lightly her bare feet never touch the ground—and orbits Miriam. "I don't know exactly what you want, but you want the same thing everyone else does. You want to find something, or someone, or somewhere. We're all looking for these things."

"And you can help me find them."

"It's what I do."

"You're the real deal. Not just some hokey string-puller."

"I found you, didn't I?"

"She could've called you. Gina, I mean. Just because you're saying she didn't doesn't mean—"

"You're psychic, too," Sugar says. "Aren't you?"

"How'd you know that?"

"It bleeds off you."

"Sorry, must be my time of the month."

"You defend yourself against engaging with people in a real way by being witty. And cruel. It affords you distance."

Miriam snorts. "Your psychic abilities tell you that?"

"No." Sugar smiles; it's like warm honey spreading on toast. "That one I can figure out on my own."

Miriam and Sugar pace around each other. Incomplete circle against incomplete circle. The woman stares at her. Smiling. Almost smug. Like she thinks she understands Miriam in a way that Miriam doesn't or won't ever. Miriam feels suddenly on guard. Cagey. *Caged*.

"Tell me what I want to know, then," Miriam says.

"You're looking for someone, is that right?"

"Don't you need to touch me to find out?"

"I only need to look in your eyes."

"And what do you see in there?"

Miriam realizes suddenly that Sugar doesn't blink. Her eyes are open, wide open—each a whirlpool of gray water drawing her in. "I see in you a lot of things. I see rage. I see death. I see a sky full of carrion birds, I see a bandolier of skulls, I see a well of darkness—and in that darkness I see a tiny, almost insignificant, light. Like a firefly at the end of a stick. And I see who you're looking for and where he is—"

"Tell me."

"Not yet."

"Fuck you. Yes *yet*. I want to know."

"And if you're not nice to me, I'll never tell."

Miriam thinks, *I'll beat your wifty gossamer ass until you bleat like a llama.* Instead she says, "I can be nice when I have to be."

"I want to tell you a story."

"I don't want to hear any bedtime tales. I'm not tired." Miriam fishes around for a cigarette. She finds one, thrusts it in her mouth. "I have work to do."

"Is that what the trespassing specter in your head tells you?"

The cigarette hangs from a dry patch on Miriam's lip. It dangles there like a mountain climber hanging on for dear life. "The Trespasser."

"That's what you call it?"

"Yeah. You have one?"

"I do."

"What do you call yours?"

"The Ghost."

A chill runs up Miriam's neck: a cat with icy feet. "So it's real. It's a ghost. We're haunted."

"I don't know. Maybe not. In this I have no answer, Miriam Black. Maybe it's a part of my psyche that breaks off and screams in my ear. Maybe it's the ghost of what I've lost. Maybe it's a delusion—a derangement. I've grown comfortable in not knowing."

"You're a better person than I am."

"Probably," Sugar says, but the way she says it doesn't sound smug or mean, just cruelly honest. Miriam can't fault her for that.

"You can start your story now."

Sugar smiles and tells the tale.

SUGAR'S STORY

My father was Cuban. My mother, American.

I never met my mother. My birth meant her death.

I have since met my father, but he gave me away when I was born. He didn't speak English, didn't understand it, either, and so he took me to the hospital in Marathon and left me there.

My father named me. Even though he could not speak English, he wrapped me in a ratty blanket and pinned to it a note in shaky scrawl:

Dulce como el azúcar.

Sweet as sugar.

I lived in a foster home with seven other children.

I was never adopted out.

My foster "parents" were not particularly nice. They were not cruel in the way that some parents are: fast with a striking hand, quick with an awful word. Their cruelty was in how they paid no attention to me at all. Not me, nor my so-called brothers and sisters. We were not a family. We were just a collection of people living under a single roof.

They got paid for it.

I was paid nothing but, I suppose, the chance to live.

I did not play with the other children. I instead invented a child to play with: a little girl my age who, in the logic given over to the very young, was also my baby girl. My imaginary friend was also my daughter who was also my age—it made no sense, but who said children had to make sense?

Some little girls always think about their wedding day.

I always dreamed of the day when I'd have my own daughter. A daughter I'd love. A daughter I'd never give away.

At first I thought I'd name her Beloved. But then I read that book.

Later in life I thought I might name her Precious.

But then I read that book, too.

So I decided that I would have a daughter and name her Cherish.

And that's exactly what happened to me ten years ago. I met a man. We did not love each other, but we liked each other. He was Cuban-born but American. He was not a drunk or a drug user or an abuser.

He was a cheat.

I knew this about Javi, and I married him anyway. Because I was pregnant with my little girl and she was his.

We rented a small apartment in Key Largo. I worked as a waitress at a dive bar that lied about having the best conch fritters in the Keys. They were not the best. They were not even fresh.

Javi worked as a boat mechanic at a marina across the street.

We had our daughter. I loved her very much. I think he tolerated her. But he was nice enough. There for birthdays and Christmas.

I didn't care. I figured he could go and do what he wanted as long as he was her father when he needed to be.

One day I was on shift. He agreed—reluctantly—to babysit.

He got bored with her. He would say, a man can only sit and play Tea Party Pirates—Cherish's favorite pastime—with his little girl so often.

So he took her to the marina. He had a boat he was working on. Or so he said.

He did take her to the marina.

But he went there to play with his other little girl—a nineteen-year-old tourist. A rich white girl. He told Cherish to go play, which she did. While she was off throwing bread crusts to seagulls, he fucked his girlfriend on a boat he was fixing.

I got off shift early because we ran out of conch that day. People thought it was because we were all fished out, but the conch at the restaurants here are really from the Caribbean, and the shipment didn't come in. We were out. So I went home.

Or, rather, I went to the marina to pick up my little girl.

I went. I looked for them.

I finally found Javi. With that girl bent over a drink cooler.

I asked him where Cherish was.

And he said, outside, just outside, throwing bread to the birds.

And I said, "No, she's not."

He laughed at me like I was stupid, and we went outside so he could show me how dumb I was for missing what was right under my nose. But she wasn't there. And he said, oh, she's over here, then, on this other dock—and we went among the boats and all the sails and she wasn't there, either.

She wasn't anywhere.

It was like she just disappeared.

Into the water, maybe. Or onto a boat. Or into a car. Or, or, or. Cherish was gone.

I'd lost her. Because I did not cherish her enough. And because my husband did not cherish her at all.

The police didn't know what to do. They found no body. They found no signs of a struggle. And I was half Cuban, my husband Cuban, and they didn't seem to care very much.

I lay awake every night, thinking about where she could be.

Caught in the darkest waters. Fish sliding in and out of her dead mouth. Or maybe taken by an evil man and used for whatever purpose such a monster would want a darling little girl for.

Maybe she was alive. Maybe she was dead. And I confess my guilt over the fact that the most horrific scenario I could imagine was the one where she'd been found and taken in by a new family. A new family that loved her more than I did.

That guilt became too much.

So one night I took myself to the docks. The same docks where Javi worked. I was drunk and I dove in. I let the dark water take me. I opened my mouth. I breathed in, and it was like inhaling ice and shadow and I remember panicking and thrashing, but it was over so quickly, almost painlessly, really . . .

That night, I died.

I didn't see any tunnel of light.

I didn't see Hell and all its devils.

I didn't see anything. I wasn't there anymore.

And then, suddenly, I was again.

I woke up screaming. In the same hospital where my little girl was born. In the same hospital where my father had given me up and named me Sugar. The same hospital where I was born and reborn.

Javi found my body floating.

He did some inexpert form of CPR. It worked, though I don't remember it; he said I gasped and threw up a rush of water but did not regain consciousness. He feared I was brain-dead, so he took me to the hospital, where I awoke.

He divorced me the next day. I didn't protest. I signed the papers.

I came back different.

Something had come back with me. My ghost. My little ghost—the little girl who follows me around when nobody else is with me. Cherish. My beautiful angel. My smiling demon. Sometimes she speaks like my little girl. Sometimes she says things no little girl would say. Horrible things.

And I came back with power.

The power to find things for people.

An irony, of course. Because while I can help others find what they want, I'll never find what I want. I'll never find my real daughter.

But I can help others.

That's what I'm going to do for you today, Miriam Black. I'm going to help you find two things, because I always help people find two things. I help them find the thing they're looking for.

And I help them find the thing they don't know they need.

Always two things.

FORTY-ONE
TWO THINGS

Miriam lights a cigarette. It feels like a cannonball just punched its way through her middle. She tries not to show it. Tries not to think about how she lost something she didn't even want—a child unborn, a life she misses only in retrospect. What this woman lost is so much worse. Sugar wanted that little girl. All her life. To fix what had been broken in her—to bind a broken wheel, to make it all whole again.

She lost what she thought she would never lose.

Sugar reaches over, plucks the cigarette from Miriam's lips.

Miriam scowls as the woman flicks it out of sight.

"No smoking," Sugar says. "You should really quit. It's bad for you."

"Everything's bad for you. Life is bad for you."

"That attitude is bad for you."

Miriam licks her lips. "Thank you, Mystical Life Coach. I'm sure you think it's cynicism, but I think it's realism."

"A saying that has long been the shelter of the cynic."

"Well, what the fuck? How are you *not* a cynic? What you've lost . . . it's horrifying. You're no optimist."

"I'm only an optimist. Because even in dying, life finds a way. An insignificant light is still a light, after all."

"You're sick in the head."

Sugar smiles a soft smile. "Maybe I am."

"Fine. So tell me my two things, then."

"I'll tell you about the thing you don't know you need first—"

"No, tell me about the—"

"Because if I do otherwise you'll run off."

Miriam stares.

Sugar winks. "The thing you're not looking for is a metal box about this big—" She holds out her hands about a foot apart lengthwise, six inches from top to bottom. "Like a safety-deposit box. It is beneath the water, as so many things around here are. Long Point Key is like a finger—its peninsula points the way. Somewhere out there, beneath the tides, this metal box awaits."

"Great. Metal box." *Worthless.* "And the next thing?"

"So impatient."

"You have no idea."

"The person you're looking for is on Summerland Key. South of it, actually, on the far side of a small island. He's camping there. You'll know the island because of the two wild tamarind trees that look like a pair of hands beseeching the heavens for favor."

"Poetic."

"I thought so."

"I'm going to go now."

"I figured as much."

"What do you want for . . . this?"

"For what?"

Miriam rolls her eyes. "For the whole . . . psychic thing. You gave me a vision. What do I give you in return? This was an exchange."

"I don't do this for gain."

"So why *do* you do it?"

"I don't really know. Why do you?"

Miriam narrows her eyes. "Do you see them? The visions? Every time, I mean. Do you know what everyone needs to find?"

"If they look into my eyes, I know."

"Do you tell them?"

"Almost never. Not unless they want to know."

"Is it hard? Seeing all that?"

"Not as hard as it must be for you." She brings the lantern close, bathing one side of her face in the artificial glow. "But it's still pretty strange. Oh—don't forget to buy some suntan lotion."

NOW

"So," Grosky asks, "what's in the box?"

He knocks on the metal box beneath his hand. *Clunk clunk.*

Miriam sneers. "I don't know, genius. You interrupted me before I could open it."

The big guy smiles. "We're good at that."

"I noticed."

"This other woman was a, you know"—he touches both fore-fingers to his temples, whistles the *Twilight Zone* theme—"psychic lady. She has powers like you. Shit, maybe we shoulda been talking to her this whole time."

"Why *are* you talking to me?" Miriam asks. Vills watches her the way a cat watches a cockroach and Miriam thinks, *It should be the other way around, asshole.* "What's your endgame? Because I'm not seeing it."

"We'll get there—" Grosky starts to say.

"We have no endgame with you," Vills says by way of interruption.

Grosky gives his partner a surprised look.

Vills says, "Christ, Richie, this girl is just stringing us along. Don't you see that? Admitting to all this like it's no big thing. Pretending she's a, a, a goddamn psychic? We're being played, Richie! Let's just pack up our stuff and hit the bricks—"

"Catherine, lemme handle this. At the very least, we get to sit here in a shack by the beach, a nice breeze coming in through those beautiful broken windows over there, and Miriam here tells us a little story."

"Richie, sometimes I swear, you have your head up your—"

"Uh-oh," Miriam says. She affects a little girl's voice. "Mommy and Daddy are fighting."

They both shoot her an *eat-shit-and-die* look.

"Cath, just sit down. You gotta remember, I'm the top dog here. I been here longer than you—"

Vills rolls her eyes. "This crap again."

"It isn't crap. Don't call it crap. Don't diminish what I'm saying to you. Don't *take away* from my years here in the behavioral unit—"

"Like you're some kind of *flawless gem* of behavioral analysis. You don't even have a degree—"

He barks a hard laugh. "*You* don't have a degree, either!"

"At least I've been out there. With the *bad guys*. You totter out into the field with your tracksuit or that ugly Hawaiian shirt with the mustard stain on the collar while the rest of us show up for work dressed for success. When was the last time you even fired your pistol?"

Grosky turns suddenly toward Miriam: the parent beseeching the child to turn against the other. "See, Vills here has only been working with me for a couple years. She got transferred to me—"

"As punishment!" Vills shrieks, face a rictus of inconsolable fury.

"She got transferred to me from—"

Now it's Miriam's turn to jump in. "Ooh-ooh, lemme guess: vice. Or whatever the drug unit is for you FBI types."

Grosky nods. Vills keeps shouting.

"I worked for the Organized Crime Drug Enforcement Task Force, and I lent support to local law enforcement in the country's HIDTAs—the High Intensity Drug Trafficking Areas. Albuquerque, Phoenix, New Orleans—"

"Miami," Miriam adds. Then she taps her head. "See? Psychic."

Suddenly Grosky is pounding on the table with the side of his fist, *wham wham wham*, the metal box jumping with each punch.

"Shut up," Grosky says. "The both of you."

He sits back down. He's broken out in a sweat. His cheeks are flushed like red water balloons. He takes out a white handkerchief, dabs the perspiration on his upper lip, licks it, then dabs it again.

Miriam whistles a low *uh-oh* whistle.

"Vills," Grosky says. "Siddown. We're staying. I'm seeing this through, and then I'll decide what we're gonna do with Miss Black. And you, Miriam—"

"Sit down, shut up, watch your mouth. Blah blah blah."

"Yeah, pretty much."

"Fine." *I got what I wanted out of this*, she thinks. Vills's cage has been successfully rattled. "You wanna hear the rest of the story, or what?"

Grosky nods but then says, "Hey, by the way, I'm real sorry about your mother."

Miriam's stomach drops out of her. She feels suddenly unfixed from the earth, as if she's on an elevator going up and everything else is going down.

"Thanks," she says.

Vills looks at her watch.

Miriam continues the story, starting with, "I needed a gun."

FORTY-TWO

LITTLE LADY HANDS

Miriam needs a gun.

She's got money, but no gun. She ditched the .38—the one she used to shoot that robber. Or mugger. (*That poor kid* is who he was.) There's a difference between the two, isn't there? Whatever. She can't be bothered by that right now. And she can't be bothered by that dumb kid, either—even now, with his face leering back at her, reflected in the streetlight flashes on the windshield glass of the Malibu. His blood-streaked, ashen mouth. He was a murderer. (*You're a murderer, too*, a small voice reminds her—a voice carried around the inside of her head, a ricocheting bullet.)

She can't mourn him.

He made his choices. She made hers.

That's how she hardens her heart against it.

Because she has no time to do anything else.

Getting that gun (*don't you mean the murder weapon?*) took time. She saved up some money from her little will-psychic-for-food experiment. Then she went to a gun show north of the city in a place called Oaks. Table after table of people selling ammo, ammo cases, knives, Nazi propaganda, KKK propaganda, Vietnam-era artifacts—

And oh, yeah, *guns*.

Buy from a private seller, slip through the loophole. No

background check. No signing anything. Fork over cash, get handed a gun.

Guy at the table was all bro-macho about it. "What's a little girl like you need with a gun?"

And she got cocky with him. "To make sure I don't get raped by flannel-wearing survivalist assholes like you."

She thought: *He's either gonna get mad and try to break my jaw or he's gonna tell me to fuck off and buy a gun from someone else.* But all he did was shrug and say, "Whatever, bitch. Your money's still green."

That's how she ended up with a little .38 Smith & Wesson snubnose.

Guy who sold it to her got one last jab in: "Little gun for little lady hands." She let it slide without pistol-whipping him, a fact she still upholds as a significant achievement and a clear watermark for personal growth.

Now, though, parked in the shadows of a long highway cutting down through the Keys, she doesn't have that option. No gun show here. Not tonight. And tonight's when she wants to do this.

No waiting.

Because time's the wolf at her door.

So, what to do, what to do?

No gun shows right now. But this is Florida. It's like a hillbilly Hawaii down here. Every time you see the news it's *Florida Man Did This* and *Florida Man Did That*. Florida Man gorges on bath salts, eats some lady's face. Florida Man tries to fuck an alligator, gets his dick stuck. Florida Man tries to hang glide onto a cruise ship and take a shit on the shuffleboard deck. Plus, down here it's like everyone thinks they're Charles Bronson from *Death Wish*. So, they have gun shops.

She just has to hope that one of them is open after 10 at night.

A pawn shop, maybe.

For this, she needs to go back to the motel and grab the phone book she saw sitting on the bedside table. That's not too far from here—another twenty to thirty minutes. Won't kill her plans.

At the motel, everything's quiet. Moths and flies and mosquitoes gather around the glowing light of a Coke machine under the stairway to Jerry's office. Miriam heads around the back end of the property, following the path until she gets to her door—and someone clears his throat behind her.

She wheels.

It's the burnout. Sitting on his lawn chair.

Behind him, a zapper sends bugs to their crispy, crackly dooms.

"They call these islands *Los Martires*," he says, like they've been in conversation for hours, like their last conversation never really stopped. "The Martyrs. When explorers came up in the night, they saw these shapes in the moonlight looking like suffering men hunched over the water. Like, prostating themselves before their god and shit."

"I think you mean *prostrating*."

"I don't think there's a difference."

"There's a pretty big fucking difference."

"Oh. Okay. Anyway, so, I think that's pretty cool. Because this place is all easy like Sunday morning and shit, but even in paradise we suffer, you know? We suffer."

"That's great. I have to—"

"Gotta lot of great names for some of the Keys, too, you know. Shelter Key. Knockemdown Key. Soldier Key. The Ragged Keys—"

"I really enjoy our time together, Florida Man," she says, suddenly realizing *this* is the guy eating faces and fucking alligators and hang gliding onto cruise ships to take shuffleboard dumps. "Lemme ask you something else. You know where a girl can buy a gun?"

"A gun? Whoa."

"That's right." She mimes a gun with her thumb and forefinger and makes *pchoo pchoo* sounds.

"Most places are probably closed. I know Billy's Pawn up in Key Largo would be open, but shoot, Billy's on a fishing trip and the shop's closed while he's out there."

"That doesn't help me."

"South of here is Kitty's Range and they sell ammo there, and sometimes you can find fliers and whatever on the corkboard, but Kitty's is definitely closed by now."

"That still doesn't help me. Listen, Florida Man, it's been supercrazy-fun-times hanging out, but I gotta—"

"You could have my gun, I guess."

"Your gun?"

"Uh-huh, yeah. It's a Springfield knockoff of the Colt 1911 .45. Or maybe it's a Colt knockoff of the Springfield. Shit, I dunno. I'll go get it." And then he gets up out of his chair—an act so slow it's like watching a glacier form over the epochs of time—grunting and groaning and moaning as he does, before tottering off to his double-wide.

Miriam stands out there. Bugs biting. Sunburned skin growing tighter and tighter—so tight she thinks it might split like a sausage casing.

Two minutes. Five minutes. Fifteen.

He went in there and . . . well, she has no idea what. Fell asleep on the toilet. Drowned himself in the bathtub. Got eaten by the alligator he was trying to cornhole.

That was fun while it lasted.

She turns around with her keys—

And sure enough, here comes Florida Man.

He's got the pistol in his hand like he's ready to start shooting people. He strolls up, walking less like *a person* and more *a self-propelled collection of dirty rubber bands,* and he points the gun right at her.

"Here you go," he says.

She stares. "That's maybe not the best way to hand someone a gun."

"Huh?" He looks down. "Oh." He gingerly uses both hands to turn the gun around so the grip is facing her.

As she takes it, his finger brushes her finger and—

He's 105 years old and looks like some kind of sun-baked beach mummy. He sits on a dock with a can of Schlitz in his arthritic claw and his body just . . . gives up. Everything goes slack. All his organs power down like someone turned off a breaker somewhere. The can drops out of his hand and rolls into the ocean, beer foaming over the edge. He laughs and farts a little fart and then it's a slow, comfortable brain death.

—and she pulls back, honestly surprised. No bath salt cannibalism. No hang glider defecations. Zero alligator fucking. She's almost disappointed, but she finds solace in the fact that Ashley doesn't find *him*, too.

"You die well," she says.

"Thanks." He nods like he understands, though he surely does not. "My name's Dave."

"My name's Miriam."

"Cool. You gonna shoot some cans or something?"

"Or something."

"Cool."

FORTY-THREE

MURDER WAS THE CASE THAT THEY GAVE ME

Gun in her lap. Foot on the pedal.

She tried to give Dave the Florida Man a couple hundred bucks from her stash, but he didn't want it.

So she took the money, hid it under the motel bed, and hit the road.

Now she's out on the highway.

She tastes blood. Her trigger finger aches.

In the seat next to her, the thug with the blown scalp covers up a laugh with his hand. "You gonna kill the right motherfucker this time?"

"I am," she says.

And she is.

FORTY-FOUR

SUMMERLAND

Midnight.

Moon in ribbons on black water.

Miriam stands at the edge of someone's yard at the southern-most point of Summerland Key. An abandoned white house sits, lights out, fifty yards down. Around her are half-collapsed deck chairs and rotting picnic tables. Unlit torches. Swaying palms like black fractal shadows.

She doesn't know who owns this place. The fence has long blown to the ground, the white paint peeling off the pickets, the wood rotting.

Easy entry, then.

Pale gravel grinds under her boots. *Like little knucklebones.* Like the ones Ingersoll kept in that pouch of his.

A minivan sits parked nearby. Also dark.

She steps up past all that, walks right to the water's edge.

There, in the distance, a small island.

Two big trees stand above all the others like hands reaching for the sky. As if hoping to grab the moon and forever failing to do so. What was it Sugar said? *Beseeching the heavens for favor.* That's it. That's the island.

And she curses herself. She didn't even think of how she'd get there. All the other islands seemed connected—bridges and roads are the thread that stitches this crazy archipelago together.

But this island is just . . . out there. Across the water.

At least a quarter of a mile out.

Even thinking of dipping her *toes* in that water gives her the shivering fits. As the thought crosses her mind, she thinks of the waters of the Susquehanna—turbid mud stirred by the angry current, voices carried along with it. Bubbles and ghosts and terrible thoughts.

Eleanor Caldecott's corpse—a finger pressed to dead lips.

Shh.

Miriam presses the heels of her hands against her eyes.

The river was bad. The ocean is worse. A big hungry mouth. With coral for teeth and sharks for tongues. Wanting to swallow her up.

She won't swim.

Won't do it.

Can't do it.

She shudders.

Wait. There—

A shape bobbing in the water past the house.

It's a kayak. Just past a boat ramp. The paddle floating next to it, tethered there with a dark cord.

She goes to the boat. Takes her knife, cuts the rope holding it to the post next to the ramp. Then she slides down the concrete and—

Don't get in the water don't do it just go home fuck this you still have time maybe you can wait and spring a trap and catch him leaving—

But then she sees her mother. Stab wounds like little bloody mouths opening on her chest. She sees Jerry and his dead bird. She sees Peter and his squirting jugular. And over all of it: Ashley's leering face. That boomerang smile. Those shiny nickel eyes.

Miriam gets in the boat.

FORTY-FIVE

DARK CROSSING

She sees faces in the water.

Not just tricks of the light, either. Corpse faces. Brined and swollen like tumors. The boat thumps against them.

They're not real. It's just the Trespasser.

Dead mouths drift open. Silvery bubbles burst to the surface, carry with them whispers that crawl into her ears like snakes—

Chooser of the slain . . .

You don't know what awaits you . . .

You're not prepared . . .

Turn back, go home, give up . . .

The faces of those she's killed stare up at her.

Edwin Caldecott's prim, pursed-lips. The cop, Earl, his tongueless mouth sucking in seawater. Beck Daniels—really, Beck Caldecott—on his face is painted a twin-tailed swallow tattoo, the lines distorted and wings bulging from the bloated, waterlogged flesh. Other faces swim in and out: the Mockingbird Killer, Ingersoll, Harriet, the ATM thug. The faces, too, of those whose deaths she did not cause but that feel like hers just the same: Del Amico, Ben Hodge, Jack Byrd, Hetta Gale, Steve Lister, the little boy named Austin with his red balloon, a balloon she sees float to the surface like a fishing bobber—

They all tell her the same thing:

You're not ready for this. You pushed and pushed and pushed.

Eventually something was going to push back.

And then she's almost there. Almost to the island of the pleading trees with the reaching, desperate branches.

FORTY-SIX

TWO TREE KEY

The kayak bumps against the rocky shore. She curses even the slightest sound and tries carefully to clamber out of the boat—but she's not used to boats, doesn't know how it all works. It's not like getting out of a car. Her foot presses back and suddenly the boat drifts away. Leaving her here. On the island with the two skeleton-hand trees taller than the rest.

She tells herself, *I don't need the boat to do what needs to be done.*

Everything is dark. The cover of the trees above blots out the moon and stars. She draws the pistol. Checks it for ammo. Pops the magazine back in, then thumbs off the safety.

She creeps into the tree line. The island isn't big—but it's big enough. Walking its circumference might take her a half-hour. Better to cut through the middle. Sugar said that Ashley was on the far side.

Miriam descends into the brush. Gentle steps through sand and tide pools. Water soaking boots, socks. Clouds of flies parting like mist.

It's then she smells it: food. Something sweet and savory.

Baked beans. Like her mother used to make.

She follows the scent like it's something out of a cartoon, the vapors tickling the underside of her nose and drawing her closer, closer.

By some small favor, she's as quiet as a priest's whisper.

Ahead: an orange, fickle glow.

Firelight.

Now the smell of food is joined by smoke. The firelight plays off metal—the bottom of a small boat. A boat brought to shore and overturned. The boat Ashley must use to get to and from this island.

Gently, carefully, slow as a praying mantis, she parts a nest of mangrove branches with the side of the gun—

And there sits Ashley Gaynes.

His back is to her. A small campfire crackles and pops ahead of him.

The gun feels suddenly heavy in her hand.

Gingerly, she raises the .45.

The back of his head lines up between the two iron teeth of the pistol's sights. Her finger coils around the trigger.

"I see you got my messages," he says, setting down a can of baked beans swaddled in foil. He drops a spoon into it with a clank-and-rattle.

Her hand shakes.

"Go ahead," he says, still facing away from her. "Pull the trigger. Lemme make it easier on you." He scoots on his butt in a circle until he's finally facing her. It's him. Just like in the visions. The fire lights him from behind. He's just a shape—the silhouette of a paper target she wants to perforate with bullets. *So why won't you shoot?*

"You just couldn't leave well enough alone," she says.

He smiles. Runs his hands down along his jeans, then pulls up the hem on an ankle to show off a glimpse of the metal prosthetic beneath. "I was going to. I really was. But I've given myself over to it. This isn't my idea, Miriam. It really isn't. I'm content to live and let live here. My hands, though, they're tied." He holds up both hands. He wiggles the fingers. Taunting her.

"I could just shoot you."

"And I'm sure you will. You've got the jump on me. I'm just a crippled asshole, can't outrun a bullet. So why not take a second? Let's have a conversation. I've missed you."

She bares her teeth. "Die in a car fire."

"We were good together, you and I."

"You were a manipulator."

"Like you're any better."

"I am. I'm honest."

"Like when you told Louis that I was your brother?"

"That was *your idea*." She punctuates the last two words with a thrust of the pistol. "I came clean. I've changed."

"You have. You're right. You figured it out." He starts patting the side of his jeans and she growls, waves the gun. He holds up his hands in plaintive surrender. "Just looking for my flask. Got a little rum in it if you want. I see you like rum now."

"When in Rome," she snarls.

"When in Rome, eat Roman pussy?" he asks.

Gabby. Of course he knows about her.

He pulls a flask. Spins the top off and takes a swig. He offers it to her. Part of her wants a taste. She wants that fire in her belly.

She shakes her head.

"Here's what's changed," he says. "You've started to figure out your gift. After years on the road, watching people die, you've suddenly become illuminated." He licks the top of the flask and makes a small *yum* sound. "You went from being the thief robbing fresh graves to the killer filling them. So now you've got your grim purpose. Good for you."

"You're the killer. Not me."

He ignores the comment. "What surprises me is how long it took you to figure it out. Nobody gave you an instruction manual. And that's sad. Me, though, I'm playing for the home team. I didn't have to wander around, pulling on my dick, hoping I'd get some epiphany shined in my eyes. They told me everything I needed to know. They still tell me. They're talking to me even now." He swats his arm. *Smack!* The short sharp shock of the sound almost makes her blow his head off. "The bugs here. They're bloodsuckers. What was it you used to say? *It is what it is.*"

"What the hell are you talking about? Who is *they*?"

"The voice, Miriam. The gods. The *fates*. I fell out of that car, my leg carried farther and farther away by a white SUV and . . ." He takes a deep breath. "I bled. I could smell it. The blood. The piss. Christ, I shit my pants. How awful is that? One leg gone, the stump pouring blood, and all you can do is roll around on a New Jersey back road with shit in your pants. Eventually some-one found me, but I'd lost so much blood by then I must've looked like your toes after they spent too long in wet shoes: pale and wan. Sad little things. Some campers found me and got me to the hospital but the storm wasn't over. Weeks of infections. Scraping bad tissue. Trying to grow good tissue. The fevers. The hallucinations. And the pain—whoof. I couldn't click that little morphine rocket booster button fast enough. But then in the midst of all that . . . They started talking to me."

"You're telling me you've got some . . . power?"

"Like C&C Music Factory, baby."

"And what power is this?"

"Oh, you'll see."

"Not if I put a round between your eyes."

A wicked grin cuts across his face. "That's *exactly* when you'll see."

Fuck this.

She pulls the trigger.

FORTY-SEVEN

THE HANGED WOMAN

The stink of gunpowder. The high-pitched whine like a fly caught in the bell of the ear. The taste of mud and seawater.

The gun is no longer in her hand.

Miriam tries to breathe through pancaked lungs. Her hands claw at the wet ground beneath her, only pulling up dirt and sand.

What the hell happened?

The memory of only moments ago comes back in fits and starts—

She pulls the trigger but Ashley's fast—too fast, shockingly fast. He jerks his head to the right before the bullet even leaves the gun, and it throws up sparks and punches through the bottom of the overturned rowboat behind him—

She does a clumsy push-up, but Ashley presses down between her shoulder blades with the base of his prosthetic foot. He laughs. Says something about being like the Terminator.

—Already she's tracking him again, following him with the gun barrel, but it's like he's ready for her. He jerks left and then lunges backward, scooping up a fistful of hoary ash from the campfire's margins and flinging it toward her. Suddenly she can't see, her eyes stinging, her mouth tasting of char and cinders. She starts coughing, fires the gun once, twice, bullets biting off bits of trees but finding no part of Ashley Gaynes—

The knife. She needs to get to her knife. In her pocket. But before her hand can even twitch, Ashley kneels on the small of her back. His hand thrusts deep into her back pocket, snatching the blade like a thieving magpie. He says, "Miriam loves her little knives, doesn't she?"

—*She steps forward and even before her foot hits the ground, Ashley says, "Watch your step." But it's too late. Of course it's too late. Her foot falls into a short hole dug out and covered in leaves; the ankle twists and a sharp pain pistons up through her leg to her knee, to her hip. Miriam cries out and starts to fall—*

"Is this a knife in your pocket or are you just happy to see me?" Ashley says. He follows that with a mad cackle. He flicks the blade open and thrusts it up under her chin. "I could kill you now, you know. But that's not the point of all of this. The point is to teach you a lesson first. The point is to make an *example* of you. You don't die here. But I'm sure nobody will mind if you get a little hurt, right? By the way, I'll need this back later—" And he plunges the knife into the back of her thigh. Miriam screams.

—*As soon as she hits the ground, Ashley swings out with a kick from his good foot, kicking the gun out of her hand. She scrambles fast, grabbing at the lip of the boat and giving herself the leverage to stand, but he pumps a fist into her solar plexus once, twice, a third time, the breath robbed from her. In its place blooms a mushroom cloud of terror—*

His hand curls under her chin and clamps her jaw shut hard enough that she bites her tongue. Blood fills her mouth. "Fuck you," she growls through gritted teeth, and in response he shoves her face into the sandy mud. She tries to breathe but can't. *You're not ready for this. You pushed and pushed and pushed. And now something's pushing back.* Her body spasms. Panic throttles her.

—*Gasping for air, she pitches a clumsy fist at him, but it's like he knows it's coming, because he's not there when it should land. She snaps a hard kick toward his head but it's like he anticipates that, too—he's already dancing out of the way before she even lifts her foot. And he's having fun doing it, smiling and laughing like a kid on the playground—*

He lifts her head back up. She cries out. Then snaps back with her head, hoping to connect with his nose. But when she does, he's not even there. He's hobbling around to her front, and he drives a boot into her cheek. All she sees is a rain of stars falling in the dark of her eye and she thinks, *He's gotten me. I can't do this anymore. I can't get up. I can't move.* She feels his hands on her ankle, dragging her somewhere . . .

—He cracks her across the mouth with the back of his hand, her head reeling. She tries another kick, but he slaps it away like it's nothing more than a jumpy dog, and in return he drives his knee up into her gut, again robbing her of breath. He says, "Have you figured it out yet?"—

Her world, upside down. Something around her ankle. She's going up, up, up, hair dangling, hands reaching toward earth. He's got her tied by the one foot and she sees him now, using one of the branches of the tamarind tree as a makeshift pulley as he grunts and shows his teeth, hoisting her into the air by one ankle. And there she is. The hanged woman. Dangling. Swinging. All the blood rushing to her head. Her brain is a giant blister, throbbing with each beat of her heart. Ready to split like a snare drum.

Ashley says, "Whew!" then wipes sweat from his brow with the back of his hand. He holds it up, and the hand is bloody. "Yours, not mine."

"Come closer and you can show me yours," she hisses.

"You're being tough-ass Miriam, I know. I get it. Quick with the quips, fast with the threats. And sometimes you can back it up, too. But you have to admit I got you. I got you trussed up like a deer at hunting season. I could do what I want with you. I could come over there. Cut your clothes off. Stick my dick in your mouth—"

"I'd bite it off."

"You think I don't know that? That's why I'd have to knock all those teeth out, first. All gums, baby. Then I'd take your own knife. I'd cut you up. Nothing vital. Just a slash here, a slash there. Blood makes a helluva lube for whatever I want to stick up your ass or your cunt. My fingers. The gun barrel. Your knife, heated in the fire—I could cauterize all your holes shut. Wouldn't that be something?"

"Men. Always so threatened by women." She spits out the words with as much acid and iron as she can muster; anything to hold back the tears. "Pretending like you have power. Holding your dick like it's a gun. It's barely that. A clumsy little water pistol. The vagina—now, that's power, boy. Like an oracle's cave. Heady vapors to bring even the brawniest sonofabitch to his knees. Give him visions. Give him dreams. And give him *life*, too. Because without what we got going on downstairs, you wouldn't even have been born. We're the ones with the power."

He slow-claps. "Nice speech. You practice that every time some boy has you hanging from a tree?" Before she can say anything he walks over to her like a hunter admiring his kill. "Besides, for all your talk of power, you can't even have kids, can you? Where's your power now?"

She swipes at him with her nails out—

And it's like he's ready for it. He bows his back, lets her meager swing find nothing but air.

"You still don't get it," he says. "You still don't see what I can do."

"Your precious power?"

"They tell me what you're going to do next. I don't need to see it. I just *know*. I knew when you were going to pull the trigger. I could see every punch and kick you were going to throw at my head. I knew you'd step forward and so just an hour ago I dug that hole and covered it with leaves. And I *knew* that when you stepped in it you'd twist your ankle up something fierce. Does it hurt, by the way? I bet it hurts."

"You can't hurt me," she says.

But he's lost to her answer, swept away by his own thoughts. "Sometimes They whisper what will happen to me. Sometimes I see it written across the sky, or carved into a tree, or dripped on the blade of a knife in little black beads of blood. They send me messages. And it's not just you. Everybody's connected. They're all—" And here he laughs madly, and she can see the tears in *his* eyes like this is sublime to him. He's a man given over to the ecstasy of his faith. "They're all *singing the same frequency*, these low-level harmonics that my bosses let me hear. I know what everyone is going to do just before they do it. And sometimes I can see much further than that. I knew you'd come here tonight. I knew you'd go to the motel. To Miami. To your mother's house. It's like—"

"It's like you've lost your fucking marbles, like you're crazier than a nest of yellow jackets—"

He talks louder to speak over her. "*It's like* I can see the possibilities exploded out, like a mirror shattered into a thousand pieces, and in each little piece of reflective glass I can see what will happen. If I do X, then I see that Y will be the result. If I do A, then B is what happens. I know even before I make my choices what the results will be. It's amazing. It's really amazing. I know your power is a curse, but mine, Miriam, mine is a *blessing*."

He means it, too. Gone is any pretense of sarcasm. He's caught in the river of his own power and dragged along by it.

By now every inch of Miriam's head feels like a balloon— a red balloon full of blood, a balloon not lifting toward the sky but falling toward the earth, heavy with inevitability. Given over to grim, inescapable gravity.

Darkness licks at her vision like black flame.

Ashley rubs his face. He's smiling so big it must hurt his cheeks.

"I was thinking about something," he says, "and this is going to really bake your noodle, but here it is. You're Little Miss Free Will, right? Bucking the chains of fate, standing triumphant against the oppressive tide of destiny. Blah blah fucking blah. You say that things are predetermined. *Preordained.* And yet, somehow, you got beat to shit way back when. Lost your baby. Got this . . . curse of yours as a result. Who do you think gave you that curse? If all things are written in the book of fate, wasn't that a preordained event?" He claps his hands like an excited child. "Fuck, how crazy is that? The fates gave you your fate-breaking gift. It's like they were setting you up to fail. How sad is that? Pathetic, really."

Suddenly he swats at his arm. Again and again. His giddy rub-your-nose-in-it rapture is lost beneath a surge of rage—eyes bulging, teeth bared. He swipes at the air, parting the cloud of gnats.

"I thought you were so cool once," she says. Consciousness bleeds from her like ink from a pen dropped in a glass of water.

"These fucking bugs!"

"But you're just a lost little boy."

"I have to go now," he says. "I love you, Miriam. I do. I wouldn't do all those horrible things I said earlier. You're precious to me. You enjoy your time here. This won't kill you. But it'll keep you from stopping me when I go and visit your little dyke friend in Key West. Teach her what it means to get close to Miriam Black."

And that does it. A surge of adrenalin sets fire to the encroaching darkness, and now Miriam's the one caught in the throes of rage—she swipes at him, hissing and spitting. "You leave her alone, you motherfucker—"

"Hey, Miriam. I have a joke. Wanna hear it?"

"I'm going to take you apart piece by piece, Ashley, I swear—"

"What do you say to a girl who has two black eyes?"

"Fuck you!"

"Nothing you haven't said to her twice already."

He pops her with a fist. In her right eye.

Then again in her left.

She sees fireworks as capillaries break. As her brain rocks against the back of her head. And then the fireworks show is over and all she's got left is the dark.

YELLOW JACKETS IN SEPTEMBER

Everything hurts. Her body is a road map of little welts—like her skin is Braille for the blind to read. She tries not to cry. But she keeps crying anyway even as Mother hunches over her, using big cotton balls to blob globs of pink calamine lotion onto the red welts.

"I told you not to run back there," Mother says.

"They never bothered me before," Miriam says, sniffling.

"They're yellow jackets in September. They know their time is coming what with winter approaching. They grow agitated."

"My fingers feel fat."

"Because they're swollen."

Miriam sees a little rabbit's tail of goopy cotton stuck to a calamine smear on her arm. Idly she moves to pick it off.

Mother swats her hand.

"Ow!" she cries, pulling her hand away.

"Don't mess," Mother says.

"But they stung me there and you hit my hand."

But Mother just frowns and keeps dabbing lotion all over.

Miriam had run back behind the house into the woods. Under a rotten log she'd found a hole and yellow jackets—which always made her think of little jet planes, little *evil* jet planes like out of one of those cartoons Mother says is *for boys only*—and she kept hurrying over and shoving things into the hole to stop the

yellow jackets from coming out. She was laughing and having
fun, watching them try to push past her roadblock of mulch and
twigs and fallen ash tree leaves.

But then suddenly the air was filled with them—and they
were all over her and under her shirt and then came the buzz of
wings. The dance of little feet. The biting. The stinging.

The screaming.

And now here she is.

"You mess with things you shouldn't mess with," Mother says.

"It was fun."

Mother grunts. "There is an apocryphal gospel—the gospel
of the Nazarenes—in which Jesus says, 'Woe unto the crafty
who hurt the creatures of God. Woe unto the hunters for they
shall become the hunted.' You think you're crafty, but you're not.
You were the hunter who became the hunted."

"I'm sorry."

"Sorry doesn't change what you did. Sorry is a poor man's Band-
Aid." Mother pauses in her ministrations, then sighs. "We're not
going to the carnival tonight."

"But Mom!"

"Shush. You're going to swell up like a balloon. You look like a
mess. I can't show the other ladies from the church my bee-stung
daughter. The evidence of your sin is for you, not for me. You'll
sit at home."

Miriam starts to cry. "But tonight's the last night!"

"It is what it is, Miriam."

FORTY-EIGHT

TWO DAYS LEFT

Miriam wakes.

She can hear her own breathing as she swings upside down from the tamarind tree. It's a raspy, whistling sound—like wind keening through the broken shutters of an old window. Her nose is full. Her sinuses ache. Opening her eyes is a bitter acid misery.

Everything hurts.

Eventually the calendar clicks over and from her vantage point the sun falls from the horizon like a lightbulb dropping from its fixture in slow motion. It isn't long before the air grows hot and the sun's kiss turns from something pleasurable into something torturous.

When the sun lights the world she sees it—farther down the shoreline sits, of all things, a submarine. Not a real one, like, some huge nuclear Navy sub. But a small thing. Bigger than a rowboat, but not by much. The narco-sub sits painted in blue camo.

The front is torn open.

A red, dead hand rests on the torn metal. Gathering flies. One of the transporters. One of the Colombians Tap-Tap said went missing.

I have to get down.

Ashley is going to kill Gabby.

Gabby may already be dead.

That realization nearly causes her to black out again so strong is the rush of grief and horror. It's not like she loved Gabby. She's not sure that what they had was anything at all besides two people crashing together before pulling themselves apart. But it was fun and Gabby was nice and she deserved more than what Miriam gave her.

Miriam's legacy of pain.

The pain is all over her. Swaddling her: a blanket of nettles for a troublesome infant. Her face pounds. Her middle aches. Her ankle feels like it's a toothpick cracked in half. And whenever she tries to move, the knife in her thigh gives her a mean twinge. If the rest of her leg weren't numb she'd probably feel fresh blood trickling.

The knife.

She has to get the knife.

She can cut herself down.

She bends her body at the waist—

Her whole body is a powder flash of hot pain. Miriam cries out. She lets her body go slack.

Again. Try again.

Another hard bend at the waist, and more pain crashes through her—a big rock in a little pond, a train through a preschool, a 747 into one of the Twin Towers. But this time she reaches up and catches a fistful of her own jeans. It anchors her, lets her stay bent.

Blood moves around her body, rushing this way and that. Filling spaces it had fled. Leaving spaces it had pooled. Her muscles scream. Her skin tingles like it's being poked with safety pins.

Keep going. Move, you crafty bitch.

She pulls herself farther. Hand sliding along the back of her thigh. She bumps the tip of her ring finger into the base of the knife and it's like flicking a car antenna. A frequency of new pain runs through her, and she thinks, *It's like a Band-Aid, just rip it off fast.* She grabs the knife with her fingers and wrenches it free with a splash of blood—

But her fingers are numb—

Blood makes a helluva lube—

The knife drops from her hand.

The blade sticks in the ground.

She tries not to sob. Tries not to scream.

Miriam reaches for it.

It's too far.

Fuck. *Fuck!*

She stops struggling for a while. She tries not to weep, but it's too late. The tears come, spilling up toward her brow, dampening her hair. It feels weak. Meager. *Crying is for girls,* she thinks. *You're no girl. You're a badass woman. You're a hunter. A killer. You're the river breaker. You're fate's foe.*

And yet, the tears keep coming.

Until a shadow falls over her.

Louis.

He found her.

He's here to save her.

Of course he is. He always is. He's always the one standing between her and death—the one keeping her sane, keeping her balanced—and the wave of realization crashes down on her shores: *I need Louis to balance me out. I never would've killed that boy in Philly if he were around.* She holds his arms and he shushes her and tells her it's going to be okay, and she says, "Oh, God, Louis, please help me—" And she reaches out and he reaches back and his massive hands clasp her arms at the biceps, and they could squeeze her and wrench her arms out of the sockets, but his touch is as gentle as it's always been.

"I had a dream about you," he says, "and so I came."

But then she sees something move—

A yellow jacket crawls from beneath his arm.

Then a second. And a third. And four more after that.

Soon his arms are a swarm of them, some alighting into the air before landing again on his skin. Miriam says, "No, no, no, now is not the time, don't fuck with me, quit fucking with me," but the Trespasser leans forward and whispers into her ear.

"You messed up. You weren't ready. You went off like a gun half-cocked, and now what? Now you've lost your shot. And Gabby's dead. And your mother's going to die, too. You've failed."

Miriam screams.

Her scream echoes out over the water.

Loud enough, she thinks, to churn the seas. To rip the sun out of the sky and cast it into the water. To tear up the shore. To part the clouds.

It's enough. A jolt of adrenalin lights her up like a city skyline and she reaches, reaches—her fingertips tickle the end of the knife.

—almost—

—her fingers slide off, finding no purchase—

—the angle's all wrong on the knife—

—*goddamnit goddamnit goddamnit*—

Then she falls. Not her body. But her mind. It feels like her brain slips a gear and lurches out of sync and—

She sees herself. Hanging there. Looking like fresh hell. Like a dirty sock that's been run through a mud puddle and then a pile of roadkill, then hung up in a tree to dry. She feels little feet beneath her. Feels the taste of worms and sand and fish in her mouth. She tries to move toward herself and the little feet go hop hop hop *and then it hits her—*

Oh fuck, I'm a fucking bird.

It worked. Now. Beaten to hell. Beaten down. It worked.

The bird as Miriam, Miriam as bird, hops forward.

Hop hop hop.

To the knife. A little beak—her beak—thrusts out and taps the knife handle forward, tap tap tap, *putting it in reach—*

A sound of rushing wind. Like cars in a mountain tunnel. And then Miriam's back in her own body. She gasps. Still tastes the sea water, the fish brine, the worm guts. A little gray-and-white plover bird stares up at her and shakes like a dog trying to free itself of rainwater before flying away.

Her fingers pinch the bottom of the knife.

She has it.

I have it!

Triumph tastes sweet. At least until she again has to bend at the waist—misery throttling her body, *bend don't break*—and saw the rope with the blood-wet blade of the small knife.

The rope frays. Cuts. Miriam drops.

She lands hard on her shoulder, but the ground beneath is soft.

For a while, she lays on her side. Curling up like a baby in the crib. Her body shudders as if she's crying, but no tears appear.

Then eventually she sits.

She looks around: no gun anywhere. And her cell phone is back in the car where she left it.

Out there, the ocean. The line of black water. Bright at the top with the cresting sun. The hungry water. The consumptive deep.

She's going to have to swim.

I'm going to have to swim.

She doesn't have the strength. The water terrifies her. Her muscles will fail out there. The ocean will suck her down. Chew her up. Her and Eleanor Caldecott: bowels for fish, throat for eels, eyes for minnows.

Then comes a heavy flutter of wings.

Followed by a piggy grunt.

A green-eyed cormorant lands by her side. And stares up at her.

Grunt, grunt, squark.

Miriam tries to spit at it, but she can't summon any *moisture* into her mouth. "Go away," she croaks. "Trespass somewhere else."

The cormorant pecks at her knee. Peck, peck, peck.

Then: footsteps. Splashing in water. Crashing through brush. "Miriam?"

She blinks.

"Miriam?"

And that's when Jerry Wu comes running full steam up the shore.

FORTY-NINE

HOBBLE AND LIMP

The world seems askew, unfixed, like a paper boat tossed about in a river. This feeling is magnified upon getting into Jerry's rowboat—with Corie the cormorant sitting proudly at the bow, the ugliest mermaid you ever did see—as the water shoves and slaps the little boat along.

Her legs and feet are still numb. Her skull feels like aquarium glass tapped on by an unruly child: *thoom thoom thoom, hello little fish.*

Jerry doesn't say much. He mostly just stares at her, face a pair of masks fused together: not comedy and tragedy, but confusion and horror.

Miriam looks back at the shore. Sees the little island with the two reaching, beseeching hands disappearing slowly. The boat motor growls.

"I need to—" It feels like she's trying to talk past a wad of bristly hay in her throat. She coughs, and Jerry quickly grabs for a small thermos behind him and hands it over. She opens it, takes a long swig—coffee. Cold. Doesn't matter. It's perfect. "I need to get to Key West. A friend is in . . ." *A body bag.* "Danger."

"Sure, sure, but maybe you oughta get to a hospital first."

"No time." She levels her gaze at him. "How'd you find me?"

"You really wanna know?"

"I hate that question because, yes, I—" She breaks into a hard, raspy cough. "I really obviously want to know."

"The bird led me here."

The cormorant grunts.

Miriam says nothing but raises an eyebrow.

"I was getting ready to do some morning fishing. I drove the truck and the boat down to the bay. But then Corie here started . . . you know, freaking out. Flapping her wings, beating them against the side of the boat. Squawking. Then she flew away and landed on the hood of my truck and I kept trying to wrangle her away, but she kept flying back."

"And you were okay with that."

"No, I wasn't. I wanted to get out in the water while the fish were still jumping. Then like that, she flew away. And not toward the water but toward the road. No way was I gonna keep up with her on foot so I got in the truck. She'd fly. I'd follow. I'd lose her—but the highway's a straight shot so I kept driving and looking and then I'd see her sitting there on top of a DON'T DRINK AND DRIVE sign or on somebody's mailbox. Then, soon as I got close again—" He claps his hands. "She'd take off again."

"She led you here."

"She led me here. You got it."

Holy shit.

She turns toward the bird. "You're a good bird."

Corie oinks at her. The bird's beak opens and closes with a clack.

Jerry says, "I gotta tell you, the last thing I expected to see was you hanging from that tree."

"Things didn't work out."

"With your perp?"

"Yeah. With my perp."

"So now what happens?"

Now he hurts those people who fell in with me. Including you, Jerry. All because I fucked up. All because I took my shot and I missed it.

FIFTY

THE MONSTER WE MADE

Back at the Malibu she tells Jerry that she appreciates his help. She even leans forward and gives him a small, probably unpleasant hug. Her arms don't quite touch his, don't quite *complete* the embrace, but hugging is not a skill she has practiced very often in this life.

The hug hurts. Literally. Not in the way some people use that word now—literally as figuratively—but literally, actually, honest-to-all-the-gods-and-devils it hurts her body from top to bottom just to give a half-ass hug.

He tells her to go to the hospital.

He tells her to call the police.

She makes all the right noises—mm-hmm, yes, sure, it'll be fine, right, right. And then she gets in the car and does none of those things.

From inside the glove box, she fetches her cell. She grabs Gabby's number and starts to punch it in even as her tires are kicking up pebbles and the car lurches forward like a drunk off a barstool.

It doesn't even get to one ring before someone answers.

"Miriam," Ashley sings. "That's such a pretty name."

"You leave her alone."

"File that one under *too late*."

"Then stay right there. Because I'm coming for you."

He laughs. "You came for me once already. How'd that work out for you? I admit, you got away much faster than I expected. But once I was done with your girlfriend here my friends gave me a message—I saw it written in her blood across the bathroom mirror. I saw the words drip together and tell me that you were on your way and that I was to expect a phone call. So I sat by the phone. I felt the familiar tickle, heard their little whisper—and sure enough, ringy-dingy. Here we are."

"I'll find a way to hurt you. To whittle you down like a stick."

"You're on the losing side, Mir. The side of the scrappy under-dogs."

"The scrappy underdogs always win."

"Only in the movies. In the movies, the underdogs pull it out of the fire in the final game. In the movies, the killer's victim makes it out alive—the final girl who kills the big bad boogey-man. But this isn't the movies. This is life. And in life, the monsters prevail."

She screams into the phone.

But he's already ended the call.

"The girl is expendable," says a voice. Miriam turns. Her bowels go to ice water. It's Harriet. Harriet, the grim assassin. An evil little teapot, short and stout, here is her handle, here is Harriet cutting off all your fingers and toes because she wants to prove her dominance over you.

Miriam knows it's not her. She tells herself that again and again. *It's not her, it's not her, it's not her.* But still, she feels her innards loop like a noose at the sight of her. "You're not real."

"You should've died that day in the Pine Barrens. I gave you a gift. I gave you my gun. Think about it. If you had used it, we wouldn't be here right now. Gabby would be alive. Your mother would not be next on the chopping block. You have less than two days now, you realize."

"I chose life."

"You chose complexity."

"I *chose*. You're always telling me there's work to do. Well, I choose to do it. I chose that day to put a bullet in your ugly-ass haircut and my life is now my own no matter how you haunt me or mess with my head."

Harriet smiles. "Good. Then maybe you're ready for this. Maybe. Because you didn't listen to me before. I said you weren't ready, but did you listen? The forces working against you realize the power you have. You're the penny on the tracks—small, but still able to derail a train."

"That's a myth. The penny just gets squashed."

"I prefer my narrative. Though maybe that's what will happen to you. Maybe you'll get squashed. Maybe this is all just a trap and I'm not really here to help you. Maybe I'm here to hurt you. Maybe everything I tell you to do has just led you to deeper, wider circles of misery. You're Dante in Hell. You're Sisyphus pushing that boulder up and up and up until it falls back again and again *and again*. Or maybe you're Prometheus. You stole something precious from the gods, and now they punish you. I'm the eagle pecking out your liver for all of eternity."

"Just shut up. I'm tired of hearing you speak."

"It's like I told you. Nature is brutal and grotesque. If you see yourself as a part of nature—as you must, dear Miriam—then you too must be brutal and grotesque if you are to persevere. Once I told you to be docile. Now is not the time to be docile."

"I said *shut up* and *go away*."

"Not without leaving you one last gift."

Then Miriam turns—

Harriet has a gun pointed at her head.

The gun barrel is a dark eye, unblinking.

Trigger pull.

Bang.

The vision hits Miriam like a bullet to the head.

HOW GABBY DIES

Fast forward: She and the other woman are bolting down Duval Street past the drunks and pirates and cruise-ship tourists and the blonde pulls Miriam into an alcove between an art gallery and a Cuban food joint and Miriam starts cursing about those thin-dicked shit-birds, those assholes who think they can saunter into a bar and jam their nickel-sized cocks into whatever coin slot they want just by using a few half-ass weak-fuck pick-up lines—

The other woman says, "You have a dirty mouth. I want to taste it."

Then it's her mouth on Miriam's—

It's five years later and it's night in Key West and the air feels like the breath from a panting dog and she tosses and turns, but her skin crawls and her heart is a jumpy mouse. It's another panic attack where she feels oh so small in a world so big, like she's nothing at all, just a bug under a boot, like all eyes are watching, like all eyes are judging—

And she gets up and goes to the bathroom and turns on the light and the scars that criss-cross her face like the clumsy lacing of a crooked boot are puffy and pink and long-healed but still horrible, Xs and dashes of ruined skin. Across the nose. The brow. The cheeks. Lines cut into her cheeks. Her face is monstrous. Like when a child breaks a vase, then sloppily glues it back together again.

The panic seizes her. She's ugly. Mauled. Nobody will love her. Nobody could love her. Her breathing goes shallow. She feels woozy. Sick with self-hatred, like it's an infection whose tendrils grow long and dig deep.

This is it. She can't do this. Can't handle it. The horror and dread and disgust are a meteoric fist punching her into the dirt—

She flings open the medicine cabinet.

Oxycodone. Old prescription.

She grabs that.

And Ambien. Her sleeping pills.

That, too.

And Ativan. For the anxiety.

She puts a bunch into her mouth. Not even sure how much. Not too many. She's sure of that. The wrong amount is the right amount.

She scoops water into her mouth from the faucet.

The pills go down, and she goes back to bed.

Soon she stops crying. And shaking. And sweating.

And breathing.

FIFTY-ONE

STILL ALIVE

Gabby is still alive.

The vision says she dies in five years.

Which means today, she's still alive.

But I bet I know who's gonna carve up her face like that.

Miriam slams her foot down on the pedal. She knows that it means a cop could stop her. Let them. Anybody tries to stop her, she'll cut a path through them all.

FIFTY-TWO

PRETTY PRETTY CICATRIX

The door is ajar.

Blood on the inside doorknob. A handprint.

Miriam hurries inside.

She goes room to room—a small house, not a long journey—open kitchen, living room, bedroom. She smells a mix of perfume, piss, blood, and it's in the bathroom that she finds Gabby.

No no oh no I'm so sorry—

Gabby, curled up in the well of the old clawfoot bathtub there. Lying in her own sticky blood. Her face vented, sliced, each cut like a fish's gill, and as she sits up and cradles her head against Miriam's thigh, the dry blood crackles and some of her cuts open anew—

Fresh red soaks Miriam's jeans.

Miriam fumbles with her cell phone. She calls 911.

She strokes Gabby's hair. Kisses the back of her head. Tries to soothe her with shushes and coos but then worries that it sounds like she's trying to quiet Gabby's whimpers and cries and so instead she just tells her how sorry she is, how this is all her fault, how she's going to get the guy who did this.

Gabby speaks, then—with stiff lips where the words slip out broken and half-uttered but clear enough to hear. "Not all about you."

If only you knew.

Gabby looks at Miriam. "He got you too."

Miriam nods. *And I'm going to kill him for it. Somehow.*

"Don't have . . ." A pause. "Health. Insurance." And that brings on a new wave of tears. Out of all this, that's what makes Gabby cry the hardest: that she doesn't have health insurance. Miriam thinks, *Welcome to America*, and finds that all the more heartbreaking.

FIFTY-THREE

THE ARROW THROUGH THE HEART OF THE APPLE

They take Gabby into the ambulance. Gabby cries, wants Miriam to come with her—but here, too, are the cops, and they want to talk to Miriam about what happened. And she thinks, *I don't have time for this*, because two days left is rapidly about to become *one* day left as time bleeds out as if from a throat-slit pig. So she does the only sensible thing.

She runs from the cops.

There's only three of them. And they're inside, looking over the place, and she tells them she needs to go to her car to get her driver's license—a lie, because she has no driver's license—but she *does* go to the car.

Then she gets in. And starts it.

And drives away.

Again, she finds herself with the windows down, the Florida air now trying to *steal* her breath instead of filling her with its own. Again she finds herself stripped down, scraped raw, haunted by trepidation and indecision. The highway ahead is a straight line and the future wants to be, too. Fate knocks over the dominoes and it all falls in the expected direction: Her mother dies, Jerry dies, that asshole Peter dies, maybe Louis, maybe Wren, whoever else Ashley has on his *list*. All of them, murdered.

All because she doesn't know what to do next.

Everything feels like it's falling through her fingers. She

thought she'd hunt Ashley but he beat her down, owned her ass like a man owns a kicked dog. And now, this. Gabby. What about Mother? He could already have her by now. Could already be torturing her somewhere. With his power, it'd be easy. He knows her moves. He knows what comes next even though she has no idea at all.

Fuck!

Sugar told her that there was something else—something she wasn't looking for. Something under the water: a box. She thinks, *Maybe it's a secret weapon. Maybe it's something I need to kill Ashley.* But, then again, maybe it's a big box of nothing. Seashells. Or money. Or just a pile of sand. And then what? What could she possibly find there that would save her own mother from extinction at the hands of a vengeful ex-lover—an ex-lover with the psychic power to see everybody's next move before they even make one?

No. That's not an option. She can't waste time looking for something that maybe won't help her kill Ashley.

That means she has to do what she didn't want to do—go to the source of the next kill.

Go home. See Mother. She's gotta try. She can stand her ground there. Leaving home was a mistake all along.

When Ashley shows his smiling face, Miriam will be waiting.

FIFTY-FOUR

CURTAINS

Miriam doesn't think anything of the gray car parked just down the block. All she can think about is Mother. In that little house. Unprotected.

She pulls up across the street from Evelyn Black's cottage and gets out of the car. Right now everything about Miriam feels like a fishing line pulled taut—she feels every little vibration, every jagged little worry, every small bite of pain magnified. Beaten up, but not beaten down. It occurs to her that inside her lurks an urge to kill, fierce as a house fire and twice as hot. Like that's a thing now: a thing she not only *does* but a thing she *is*. She doesn't like it. *But,* the thought strikes her, *I need it just the same.*

Strange now that she cares. About that woman. About her *mother*. For years she's been wearing that emotional metaphysical colostomy bag around her hip—full of the thousands of angry, shitty thoughts wasted on that woman—and now she's marching toward the house to save her.

Life can be pretty fucking twisted, she decides.

Ahead, the curtains at the kitchen window part. She sees her mother's face there at the window. Maybe she's imagining it, but she likes to believe the woman's face brightens a little when she sees Miriam. Maybe *brightens* isn't the word—maybe it's just a shadow that lightens, but it's enough.

But then, another face just behind her.

Ashley.

Grinning, almost skeletal rictus. Bright eyes. Like he's laughing.

His hand wrenches back her mother's head. The curtains flutter and fall closed. Miriam screams, breaks into a run—

And that's when she hears the scuff of a boot behind her.

Her mother's eyes go wide. She starts to shout from behind the glass.

Miriam thinks, *I've fallen into another trap.*

She spins around—

Grosky grins. "And that's when you met us."

Miriam clucks her tongue and nods.

"The first time, at least," she says. "You screwed it all up for me."

And I'm gonna screw it up for you.

Vills paces, nervous.

FIFTY-FIVE

LOST TIME

She's like a cougar in a cat carrier—snarling and screaming behind a duct tape gag and shouldering the car door and trying to kick at the windows. The heavyset guy driving has a gold watch biting into the meat of his wrist. The woman next to him is tall and lean, her hair wrestled into a wasp's nest by all the humidity.

They showed up just outside her mother's. The woman had a gun. The man had a badge. Said they were FBI, they needed to speak to her.

Miriam ducked, tries to run—

But her body hurt. Sore all over. Her leg, still throbbing from where the saw cut her. Where her own knife stuck in her leg. And the rest of her—a body bag worked over by a young, eager boxer.

That means she was slow.

She screamed for her mother.

But the big fuck and the skinny scribble of ink grabbed Miriam and wrestled her into the car. She kicked and hissed, but one of them clipped her on the back of the head with a gun. The strength went out of her, and then the reality slammed into her like a truck: *They could shoot me, and then how will I save my mother?* (Though there a grim thought entered her mind: *If I let them shoot me, will that be the thing that ends Ashley's fucked-up quest for vengeance? Could my death end all the other deaths?*)

No! No. She can't think that way. If she dies, that just means Ashley gets to go on living. That can't happen. That is *not fucking allowed.*

Her only thought is:

Maybe I can use them. Somehow. Some way.

Now here she sits. In the back of a car driven by people she's pretty sure aren't Feds at all. They haven't read Miriam her rights. They haven't told her anything about lawyers. She's got white plastic zip-ties binding her wrists at her back. She growls and struggles.

Tap-Tap's people? Maybe. They don't look right for Tap-Tap. But a drug dealer like him probably has all kinds of mother-fuckers in his pocket. And she owes Tap-Tap. She owes him what she'll never pay. Wouldn't be a surprise to have him snatch her off the street to take what he tried to take the first time: one of her limbs.

If only she saw how one of these two will die.

So many clues in death. So often that death reflects life in some way. Addicts overdose. Fat fucks like this one in the front seat overeat. The violent die violently. Even good people so often die in service to their virtues: Martin Luther King Jr. catches a bullet. Woman trying to rescue a kitten from a tree has the branch break beneath her.

How you die is who you are.

Unfortunately, when these two shoved her in the car, neither of them touched her in a way that afforded her that precious *skin-on-skin* connection—hands on shirt, on sleeve, on hip, no touch of the neck or arm or hand. She was *sure* when they zip-tied her hands that she would see *something*—but oh no, those things are like designed for cuff-use now: two holes for the hands and a ripcord to pull to tighten it.

And now here she is.

An hour later.

In a car heading . . . she has no idea where. But she sees signs—Palm Beach, Port St. Lucie—that tell her they're heading north.

She screams behind the gag.

It's killing her. Because every hour in the car is another hour it will take to get back. Time taking two steps forward instead of one.

She replays it again and again: Her mother's face at the window. Ashley behind her. The curtains closing.

Her mother, on a boat.

So many plunges of the knife.

Water and blood and the underside of a boat.

As she watches from a porthole only six feet away.

The heavyset driver nods to the woman, who reaches back and rips the tape off Miriam's mouth. The very moment it's off, Miriam explodes:

"Fuck you! You fucking animals! Who are you? *Do you know what you've done?*" She howls at them. A primal velociraptor shriek.

"Where are we going?"

"Calm down," the big fuck says. "We're just going somewhere to sit awhile, maybe have a chat."

"Just a chat," the woman says.

Miriam thinks, *I need to get out of this car.*

A car going 75 mph on I-95?

Miriam then thinks, *I need to stop this fucking car.*

But how?

For now: delay.

Use them. Abuse them.

"We can chat now," she says.

"I'd rather get more comfortable somewhere," the big guy says.

"It'll just be a few hours," the woman says. "Sit tight. You want some music on?" She reaches for the dial but Miriam barks at her like a dog.

"No music. How'd you find me anyway?"

"You gave your name at that crime scene down in Key West five hours ago. Then we caught you on some traffic cams. Checked the car, saw it was registered to Evelyn Black—so we showed up and waited."

"What do you want from me? You're not Feds. No way you're the Feds."

Big guy laughs. "We're FBI, I promise."

"I've been told that before." *Find out more about them. Take something from them.* These people, she decides, are tools. Tools handed to her for an unknown reason. Fate is trying to fuck her over, and that means it's time to fuck right back. Hell, she's *seen the future.* She knows what fate wants. Fate wants her on that boat. She just has to figure out how to earn that particular outcome. *Concentrate on the boat.* So she says, "Prove it to me."

"Prove what?" the woman says.

"That you're the real-deal Feds."

"You saw our IDs," the big fuck says with a laugh.

"I stole a boat," Miriam lies. "A good-size fishing boat. I stole it from somewhere down in the Keys. Tell me where I stole it from."

The woman turns around and puts a crooked Ichabod Crane finger to her thin earthworm lips. "Honey. Shhh. We'd hate to have to gag you—"

"Nah, nah, nah," the big guy says, waving one hand off the steering wheel. "Let's humor her. Maybe she'll play nice if we pony up. Am I right, Miss Black? If I give you what you want, you'll give us what we want?"

"You betcha," she says, putting on her best golly-gee-sure-officer-always-happy-to-help-an-officer-of-the-peace voice.

The big guy pulls out a crusty old flip phone, pops the clam-shell and hits one button. He has a one-sided conversation:

"Yeah, hey, Tony. Grosky. Right. No, I don't . . . Hold up, listen. White fishing boat. Stolen from somewhere in the Keys. Got any data for me? Yeah, I'll hold." He gives Miriam a patronizing little smile-and-nod. His neck fat jiggles. "What's that? Uh-huh. Mariposa Marina. Ramrod Key." Now he looks back and gives her a cocky, *See, I told you I could do it* look.

But she interjects: "Name of the boat."

Him, holding his hand over the phone. "What?"

"I said, *what's the name of the boat* I stole?"

Back to the phone. "Tony. What's the name of that boat?" He holds up a placating finger. "Ah. The *Swallow*? The *Swallow*."

The *Swallow*.

Of course.

Ashley knows about the Mockingbird Killer. About the Caldecotts. A family of killers who shared the common characteristic of a naval swallow tattoo. Who shared the duties of murders done in service to their mother's twisted visions.

He's mocking her.

She should have figured that out. It's no surprise he chose a boat not just because of its functionality but because of its message for her. And suddenly she feels slow and stupid and behind the eight ball, because no matter where she goes, he's out there messing with her.

One step ahead.

It makes her angry.

Angry at herself. Angry at him. Angry at everyone in this car.

The big guy turns back around, the ruddy mounds of sweat-shined cheeks pulled back to show the wide white veneers of his smile and he's about to gloat and say something—

Miriam wrenches her body upward at the hips—

And kicks him with both feet in the face.

His head rocks back and he's already turning and pawing at the steering wheel like a housecat trying to claw through a closed door—and already the car is losing control and careening left, then right. Then his heavy foot is punching down on the brakes and she hears the tires skid beneath them and the tires of *other cars* skidding—

She awaits the sound of shearing metal.

She awaits the car being split in half like a soda can hit with a shotgun.

She awaits death and all its accouterments: blood, fire, piss, shit, screams, this time all her own—

But the thought strikes her fast as a lightning whip. *I don't die here.*

Fate wants her on that boat.

Ashley wants to give her a show.

The thought strikes her again, this time giddy, mad, a flurry of lunatic bubbles rising up from her heart and into her brain. *I don't die here!*

As the car slides to a complete stop, Miriam cries out and pushes past the pain to kick at the back passenger-side window—

The big fuck in the driver's seat is looking around, woozy, trying to get a measure of what's happening. He tries turning the key again, but the car's engine bitches and moans but doesn't turn over.

Cars zoom past outside. Honking.

The woman is fumbling for something—

The gun! She's got the gun pointed over the back seat just as Miriam's feet crack a spiderweb in the glass and knock it out of its frame—

"Stop!" the woman screeches, and Miriam wants to reach up and grab that gun and slap her. But the whole hands-bound thing makes that hard, so she works with what she has, and what she has is her skull.

Miriam moves her body like she's a dolphin trying to get back into the ocean and tries to smack the top of her head into the woman's gun hand. But she discovers a better opportunity instead—she bites down hard on it. *Crunch*. The woman shrieks. At the same time, the big guy grabs Miriam by the scruff of the neck—

"Wait wait wait," Grosky says. "So you *do* know how we bite it."

"Bite it. Is that a pun? Because I bit your scarecrow friend here?" Vills looks down at her own hand and frowns. Miriam hisses, "You're interrupting my story, and that's very impolite. You're rude and unpleasant. Like a soccer mom, or a dog fart."

"We already *know* this part of the story," Vills says.

"Apparently not, because Big Boy here has questions. And yes, Agent Grosky, I do know how you both die."

"Come on. Give us a taste."

"*You* die by choking on a canned ham—still in the can, actually. *So impatient.* She chokes, too, but on a horse dick. Awkward! They're very big. I think her eyes were bigger than her stomach, don't you?"

"You little twat, I'm done with—"

But Miriam turns her volume up to drown out Vills. "No, wait wait wait. I remember now. Grosky, you crush your wife during sex—she explodes like an overcooked sausage, it's totally gross—and the guilt drives you to take your own life. And Vills, you fuck a nasty old zoo chimpanzee and get some kind of zoo-born chimp-flu that covers you in canker sores—"

Vills slams both palms down on the table. "See? This is what we get, Richie. This is what you want to stick around for. *We have to go.*"

Grosky levels his gaze at Miriam. "Tell me how we die."

Miriam winks. "That'd be cheating. Don't you like surprises?"

FIFTY-SIX

LEAP BEFORE YOU LOOK

Vills screams and yanks her hand away. The gun drops. Miriam gets her feet under her, wrenches her head free of the big guy's meaty grip—

Then she uses her legs to push her body up and out of the busted backseat window—

—right into traffic.

She lands hard on her shoulder—*oof!*—just as a big-ass cherry-red pickup blasts past so close she can feel the tires' wind on her hair.

Not gonna die, not gonna die, not gonna die.

She's in the middle of a highway. Four lanes.

At the far side, a guardrail.

And over that guardrail—

A drop to another highway. The turnpike, she thinks. Crossing like two ribbons atop a Christmas present.

Miriam sprints across the highway. Cars don't stop. Drivers don't give one shit, two shits, a hundred shits—they've got places to go and, by golly, this is Florida, where stuff like this must happen all the time. A motorcycle nearly takes her boot off. A white sports car almost cuts her in half.

But then—*wham*, she slams into the guardrail.

She turns around. Faces the gray car. The woman is already out. Gun back in her hand.

Miriam starts sawing the zip-ties back and forth on the

ragged, almost serrated edge of the guardrail. Back and forth. Cutting into her hand.

The woman aims the pistol.

The big guy is half out of the car, yelling, "Don't shoot! This isn't on the books. *Don't shoot her, goddamnit—*"

Miriam winces, keeps sawing, feels blood crawling down the sides of her palms.

The woman hesitates pulling the trigger.

A grungy gray box truck blasting booming Reggaeton music charges past.

She fumbles with the gun.

Both halves of the zip-cuff come free.

Miriam looks down over the highway's edge.

Here's my chance.

And she jumps.

FIFTY-SEVEN

CRYSTAL BLUE PERSUASION

Boom. She cracks hard into an empty swimming pool carried on the back of a flat-bed trailer—a stack of swimming pools, actually, three piled atop one another and held to the truck with wide white straps. The horse-kick of pain transitions swiftly to a dull roar of misery throughout her body.

She gasps, lying on her back. Arms spread out, cruciform.

I really wish the pool had been filled with water first.

Still. Nothing seems broken. Moving her limbs hurts like a sonofabitch—and yet, they move. Nothing falls off. All her organs remain firmly ensconced inside her body.

She's going to have a helluva bruise, though.

It'll match all the others.

This truck heads southbound on the turnpike. Opposite to the direction she had been going in the car with those two so-called Feds.

That means she has to get off this truck. Right? She has to get back to her mother's, has to stand in Ashley's way, has to get the Malibu—

But then she thinks, *fate is a river with dark, fast-moving waters*. That's what she hates about it. The *inevitability* of it. The illusion of choice—paddle left, paddle right, the rapids will still carry you where they want to carry you. She feels a spike of pride that she's the *riverbreaker*, a big stone that parts the waters, that changes the course of the river, that turns one straight line into two divergent ones.

Today, though, she doesn't have to do the heavy lifting.

Today, fate is not her foe—it is her friend.

Why fight it? She's seen the future. She knows where fate takes her.

It puts her on a boat. With Ashley Gaynes. And her mother.

Her mother, who's probably already gone. Ashley's taken her already. Miriam feels it like a steel wire threading through her marrow: A grim certainty that she'll go back to the house and find no one there. And he'll taunt her with it. He'll leave a note. Or call her. Something to remind her that she's always one step behind—a little boy chasing a red balloon right into the path of an oncoming SUV.

Fuck that. Instead of fighting it, she's going to go with it.

Fate is like gravity. If she lets herself go, it'll always pull her down.

She'll go all the way to the bottom. Right to the boat. Right to the moment that it matters. She wanted to avoid that, but she's been struggling against it to no avail. The bottom is where she belongs.

The end is where she *lives*. And she's learned so much along the way.

Southbound it is, then.

Mile zero, motherfucker.

Besides, she's tired. Really goddamn tired. All parts of her feel weighed down—a corpse dragged to the ocean floor by heavy chains.

She curls up in the scalloped edge of the pool. Wads herself up in a fetal ball. Miriam sleeps. And for once, she does not dream.

FIFTY-EIGHT

PREDESTINATION

Coming down off the long side of a bridge, the driver hits the brakes to slow the truck. The jake brake grinds and stutters— *gung gung GUNG GUNG*—and jolts her out of the deathlike sleep that embraced her. It gets her blood hot, her heart pumping. She peeks up over the lip of the pool—

And sees evening settling in over the smooth crystalline bay. Islands—keys—in the distance. Beneath the truck is the Seven-Mile-Bridge, the massive white whale with the bowed back that connects Marathon with Bahia Honda by hopscotching Pigeon Key.

Birds sit along the power lines stretched out over the water. Cormorants. Reclining in the fading light of day. Out beyond is the old defunct bridge—a trestle of rusted bones that looks like it might collapse if even one of those birds decides to land on it.

Perhaps tellingly, no birds land on it.

The truck comes off the bridge and slows as it continues down the last straightaway. It grinds and turns wide toward a pebble-gravel entrance with a sign out front: SMUGGLERS COVE RV RESORT.

The hydraulics squeak and hiss.

And the truck stops.

Fate has brought her back to the Keys.

Now to see what else it has in store.

She grabs the lip of the pool, swings over the edge—her body cries out as she does so, her teeth reflexively gritting to bite back the pain. She uses the other stacked pools like a ladder and drops into the lot. More vibration. More pain. It rises up through her feet. She suppresses a yelp.

The "resort" is no such thing—it's an agglomeration of campers and RVs hitched to posts and racks. Folks are milling about their respective vehicles, grilling hot dogs and BBQ chicken on little charcoal hibachis. Doves and blackbirds strut around the ground, pecking for leftovers.

A girl in a tie-dyed half shirt sees Miriam and walks gingerly toward her, bare feet padding on the loose pebbles. She's got a cigarette pinched in the scissors of her thin little fingers.

The freckle-faced girl comes up, says, "You Miriam?"

"What of it?"

"Guy named Ashley's got a message for you."

"Does he now? What message?"

"Says he's . . ." She takes a moment, as if to remember. "He's surprised you're pushing it this far. Says you still got some surprises in you yet."

The girl takes a hit off the cigarette. Miriam wants one and pulls out her own pack—and before she even plucks a finger in, the girl says, "He said you'd be out and that I wasn't to give you one of mine. But I'm out, too, so I guess it don't much matter. I got some Hubba Bubba gum, though."

"I don't want the gum. Just make with the rest of the message."

"He told me to collect some things from you. Your boots. Your knife. Your sunglasses. Your phone, too."

"I'm not giving you those things."

"He said you'd say that. He told me to ask what you think Eleanor would say to that."

Miriam's hands tighten to fast fists. "Eleanor?"

"Sorry. Meant *Evelyn*." But the way the girl's smiling, Miriam thinks the slipup was intentional. The girl's not an actor. She's barely legal; this little minnow can hardly keep it together. Ashley told her to say all this. "You gonna give it over or what? Billy's got brats on the grill and Boone's Farm in the bucket so I gotta get back."

Miriam licks her lips. Starts removing the requested items one by one. Unlace the boots. Pull out the knife—still rusty with her blood. Fish her aviators out of her pocket—not sure why he wants those. Maybe he thinks she'll break a lens and use it to cut his throat. (She makes a mental note at that. Attacking people with nearby objects is becoming a fast favorite.)

Finally, the phone.

As she goes to hand that over, it rings.

"That's him," Freckles says.

Miriam answers it. She doesn't say anything.

"You're going along with this easier than I thought," he says. "It's like you don't want to play anymore."

"I don't. I want to finish this."

"You're pushing it all the way. I respect that. Cutting right to the end. Realizing that you have no power here is admirable. Brave, even. When I was a kid my mother used to take me to these air shows, and I loved it when the stunt pilots would dive toward the ground—"

"Spare me the fucking storytelling and get on with it. You want me on that boat. I want to be on that boat. Tell me how."

He laughs. "What if I told you no?"

"You won't."

"I don't like your attitude anymore."

Then he hangs up.

"Shit!" Miriam yells, and eyes turn toward her. She hits redial on the phone, and it rings and rings. *He's just fucking with me. He'll call back. He needs this just as much as I do.*

Freckles just stands there. Miriam didn't even notice the girl shoving a piece of gum in her mouth. The gum crackles and pops. She blows a big cartoony-balloony bubble. Miriam pops it with a spear-thrust of her pinkie.

"Hey!" the girl protests.

"Fuck it," Miriam says. "He calls back, tell him I'm done. Tell him he wants to kill my mother, he's going to have to do it without me. Tell him that I don't even *like* her. Fuck fate. Fuck the river! And fuck you, too, you vapid little malignancy." She flips the phone toward the girl, who barely manages to juggle-catch it.

Then Miriam turns and walks.

She heads to the highway.

The sun sets.

Evening bleeds.

She walks.

FIFTY-NINE

AT LENGTH DID CROSS AN ALBATROSS

Midnight: Miriam's hour.

After the RV park, Miriam walked south, past Bahia Honda beach, past the bend toward Pine Key, where she found the glowing lights of the tiki bar sitting outside yet another marina—the narrow masts of dozens of boats sitting out there like the wooden crosses of old, poor graveyards. She really wondered what it meant. Had she broken the yoke of fate? Or was she just slowing her descent—the stunt plane that Ashley was talking about still heading toward the hard and unforgiving earth, this time at a gentler (if still deadly) decline?

Now she sits barefoot at the tiki bar, thinking she really should have gotten her shoes and her knife back.

The bartender—a flabby black guy with man-tits poking their peaks against the inside of a hot pink T-shirt—asks her what she wants, and she says she doesn't care, doesn't care at all, but *make it big* and *set it on fire*.

She waits. Looks around. Fish nets hang from the ceiling with a bunch of one-dollar bills caught like little minnows. A few old salts mill around the back. A pair of girls sip from one giant fishbowl—which looks like it's full of Windex—quietly in the corner.

He brings her something called an Ancient Mariner. It's in a tiki glass—big ceramic mug looks like an angry Hawaiian god with a mouth made of lightning and eyes like church windows.

289

The bartender clicks a long-necked lighter.

The drink combusts.

Flame ripples. Blue blazes.

She blows it out and takes a sip. Rum and allspice and citrus and it's smooth and warm and would usually be good but beyond the heat it tastes like ash and vinegar in her mouth.

Mostly, she just lets it sit there. She idly smears streaks in the condensation collecting on the tiki's face. Her sunburn hurts. Her leg hurts—where someone tried to saw it off, where another someone stuck her with her own knife. Her back hurts—where she probably has a bruise the size of a trashcan lid. Pain every-where. Face. Ankle. Chest. Neck. Mind. Soul.

She goes to take another drink but then sets the tiki down instead.

Because someone sits down next to her.

She knows who it is.

Ashley asks, "You gonna drink that drink—"

She finishes it for him. "*Or is this just foreplay.* I know you love the classics but seriously, get a new line. It's tired. *I'm* tired."

"I need you on that boat," he says. His voice is like a piece of wood cut against the grain with a dull saw. Splintered and bristly. "I need to show you." He licks his lips. "I need to make you hurt."

"You've already made me hurt. Isn't that enough?"

He doesn't say anything but the answer is clear: *no.*

Ashley showing up is not a surprise.

What he does next is.

He sighs. "I knew you'd say no. That's the thing. That's my curse. I called it a gift but sometimes it really is a curse because I *know* what people are going to do before they do it and that—" Here his voice gets low and growly, and he speaks through gritted teeth. "*And that burns me.* I wish I didn't have to make people do things. I'd like to be surprised for once."

He drops a little snack baggy on the bar top.

Two round, wrinkly skin-colored orbs sit within the plastic.

Miriam feels her guts lurch.

No.

"Those are Evelyn's toes," Ashley says. "Just her pinky toes. I thought it better to start there. I'm going to whittle her away if you don't come with me. I've got these two toes. Then I'll take the rest. Then more of the leg. To the knee. Above the knee. Mid-thigh. To the hip. Then I'll start on the other leg. Then the fingers, hands, arms, to the face. Ears, nose—"

Miriam moves fast.

She palms the tiki glass and smashes it against his head.

Or tries to.

Even as she's grabbing the glass, he's kicking out with his fake leg. The stool beneath her goes out from under her and she falls.

The tiki glass drops from her hand.

Ashley catches it.

And smashes it against her head just as she tries to stand.

She reaches out for the stool, tries to pull herself up. People are yelling. Ashley is laughing—a loud, theatrical laugh. Then he's got a pistol in his hand and the air is full of gunshots and screaming. Miriam holds her ears, tries to scramble to the door, but his hand grabs the back of her head and lifts it up. He thrusts the gun under her chin.

"No more of this," he growls. "You come with me, or your mother will be delivered to you in slivers of lunchmeat."

He drops her hair.

Then hobbles toward the door.

On his way out, one of the girls crawls over the body of her dead friend. She cowers as he passes. He puts a round through the top of her skull. Her brains evacuate through a lower jaw that is no longer there.

Then he's gone.

Miriam stifles a sob. Then she crawls to a stand.

And follows him out the door.

SIXTY

THERE PASSED A WEARY TIME

Ashley sets up a chair for her inside the boat's cabin. Then he sits across from her on a small captain's stool.

Behind him, flies orbit the bodies of the boat's original owners. A couple Ashley introduces as "Bob Taylor and his mistress, Carla Pilotti." They lie, supine, bodies cocked halfway down the steps toward the belowdeck cabin, a black puckered crater in the center of each forehead.

Ashley swats at any flies that come near him.

The flies must irritate him. Every swat comes with a frustrated growl and a narrow-eyed wince.

The inside of the cabin is destroyed. As if by ax or hammer. The console is mostly shattered. The windows, boarded up.

"Your mother's belowdeck," he says. "Resting. You ought to rest, too—"

"Mom!" she cries out, but he grabs her face and squeezes hard enough to shut her up.

"*No,*" he says. "No speaking to her. Your time with her is done. She's unconscious anyway and gagged so that she cannot speak to you. Don't make me gag you, too." He again relaxes. "Tomorrow is a very big day."

"It is." *Tomorrow's the day I kill you.* But she doesn't know how. And she's not even sure she believes it anymore. Every move she makes, he knows it. Big and small.

He wheels the stool through a dried puddle of blood—the blood of Bob, or Carla, or her own mother, she doesn't know—and heads to the console, where he starts the boat. The engine growls. Beneath them, a propeller churns the dark, glassy waters and they begin to *slide away* from the marina, from the shore, from the land Miriam knows and trusts.

His back is to her.

While he's facing away, she begins to look for a weapon.

She looks for something—anything—to use against him. A screwdriver. A piece of window glass. A long splinter. Nothing.

Goddamnit.

She'll use her hands. Her feet. Her *teeth*.

No. Then she sees it.

The leg. The prosthetic leg. *I'm going to beat you to death with your own leg, you motherfucker.*

But even as that thought lands, even as she plans her first strike—

He turns his head toward her. The front of him is facing forward, his elbow casually resting on the wheel like he's out here ready for a fun day of fishing with his half-dead family. He rests his chin on his own shoulder and makes a pouty face. "You're thinking of hurting me, Miriam. And while I guess it's understandable, it damn sure isn't very nice."

"I . . . I wasn't."

That wolfish grin. "You were. They told me you were. I saw the words drift across the wheel as I turned it. A warning from my friends."

"Is that what they are? Your friends?"

"They've done me a lot of good. Given me a lot of purpose. They're my bosses. My masters. My parents. But they're also my friends. Because they take care of me. Like good friends should."

"I took care of you that day in the SUV. With Ingersoll. I got you free. They would've cut more of you away. I did you a *favor* that day."

"You should have *never left me*." He clearly doesn't want to talk about that because all he says next is, "You're welcome to try to hurt me again but it will only bring you more pain. It's like that old Pee-Wee Herman playground taunt: *I'm rubber and you're glue. Whatever you do to me bounces off and sticks to you.* And right now I bet you're in a lot of pain. You look like shit, if I'm being honest."

A lone, betraying tear crawls down her cheek. She swiftly wipes it away with the back of her hand and tries to scowl past it.

They stare at each other like that, not saying a thing. Him smirking. Her glowering, hoping she can hold back her tears— hoping she can figure out how to kill him with just her look.

Eventually, he winks and turns back to piloting the boat.

He steers it out into open water.

The fishing boat chugs along.

Outside, the squawks of gulls. The occasional *thump* above their heads. He looks up. "Fisher birds like gulls and gannets. They follow after boats. Looking for bait. Looking for the catch. We're all just looking for the catch, I guess, right?" He shrugs. "It's good you're giving up," he says. "Giving in. This thing you do has just brought you a lot of suck, hasn't it? A big old misery sandwich." He swats at his neck. "God. These *fucking* flies. I should've sprayed or something."

Guess you're not so psychic after all.

"I just want to say, it's nice to be with you again." He suddenly wheels the stool back around to face her. "You know, I was a real fuck-up, and I never actually managed to apologize to you. When we met I was a . . . I was a man without a purpose. I think that's what weakens us as people, when we drift through life without any kind of *meaning*. Idle hands, am I right? I was just some shitty two-bit con artist who thought he was the craftiest little trilobite the ocean floor ever did see. But real fish swam above my head. Sharks and barracuda. I had no idea. Then I saw you down there with me and I drew you in—I thought, Jesus, here's a girl just like me, somebody smart but without *purpose*— so I did what I always did. I was a user. I used you like I used everybody. Then I started using drugs and . . ." He whistles. "Ugly times. But us meeting was powerful. It was like . . . it was volcanic. *Boom.* Shook both of us up. Showed us both the way, but to fix something you have to break it first, so we had to lose things before we could begin." He snaps his fingers. "It's like losing your virginity. Right? Girl busts that cherry—" He thrusts his finger into his mouth and makes a cork-popping sound. "And there's pain and blood but then a kind of clarity. And eventually, even pleasure. I have my clarity. And this is my pleasure. But when we met each other I didn't have those things and so I am very, very sorry."

She has nothing to say to any of that. To her, it's all just noise.

Instead she asks, "The windows are boarded. How do you know where you're going?"

He smiles. "I just do. You do, too. In a way."

"The cops are going to find us. You killed people."

"I did. And they won't. I killed everybody there. Nobody to ID me. Nobody to even call the police. Too early for there to be other fishermen out at the boats. Eventually they'll come look-ing. And I'll be one step ahead. We'll be gone. Your mother will be dead."

"Will I?"

He laughs. "No, I'm not going to kill you. Not yet, anyway. I don't even know if that's on the menu. Depends on what *They*—" He points up toward the cabin ceiling. "Have to say about it. That's their call. Not mine. I'm just their man on the ground."

"You're their little bitch."

"Such a dirty mouth. You reduce everything to its components.

You're like the maggots these flies make. Breaking it all down to its basest, most . . . disgusting bits." He's angry. Good. Let him be angry. "I'm not their bitch. I'm their *avatar.* Gods used to have avatars. Krishna. Jesus. Human beings acting as the hand of the divine there in the dirt, here on the water."

She sniffs and blinks her bleary, wet eyes. "That who you think you work for? God?"

"The *gods.* Plural. The gods of order. The gods of fate and destiny."

"And who do I work for?"

He lowers his voice. "The other ones. The gods below. Gods of chaos and disorder. Free will. *Free will.*" He suddenly wheels close to her, thrusts his finger in her face. "See, you think that's a *good* thing. Free will. Like you're one of those patriot assholes who think it's all about *individual freedom*. The freedom to carry a gun or not wear a helmet on a motorcycle or the freedom to just be an asshole. I used to think that way. But see, that's the trick. Nobody uses that freedom to do good things. It's just another way to say, *I want the excuse to be a self-interested, self-absorbed monster*. Fate is about keeping things in line. About marching us toward a destination. See? Destiny. Destination." He laughs so hard his cheeks turn red. "It's in there. The one word nested in the other."

"Fate is nested in fatal, too," she says quietly.

"It is at that. Because sometimes fate is about people dying whether you like it or not. But *you* wouldn't understand that. You come along and you *fuck things up*. The people who are supposed to die—you save them from the edge of the pit. And the others standing there watching—you kick them into the darkness. You keep people in the pattern who aren't supposed to be there anymore and you put others in their place. You're *damaging* things. You can't . . . you can't go around *doing that*."

"Like you said, we all have to find our purpose."

That straight-razor smile flashes. "We do. And mine is to show you how wrong yours is. One day you'll see. One day you'll see because darkness is rolling toward us like a sky full of locusts. The death will be a great cloud of wings and teeth and it will rob from this world so many. People starving. People sick. People killing each other. The world goes through these transitional periods. Some worse than others, but people always die—and that's necessary for the pattern. For all of the people to keep going, some of the people—sometimes a *lot* of the people— have to die. You misunderstand that now. You won't, one day. Maybe one day soon you'll see how necessary it is. You'll see that sometimes to fix something, you first have to break it."

"Maybe I'm the one doing the breaking," she says.

He backhands her.

It rocks her head. She tastes blood.

A moment of chaos.

She seizes it. She launches herself toward him.

He grabs her as they fall backward.

Ashley uses her momentum and slams her forward into the console. Wood paneling shatters. He scrambles to stand and pistons a punch into her midsection—a boulder dropped in a lake, ripples of agony.

"You still have that fight in you," he says, panting, licking his lips as he stands up and over her. "But we'll squeeze those last drops out by morning. For now, I have a boat to captain, and this game is tiring."

SIXTY-ONE

I FEAR THEE AND THY GLITTERING EYE

The hours pass.

Miriam's time is punctuated by fits of rebellion.

And Ashley quieting her efforts.

She tries to go to the door—fling it open, leap into the sea—but even as she's getting up he's already on her. Her neck in the crook of his arm. Blood pounding. Legs kicking. He brings her to the very edge of unconsciousness, then drops her.

She tries to attack him. Each time he meets her efforts like she handed him stage directions. He seems to expend no effort at all putting her back on the floor. Eventually, as soon as the thought crosses her mind he stands up like a swift storm rolling in and walks over to punch her in the gut. Or kick her in the side. Or slap her in the face again and again.

None of it hard enough to do any long-term damage. But all of it erosive. *Corrosive.* Like it's whittling away at her in a way far deeper than how he threatened to whittle away her mother.

As to her mother—she hears her sometimes. Down there in the cabin. Whimpering. Crying out past the gag. Miriam tries to call to her, and Ashley storms over again, fist up.

But then he laughs. Tells her it's okay. Tells her she can call to her.

So she does.

She calls down to her mother. Tells her she loves her.

And that she's sorry.

She tells her this ten times.

Twenty times.

Fifty.

Until the words sound like gibberish in her ears, and maybe they are gibberish—words slurred and garbled beneath the great gasping sobs that come out of her.

And when she's done, Ashley comes over and slaps her again.

Outside, the gulls and gannets swoop and squall.

SIXTY-TWO

AS A SLAVE BEFORE THE LORD

Mother gently strokes her hair.

"It's okay," she whispers. Miriam moans. Tries to stand. But everything hurts. Like all that she is has been drained out of her and only ache and anguish have been allowed to fill the void. "It's okay."

"Mom. Please. Go. *Run*."

"It's okay."

Then Mother kisses her brow and Miriam feels her mouth open and grave-worms slide out in a slurry of wet sand and river silt—

She gasps and jerks her head up.

Nobody's here.

She's in the boat cabin, alone with two dead bodies caught in what little sunlight streams in through the porthole and around the faint margins of the boarded-up windows.

Her hands are bound in front of her with tape. She struggles. Cries out for her mother. She crawls over to the bodies—the carpet of flies ripples and takes to the air. She yells down into the dark of the cabin. "Mom! *Please*."

She sees an opportunity—a grotesque one, but there's no time to do differently. Since there's no serrated guardrail this time, she thrusts her wrists forward and works the tape into the mouth of the dead Bob Taylor, a man's whose cheeks are darkened with striations of purple, whose eyes are swollen grapes in his head, whose decaying musk gags her and almost makes her throw up, whose teeth are perfectly white. She saws the tape back and forth on those beautiful chompers until it wears through and the tape splits—

She realizes she's going to have to climb down past them.

Into the dark.

But then—

Tink tink tink tink.

Something at the porthole window.

Her stomach sinks.

She stands. Each step draining.

Ashley stands there. Smiling big and broad like he just got straight As on a report card. He's got a hunting knife—*the* hunting knife—in his hand, and that's what he's using to tap on the glass.

"It's time," he says.

She slams herself against the door to stare out.

The sun is up over the nearby trees and the water. She has no idea where they are. In the distance, mangroves prop themselves up on roots of stilt and peg. Little birds flit from branch to branch. Gulls swoop overhead.

Mother sits bound to a folding chair—the same chair Miriam had been sitting in—and to the deck railing behind it. Her nose is busted, streaming twin swallowtails of blood. Her lips are stretched around a tennis ball duct-taped into her mouth—the skin cracking, splitting, bleeding. And Miriam can see now that both feet are swaddled in newspaper and duct tape. Newspaper darkened with blood.

Miriam pounds on the glass.

She leaves bloody streaks behind—

She cut herself. On Bob Taylor's teeth.

She didn't even know it.

Oh no, no no no—

It's all happening, happening like in the vision—

Except this time it's not Louis in a lighthouse, it's her mother, *her mother.* And this time she's not charging up the spiral stairs at the last minute with a gun in her hand. She's trapped behind a door. With a window that she's trying to break but won't, a window too small to crawl through even if she wanted to.

And she starts to realize, she fell into this. She failed by giving herself over to it. Letting herself be swept along by the river.

Instead of breaking its current.

Again Ashley taps on the glass with the knife.

Tink tink tink tink.

Then he steps back and begins his speech.

"A tale of two Miriams," he says. "This is for you, the Miriam that's here." He sweeps his arms across the sky. "*And this is for you, the Miriam who's touching her mother and seeing her death. You came for a show, so I sure don't want to disappoint!*"

It's strange. To be in two places at once in a way. To be the Miriam witnessing up close the show she's already seen.

And to be able to do nothing about it.

Suddenly, Ashley stops and stoops his head. Conferring, she thinks, with his "friends." She wonders if he ever sees them as she sees hers. But his are not Trespassers. He *invites* them in.

He laughs.

"You know what they did?" he asks. Each word is laced with vibration—shot through with a panicked but giddy frequency. "They went to my mother. I don't know if you knew that. That's how they found us. They went to her and I'd sent a postcard to her and that was how they knew where to start looking. You know what they did to my mother? They shot her. Set one of the burners on the stove. Then turned up the nozzle on her oxygen tank." He claps his hands. "Whoosh. My mother was a hoarder.

Lot of junk in that house. Tinder for the biggest campfire the town of Maker's Bell ever did see."

Miriam pounds on the glass. She screams herself hoarse. Thinks to bite the glass. Slam her head against it. Something. *Anything*.

He takes the knife, sticks the point up under Evelyn Black's chin. Mother's eyes shine with fear. Not with resolution or peace. Not with the comfort of God and all his angels. But unmitigated fear, raw and pure and horrible. The fear of what comes next.

Mother knows what comes next, Miriam can see it in the woman's eyes.

"I'm going to take your mother from you, and you're thinking, but why? And I'm saying to you, it's because of a thing you already know. Don't you? An eye for an eye. A tooth for a tooth. Your mother for my mother. And I hear your screams from behind that window and I know we've already had this conversation, but we're going to have it again for the benefit of—" Once more he addresses the invisible witness Miriam with the knife before sticking it back under Mother's chin. "And I want you to know that I blame you for my mother dying. I put a lot of faith in you. It was because of you that I was even in the Ass-Crack of Nowhere, North Carolina. With all the Waffle Houses and rebel flags and *fixin's* and *y'alls*. I went to you because I thought you were the one for me. A partner. A real partner. And you fucked me, then you fucked me over, and they fucked me up. Fuckity-fuck-fucked. My mother died and what did I get out of it? You fawning over that bull-headed trucker. Me losing my leg and getting dumped on the road."

They pass close to an outcropping of mangroves. The little birds shake the branches. The gulls swoop and cry.

Miriam's shrieks are dulled by the glass.

She bashes her elbow against it. Fulfilling the promise of what she did in the vision, but she does it anyway like she's caught on a muddy hill, the ground slipping beneath her, carrying her ineluctably downward . . .

The glass begins to crack.

Ashley shouts. He shouts, "But now I have my own gift, you dumb cunt. Now I have a machine gun too, ho ho ho. And now I'm going to take what's owed to me."

Kshhh! Miriam's elbow crashes through the porthole—

Her arm stuck with broken glass—

—bleeding—

Ashley laughs—

Gulls cry.

And then she knows.

THE VISION

Everything stops. All things caught, as if caught like the fat black fly held now between Not-Louis's callused fingertips.

He pops it. *Splurch*. Juices run down his fingers. He flings it into his mouth like a piece of popcorn. It crunches like a cicada.

With a swipe of his tongue he wipes fly bits from his teeth.

"You figured it out," he says.

Miriam nods, staring out the porthole. Outside, she can't see anything now—just a white-hot light over the horizon. Gone are the mangroves. Gone are Ashley and her mother. Gone are the birds.

"Ashley swatting the flies," she answers.

"Ashley swatting the flies."

"And then in the vision. When he kills Jerry. He . . . he matches Jerry step for step, swing for swing."

"But the bird—"

"But he doesn't see Corie coming."

Louis snatches another fly and pops it in his mouth.

She almost laughs. She mimics Ashley's words from back on Summerland Key. "Everybody's connected. Same frequency. And he can hear them. But the beasts of the world aren't like us. They're not connected on the same frequency. And he can't hear the song they're singing."

"Look at you. Figuring it out." He shrugs. "Though pretty damn late."

"I'm going to kill him," she says.

"I know."

SIXTY-THREE

THEY SEEMED TO FILL THE SEA AND AIR

The gannet is a beautiful bird.

It's a large bird. A foot tall or more.

It has a long beak with which to catch fish. A beak that's almost silver—and outlined in black, dark lines. It has clear eyes ringed with skin as blue as tropical waters. Its feathers are white as virgin snow, but along its neck and head is a warm sunset glow.

The gannet is a *hungry* bird. The bird plunges from on high, diving a hundred feet at sixty miles an hour to catch fish deep in the ocean waters. And the gannet eats a great deal of fish.

Its name is a synonym for "glutton."

The gannet is an *impatient* bird. The massive creatures gather in flocks around fishing boats, hoping they'll bring up fish not one at a time but in great nets by the score—but if the day yields no catches, the gannets will swoop and snatch bait from the hands of fishermen.

And the gannet is a *vicious* bird. Its beak is sharp. Like a pair of scissors—*snip, snip, snip*. A man once tried to save a wounded bird on a pier. The bird took off his nose. It plucked out his eye.

In the moment that Ashley Gaynes raises the hunting knife to plunge it into Evelyn Black's chest, Miriam knows all these things about the gannet. She does not know how she knows. She cannot care.

There exists a moment—the knife held high in the air, the **307** promise of murder on the warm sea wind—that Miriam reaches out not with her arm or any part of her abused and pummeled body but rather with her mind. She finds the gathering of gannets above her head.

Her mind shatters, a fist slamming into mirrored glass—

It's as if she is drawn from her body—yanked up away from bones and skin, away from blood and muscle—

She is fragmented. Separate, carried by so many—

Miriam hears a new frequency.

A frequency of hunger. And impatience. And *viciousness*.

All of it is beautiful.

The first bird plunges hard and fast, its beak through Ashley's hand. Miriam tastes his juices. Hears his screams. But she doesn't care because all that matters is the blood. That first spray. The first taste.

The other gannets are jealous.

Miriam is both satisfied and jealous. Two minds. Twelve minds.

The birds swarm. The birds dive.

Beaks stick in the meat. Into the flesh of his biceps. Into the tender expanse of his stomach. They close in on the tendons of his neck, the splayed-out fingers, the fleshy protrusion of nose and ears and tongue—

I'm going to whittle her away if you don't come with me . . .

He turns and tries to run, tries to clamber over the edge of the boat. But they pull him back. They dissect him.

They eat what they dissect.

(*Miriam* dissects him, and *she* eats what they dissect.)

Ribbons of skin peel away in greedy, clacking beaks. Birds get great gulps of wind under wings, and they draw away carrying red ropes of raw guts. He is a fish to them—a big, strange, flailing fish. And they pull him apart stem to stern. Gill to fin. Eyeballs to asshole.

You reduce everything to its components. You're like the

maggots these flies make. Breaking it all down to its basest, most . . . disgusting bits . . .

They carry his meat into the sky. They eat it there. Two birds sharing, juggling, gulping.

Soon his bones are showing.

But even that does not last.

One flies away with his lower jaw.

Others peck at his joints. Until his skeleton collapses. They fling his bones into the water like ogres discarding their trash. They pick what flesh they can. Veins and tendons like earthworms.

When finally they are full—*such gluttons!*—they squawk and swarm and land on the railing of the boat. A line of them behind Evelyn Black. Guarding her. Standing vigilant. Watching their mother.

All that's left of Ashley is a greasy, body-wide smear of blood.

And a single prosthetic foot.

SIXTY-FOUR

MOTHER MAY I

It takes time to return.

She feels herself nesting inside the minds of these birds, broken apart like a dropped dinner plate, and it's here she finds the taste of blood and a warm, eager satisfaction—not the satisfaction of vengeance, but the simple joy of having eaten a very good meal. But eventually the hunger nibbles again because the gannet is a *very hungry bird*, and Miriam thinks, *I can go with them, I never have to be me again*—

And that horror is too much for her.

That surprises her.

And it's then she returns—thrown back into her body. The gannets, still full, take flight and circle high into the air, chattering like old friends at the bar until they're just distant caws and faraway shrieks.

Miriam sees her mother. Bound out on the chair. Eyes wide.

The door won't open. The porthole is too small. Miriam hurries to the boarded-up windows. She tries to get her hands around the wood but can't. She takes the one thing left in this room that Ashley didn't destroy—the stool—and picks it up and smashes it again and again into the wooden boards. Slowly they splinter. Surely they split.

She pulls them away. She pitches the stool through the window.

Crash.

She clambers out—trying not to cut herself, but she does anyway. She doesn't care. *Can't* care. She nearly slips on the front of the boat but catches herself and hurries around the side—

Miriam throws her arms around her mother. Rips the tennis ball out of her mouth. Undoes her bonds. Tells her she's sorry she took so long.

Evelyn Black says nothing.

Miriam peels herself away.

Her mother stares. At nothing.

Half her face is slack. The mouth drooping as if drawn downward by a fish tugging on a hook. The pupils suddenly twitch and begin to flit back and forth, and Miriam thinks, *There she is*, and she begins to help her mother stand—but the woman's left leg gives out.

Miriam catches her before she falls.

Mother mumbles. A gassy hiss erupts from her mouth.

Miriam doesn't understand. Not yet.

PART SIX

KEYS AND LOCKS

SIXTY-FIVE

THE REAPER'S TOUCH

The doctor tells her it was a stroke.

A blood clot unmoored itself from somewhere in Evelyn Black's lungs. And it fired up through her brain like a bullet leaving a rifled barrel. And just like a bullet, it did damage as it passed through.

It did damage that could have been mitigated, the doctor tells her—that word, "mitigated," so cold, so clinical—had they gotten her into the hospital within an hour. But that didn't happen. Miriam was on a boat. A boat she did not know how to pilot. She was able to start the engine and get it to the nearby shore—the tangle of mangroves—and she was able to get her mother off the boat, too. But it didn't matter.

Miriam had no idea where they were.

Her body hurt.

But she pushed on, helping her mother walk until the woman couldn't walk any more. Then she carried her until Miriam couldn't carry her any more. Miriam found a road, and there ahead a small little white building with a sign out front: KEY TO THE KEYS REALTY.

The woman inside came out, started to say that they weren't open yet, but there was an open house at the south end of Summerland—

Then she saw. Miriam, bloodied.

Then it was a blur. Police and an ambulance ride and now here, in the hospital at Marathon. Where the doctor told her that Mother had suffered a massive stroke. And that she might never really be herself ever again.

She asks the doctor, because she needs to know, "Why now?"

He says he doesn't know.

"But I can hazard a guess," says the doctor—an avuncular type with curly hair so dark it looks like he dyes it with boot-black. "The experience was traumatic. She must've already had a clot in her lung—you said she was a smoker, so—but the extreme stress of the situation probably dislodged it. Blood pressure can be a helluva thing."

He thinks the stress was what Ashley did to her.

But Miriam believes differently.

There Mother sat as a flock of birds tore a man apart in front of her. As her daughter stood at a window, watching. What did she see on Miriam's face? Rapture? Pleasure? A dead empty hungry nothing?

The days pass in the hospital. For many here, nights spent in the hospital are ones of great consequence, but for Miriam, it's just a long stretch of empty mental highway. The police come and go and they ask her questions. They want to know what happened to the killer. They tell her they have his leg and a lot of his blood. But they wonder if he's still alive. She doesn't tell them any different. What's she going to say? *Birds ate him. And I was the birds. It was weird. I've thrown up six times in the last three days just thinking about it. I can still taste the blood. Got a mint?*

Miriam convalesces. Tape for her cracked rib. Stitches for her leg. Antibiotics for the infection she didn't even know was there. One of the nurses says she's surprised Miriam didn't die. Miriam tells her she doesn't know if she *can* die anymore.

They want to know about insurance. Her mother has it. She doesn't. Another set of hospital bills Miriam will never pay.

The staff begin to whisper because they know she's the girl who was taken captive by some serial killer on a boat—a lunatic who shot up a tiki bar, who murdered the boat's inhabitants, whose tally of bodies is as yet uncounted.

The press gets ahold of it. They want to interview her. She keeps them out. Hides in other rooms when they come to hers. Last thing she wants is to be on television. And she knows that the two FBI agents are coming, too. They have to be. Surely they smell the blood in the water.

But they don't. She doesn't understand why. She's low-hanging fruit at this point: stuck in a hospital bed. Attending to a vegetative mother.

Miriam feels caged. White walls. The pharmaceutical *stink*. And the hospital has a hum to it. Even at night, a low, deep vibration. She figures it's all those machines keeping people alive, but a little part of her thinks it's something else: the chanting of souls so close to death—*same frequency, we're all connected*, Not-Louis had said.

She hates that sound.

She loathes this place.

She has to go.

SIXTY-SIX

MOTHER MAY I?

She goes to her mother and sits with her for a while and tells her that she's going to go. Mother says no real words—she just babbles. A burbling brook that *sounds* like words the way a toddler mimics the inflections and cadences of human speech. But it's nothing you can understand.

Miriam strokes her mother's cheek.

"You know, it's pretty fucked up," Miriam says. "On the one hand, I'm still so, *so* mad at you. All my life I felt like I was under your thumb. Your mean, jabby little thumb. All the things you said to me. The way you treated me. Everything was my fault even when it wasn't. And now here we are. I'm hurt. You're . . . lost. And it *is* my fault. That's where I get tripped up, because once, I think I was a good person. Maybe. But you treated me like I wasn't and I wonder, were you trying to make me a better person but by doing so made me a worse one? Or were you just foretelling the future? That one day we'd be sitting here like this. That we'd intersect again and I'd rob you of your faith and your mind and your life and . . ."

A gasping sob sneaks out and Miriam clamps it down: She squeezes her eyes so hard she thinks she might never be able to open them again, she bites her teeth and draws a deep, shuddering breath.

Don't do this, she thinks.

She sits for a little while. "It used to be that I would try to stop people from dying, and instead I'd only make it happen again." *That little boy and the red balloon* . . . "Maybe that's how it was with you. You wanted to do right so badly that you did wrong instead. It happens. I'm proof."

She stoops and kisses her mother's temple.

She represses another sob.

Evelyn Black smiles. Babbles. Laughs at some joke nobody told.

Then Miriam gets up to leave.

As she turns to exit—

"It is what it is."

She turns back.

Her mother faces toward the ceiling. Staring.

Did she say it? Was it in her voice?

Miriam isn't sure.

SIXTY-SEVEN

THAT'S SOME BUDDHIST SHIT, RIGHT THERE

She's back at the motel after a day of hitchhiking.

As she's heading up to the office, she sees Dave the Florida Man out there picking little bougainvillea flowers from the half-collapsed hedge.

"Hey," she says.

"All of life is suffering," he says.

"Oh yeah?"

"I once got high and shot a shitbucket of heroin into my body and I stood there smoking a cigarette and it fell off onto the floor and caught fire to my bungalow. Smoke and fire woke me up. Big black smoke like a, a, monster or something. I busted open the window and crawled out and it was only later I remembered that I left my retarded brother in there. Bud. Bud burned up in the house along with all his cats. I said I'd never get high again. I said it even as I got high later that night. People are stupid. Life is suffering. But once in a while someone finds a way out of it. A way that ain't heroin. A way of light instead of a big dark hungry monster." He sniffs. "I don't get high anymore. I'm pretty happy."

"Thanks, Dave."

"Sure thing, Mary."

And he goes back to picking little purple-pink flowers.

She shrugs, goes up into the office where she finds Jerry Wu.

Jerry's face is that of a man looking at a ghost. Or maybe about to be fondled by a particularly randy Bigfoot. Fear and awe in equal measure.

"I saw the news," is all he has to say.

"It's pretty fucked," she says.

He nods.

"I need your help. You and Corie."

"I . . . yeah. Sure. Of course."

SIXTY-EIGHT

GONE FISHIN'

Water dark and shadow—bubbles and kelp and little fish shining like knives turning in sunlight—the bird thumps its head against something half-buried in sand and broken coral, thud thud thud—*then the world shifts, upside down, up, up, up— surface, air, light—*

Corie hops back onto the boat.

Miriam gasps.

"You all right?" Jerry asks.

"Not really," Miriam says. *But it is what it is.*

Then she holds her nose and feels her heart try to climb out her butthole as she dives into the water—

The shock of panic is like two hands clapping over her. She immediately thinks, *I'm drowning, I'm dying, Eleanor Caldecott is down here with her corpse hands ready to pull me into the sand . . .*

But then a dark shape cuts the water next to her.

Corie swims next to her.

It gives her strange comfort.

Troubling comfort, in a way—is it uncomfortable comfort? Or comfortable discomfort? Fuck it, it doesn't matter.

What matters is that she closes her eyes and sinks to the bottom. And there, her fingers search the sand and find the box that Sugar told her about. She swims to the surface. Corie breaks through with her, gulping down a fish. And they both come back into the boat.

Later, with the box under her arm, Miriam bids adieu to Jerry.

"You're a nice guy," she tells him. "Not many of you around here. You and your rare bird are real rare birds."

"I'm going to lose the motel," he says suddenly.

"What?"

"Nice guy doesn't mean having money. They're gonna foreclose on this place. Don't know what I'll do next."

"I'm sorry to hear that."

"I owe ten grand. Whaddya gonna do?"

"Will two grand hold 'em off?" She fishes through her bag—fetched from the room where it sat on the bed—and hands him a wad of cash.

"Uh. Holy crap. Maybe."

"If it does, it does. I'll see you, Jerry."

"See you, Miriam. You ever need a room again, come by."

She salutes him, and that's that.

SIXTY-NINE

THUMB OUT

She walks and hitchhikes at the same time. Most cars pass. People know not to pick up hitchhikers anymore. Especially when they watch the news and hear about crazy motherfuckers who kill people and steal their boats and shoot up tiki bars.

She wishes she had a cigarette.

Then a car pulls up.

Gray sedan.

Back window busted out.

"Shit," she says.

"And now we're all caught up," Grosky says.

"To my credit, I didn't run," Miriam says. "So I consider these handcuffs a bit of an insult. Why handcuffs instead of the zips?"

Vills grins. "Can't saw through these."

"Ah." She sniffs. "So why *didn't* you pick me up? At the hospital, I mean. I was a flower fresh for the plucking. Why did you wait?"

Grosky hmphs. "All this is a little . . . what's the line from that movie? Off the record, on the QT, and very hush-hush? We didn't want to make a splash. We knew we could find you again."

"Congrats. You did. So now what?"

"I just gotta know. You're saying what happened to Ashley Gaynes is . . . you're telling us you . . . *became* the birds—"

Miriam shrugs.

"And they—you—ate him."

"Everything but the leg."

Her stomach lurches just thinking about it.

A sea wind comes in through the broken shack windows.

Vills says, "This is all wifty. She's pulling your cock, Richie. Mine, too. Let's get out of here. Leave her here. Call the police to come pick her up. Or just let her go. I don't care, but I'm done."

"No," Grosky says, "we ain't done yet. We have yet to make our offer—"

Just then, Vills's phone vibrates and makes a chirp.

She takes it, tilts it toward herself like a poker player looking at his cards. Then she turns the phone facedown again.

Grosky gives her a look.

"It's nothing," Vills says.

"It's something," Miriam insists.

"Who was it?" Grosky asks.

"It's *nothing*," Vills says.

"It's Tap-Tap," Miriam says.

Vills's eyes go wide.

Grosky laughs. "The Haitian? What? You fuckin' kiddin' me?"

"Forgot about him, did you? Your partner here is going to serve me up to him on a silver platter. Isn't that right, Vills? She's trying to hurry you out so Tap-Tap can roll in here and chop my legs off. Maybe my head. Because I owe him a body and I did not deliver. And *she's* on his payroll. Watch. Necklace." She tries to affect the Haitian sound: "*Tap-Tap love dat gold.*"

Vills starts to protest, but Miriam continues. "You guys leave and maybe she'll sneak back in here and put a bullet in my head. Right, Vills? Hey, lemme ask—what time is it?"

But neither of them budges. Neither of the agents speaks. Vills stares at Miriam. And Grosky stares at Vills.

Then Miriam says, "Hey, Richie. Wanna know how you die?"

That's all it takes.

Vills moves fast. She's got the gun in her hand, leveled at Grosky's completely surprised, bug-eyed face.

But Miriam moves fast, too.

She knees the table forward. Vills *oofs* like a pillow with the air punched out of it and suddenly she's leaning forward—

Just enough for Miriam to get the handcuffs and chain around Vills's scrawny chicken-bone neck. Vills kicks and grunts. The gun goes up and fires two shots in the air, punching holes through the thatch and causing dust and sand to stream down right in her eye.

The gun hand flails.

Miriam ducks it.

And she brings her whole weight down, hunkering like a gargoyle, shoulder next to the table, both wrists pulling, pulling, pulling.

The gun goes off again, and Grosky staggers, a spray of blood kicked up from the meat of his shoulder.

Vills makes a sound like *grrk*!

And then her body stops moving.

The gun thumps to the floor.

Vills is just meat now.

Miriam reaches out with a boot and pulls the gun toward her. She snatches it up and points it at Grosky.

"The cuffs. Undo them."

Grosky stands, shell-shocked.

Miriam barks the order again. "Big boy! Cuffs! Undo them!"

He looks at his own bloody shoulder and then hurries over and fumbles around before fishing out the keys and slapping them down.

"She shot me," Grosky says.

"She was going to kill you."

"She was my partner."

"Life's hard. Wear a dick protector."

"How'd you—"

"How'd I know? Because I saw the way you died. Because that's how the visions work."

"Oh. Ri . . . right. But how'd you know about . . . about Tap-Tap?"

"It was a guess but a pretty educated one. The vision of your death started with a text message. But don't forget, I saw how *she* dies, too. After killing you and presumably me, she ends up back at the car. Which is what, about a quarter-mile from here?"

He nods.

"Tap-Tap is there. With Goldie and Jay-Jay. He shoots her in the head as soon as she walks up. The other two distract her, pulling up in a white Caddy. He's hiding behind the back end of the car. Big as he is, he can still hunker down pretty small."

"That . . . that means he's there now."

"It does."

"Shit."

"Mm-hmm. You want your gun back?"

He narrows his eyes. "Why would you give it to me?"

"Because I just saved your life."

"I'm not really great with a gun."

She shrugs. "I think you're gonna need it pretty soon." She tosses him the gun and he almost drops it. "Hey, lemme ask—what was all this about, anyway? Kidnapping me. Taking me out to . . . where are we?"

"On the . . . on the beach. A barrier island. Just outside Blowing Rocks. Near, ah, near Jupiter."

"And you wanted me why?"

"I thought . . . I thought you'd be a helluva catch if what you can do is true. Way back when I started looking into the string of bodies behind you, I thought maybe you really were a serial killer. But we found your diary in the trash, and more and more I thought maybe this thing you do is real and . . . I figured your gift would be a real thing to behold. For the FBI. For the Secret Service, even—I mean, shit, imagine you touch the president of the United States and see if he's gonna be assassinated? That's a doozy."

"Well," Miriam says, "a fun idea, but count me out. Because, Agent Grosky, I don't work for anyone. Not anymore. Now give me my box. You wanna go kill Tap-Tap or see if you can get him arrested, go for it. Me, I'm walking the other way."

She grabs the metal box.

And she leaves the agent standing there and bleeding.

SEVENTY

THE BOX

She walks for a while.

And behind her she hears the distant *pop, pop, pop-pop-pop* of gunfire. She doesn't know what that means. She's not sure she cares.

Though, she admits, she might be fonder of Grosky than she thinks. Because suddenly there's a little twinge of guilt if she saved his life only to have him lose it again to a brute like Tap-Tap.

But then she remembers Goldie's death and . . .

Well. Who knows how that shakes out?

She finds a place on the rocks.

The tide comes in. The tide goes out.

The sun starts its slide behind her.

She takes the box and bashes it on the rocks until the lock pops. Like an otter cracking open a clamshell.

A bag spills out from the box. Miriam grabs it, opens up, and sees that in the bag are photos and a little ratty book.

Like a diary.

She picks out the photos. A pale, redheaded woman holding a pregnant, freckly belly. The same woman pinning clothes to a line. Sitting on a gravestone. On a porch swing. Standing again in a cemetery, this time among the graves. Miriam grunts. She's not sure what this means.

So she picks up the book.
She picks a random page and reads.
She flips back and forth between pages.
"Holy shit," she says. "Holy. Shit."

SEVENTY-ONE

BRUJA

It takes a while for Miriam to make it back to the Keys, to the concrete storefront with the shattered windows and the weeds grown up through the coarse sand. It's late when she arrives.

And Sugar is there.

Sugar sits on a pile of cinder blocks around back. Sipping noisily from a Diet Coke bottle with a bent straw. She looks up to see Miriam there. Her look is one lacking surprise.

"I'm addicted to these things," Sugar says of the diet soda.

Miriam hands her the box.

This seems to surprise her.

"I found the box," Miriam says. "The one you told me I wasn't looking for. You're right. I wasn't. You were." *Or maybe we both were.*

"What?"

"It's not for me. It's for you." Miriam, pushy as she is, reaches into Sugar's lap and flips open the box. She fishes out one of the photos—the one of the pregnant woman cradling the belly. Then she turns the photo over. "*Dulce como el azúcar.* Written in a woman's handwriting. Though this woman looks American, I guess she spoke Spanish okay. That's you, right? Sugar."

"Wait. This is my . . ."

"That's your mother. And that"—Miriam taps the round, freckled belly—"is you. There're more photos in there. And a diary. Which was maybe for me as much as it is for you. Your mother had . . . powers, too. She was connected to the dead. Like me, but different. She could speak to them. The already dead. Not quite like ghosts, maybe, but . . ." Here comes that word again: "Like a frequency. She could tap into it."

"But what we do is born of tragedy."

"Hers was, too. She lost a child when she was very young. An uncle impregnated her at the age of fourteen. Nobody would help the kid get an abortion, so she did it herself. With a hammer. And that messed her up pretty good down there and almost killed her. They told her she'd never have kids or it *would* kill her. What happened . . . it marked her. Like it marked me. Like it marked you."

Sugar stands and throws her arms around Miriam.

It's the first time they touch.

The vision sweeps over Miriam—like with Eleanor Caldecott, there's nothing there. But this one isn't a poisonous tide or a vicious crackle of hissing static. It's velvet smoke. And sad whispers. And the smell of burned caramel. Sugar pulls away, and Miriam is left feeling dizzy.

"Thank you for this," Sugar says. Tears in her eyes.

"There's something else. Your mother said she figured out a way to . . . undo her power. She doesn't say what it is but she says where she learned it. A place called Collbran, Colorado. So, that's where I'm headed."

SEVENTY-TWO

NAILS IN THE COFFIN

The next day, Miriam leaves two grand of the money on Gabby's doorstep, next to a small bouquet of flowers. She doesn't know what Gabby likes.

She doesn't even know Gabby, not really.

But she leaves a note: "This should pay for your health insurance."

She thinks but does not write, *I'm going to find a way over the next five years to give you a reason not to kill yourself. And I'm sorry.*

She knocks. And hides. And watches as Gabby comes out and takes the flowers and the bag. Her face is swaddled in gauze and tape. But even behind the bandages Miriam can see the shock in her eyes.

Gabby looks around. She doesn't seem to see Miriam.

But she waves anyway.

Miriam thinks: *This will not be the last time we see each other.* Saving Gabby's life is going to be a whole other kind of challenge. She can't kill anybody to stop this death, and yet stop it she must.

A terrifying and yet enlivening thought.

Next, Miriam picks a spot north of the Keys where she can walk, and sit on the rocks, and watch as the ocean swallows the sun.

Then she takes her phone and she calls Louis.

He does not answer, but she leaves him a message. "It's me. I love you. I need you. And you're going to help me get rid of my curse. Call me back. Did I mention I love you? I love you. I love, love, love you."

She hangs up.

She sits. And smokes. And waits for him to call her back.

And just as the sun dips below the horizon and is gone, he does.

ACKNOWLEDGMENTS

Thanks to my wife, my family, my friends. Thanks to my agent, who helps these books stay alive. Thanks to Lee Harris, for giving this book its first chance at life, and to Joe Monti, for its lifetime home. Thanks most of all to the readers, without whom Miriam Black would never have made it this far.

AN EXCERPT FROM
MIRIAM BLACK:
BOOK FOUR:
THUNDERBIRD
CHUCK WENDIG

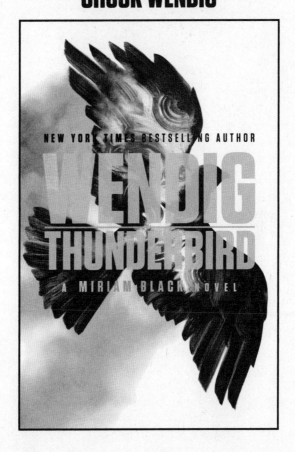

THE QUITTER

Miriam runs.

Her feet pound asphalt. Ahead, Old Highway 60 cuts a knife line through red rock and broken earth, the highway shot through with hairline fractures. Big clouds hang, clouds like the stuffing pulled out of a doll and left scattered across the sky. The side of the highway lined with gnarly green scrub brush, plants like hands reaching for the road, hoping to unzip it, rip it, ruin it. Beyond, it's just the wide-open nowhere of Arizona: posts forming electric fences that don't contain anything, craggy rocks, dusty trails, distant peaks.

Run, she thinks. Sweat coming off her hair, into her eyes. *Fucking hair dye. Fucking hair spray. Fucking sunblock.* She blinks back sweat carrying all those chemicals, sweat that burns her eyes. *Don't pay attention to that. Just run.*

Then her foot catches something—a rock, a lip of cratered asphalt; she doesn't know, and it doesn't matter, because suddenly she pitches forward. Hands out. Palms catching the macadam, bracing herself so her head doesn't snap forward and crack in half like a tossed brick. A hard pain jars up her arms, through her elbows like a flicker of lightning. Her hands sting and throb.

She gets up on her knees and then starts coughing.

The coughing jag isn't brief. She plants her hands on her knees and hacks hard, and between hacks she wheezes, and between wheezes she just hacks harder. It's a dry cough of broken sticks and dead leaves until it's not—then it's wet, rheumy, and angry, like her lungs have gone liquid and have decided to disperse themselves up and out of her mouth.

A mouth that wants a cigarette right now. Lips that would plant around the filter and suck smoke deep. Her whole *body* wants a cigarette, and the nic-fit tears over and through her like a plague of starving locusts. She shudders and bleats and laughs and cries and then, once again, coughs.

Her palms pulse with her hummingbird heartbeat. The skin abraded.

Footsteps behind her.

Heavy. Boots hitting hard.

Sweat pours off her, now—spattering on the road.

"It's hot," she gasps. "It's fucking hot. It's *Hell* hot. It's wearing-the-Devil's-humid-scrotum-as-a-hat hot."

"They say it's a dry heat."

Louis clomps up alongside her like a Clydesdale horse.

She looks up at him. The sun is behind him, so he's just a shape, a shadow, a black monolith speaking to her. *Oh, Louis*, she thinks, and then he turns just so, and her eyes adjust. And she can see the black electrical tape crisscrossing his eyes. She can see his pale face, his wormy lips, a tongue that traipses over broken teeth. And when he moves, she hears the rustle of feathers, the clacking of beaks.

Not-Louis. The Trespasser. Her companion who only she can see—a hallucination, a ghost, a fellow traveler to wherever it is she's going.

"You know what else is a dry heat?" she asks. "Fire."

"It's only April."

"It's, like, almost ninety degrees. I should've come in December."

The Trespasser stands over her. Like an executioner ready to drop the head-chopper ax down on the kneeling sinner.

"Why are we out here, Miriam?"

She rocks back on her knees, cranes her head back, eyes closed. She paws at the water bottle hanging at her hip. With her teeth, she uncaps it (and even there that small movement, that tiny moment, she thinks, *My teeth want a cigarette too, want to bite into the nicotine like it's a cancerous Slim Jim god. I want it so bad I'd kick a baby seal just to get one taste*), then drinks deeply, drinks sloppily. Water over her lips, down her chin.

Up in the sky, vultures spin on an invisible axis.

"*We* are not out here," she says, wiping her wet mouth with the back of her hand. "I am out here alone. You are—well, we still don't know what you are, do we? Let's go with *demon*. Invisible, asshole demon. You're not here. You're *here*." She taps her temple, then drinks more water.

"If I'm up there, then I'm with you, and we are still *we*," he says. A loose, muddy chuckle in the well of his chest. "Why are you jogging, Miriam?"

"It's not jogging. It's jogging when rich, limp-noodle assholes do it. When I do it, it's called *running*, motherfucker." She sniffs. Coughs again. "I do it because I need to get better. Get stronger. Faster. All that."

"What are you running from?"

You, she thinks. But instead she says, "It's funny. Anyone who sees me running asks me that. *Hur hur, is something chasing you?* Yeah. Death. Death is chasing me, and chasing everyone else, too. That's what I'm running from. My own clock spinning down. The sweep of the Reaper's scythe."

"Not like you to run from death."

"Things have changed."

Another damp, diseased chuckle. "Oh, we know. You're trying to get away from us. From you. From the gift you have been given."

"It's no gift," she says, finally starting to stand up. The sun is punishing enough it feels like a fist trying to punch her back down to the ground. "But you know that. And you don't care." She thinks but does not say: As soon as I find the woman I'm looking for, you're outta here, pal. No more trespassing for you.

"You're not done yet," the Trespasser says. As she stands, she sees Not-Louis's eyes have become black, glossy circles—crow eyes, rimmed with puckered gray skin and the start of oily feathers that disappear underneath the skin like stitches. "Not by a country mile, little girl."

She sucks in a bit of sweat from above her lip and spits a mist of it back at him. The Trespasser doesn't even flinch. Instead, he just points.

Miriam follows the crooked finger.

There, way down the highway, she sees the glint of light off a vehicle. Her vehicle—it's where she parked it. A rust-red, rat-trap pickup truck. A *literal* rattrap, actually—when she bought it, rats had made a nest in the engine, chewed up the belts and wires pretty good.

But then:

Another car.

This one coming from the opposite direction. Hard to make out what it is—the sun catches in it like a pool of liquid magma. Despite that, Miriam can see the back of the car fart out a noxious black cloud. She can hear the bang of the engine, and she can see something roll across the road—a hubcap?—that hits the tire of her Ford truck and drops. The car stops across from her truck.

Then all is still.

"What is that?" she asks. "Who is that?"

She turns toward the Trespasser, but he's gone.

And yet his voice still reaches her: "Go and see."

Shit.

NOT DONE YET

Miriam runs. Again. Because apparently she is a glutton for punishment. She tells herself that the quarter mile or so between her and the two vehicles is psssh, pffft, no problem at all, but three steps in and her feet feel like they're encased in cement and her calves feel like sausages about to split and spill their meat. Still, she runs. She tells herself it's because she has to.

Ahead, the truck and the car roam into view. Past the flinty, flashing sun. There, on her side of the road, the pickup: Ford F-250 from 1980. Rust has taken over most of the cherry-red paint. Across the highway: a Subaru station wagon. An Outback. Also old—maybe ten years, maybe more.

She hears the engines tinking and clicking. A smell hits her— bitter, acrid, sweet. A charred fan belt, cooked antifreeze.

A hundred yards away now. The driver-side door to the Subaru pops open. A black woman steps out. She's got the ragged edge of a survivor about her—a bumpy stick whittled down to a sharpened point. She's got a feral stare going on, and as Miriam slows to a jog and then to a walk, the woman points.

"Stay back!"

The woman's hand moves behind her, to the belt of her jeans—she turns just so, and Miriam sees something back there. A gun. Tucked. The driver doesn't pull it. Not yet.

Miriam holds up her hands, slows her walk. "Hey. Yo. Relax.

That's my truck right there. No harm no foul. Just gonna skootch on past, get in the truck, and go." Fifty yards now separate them. Maybe less.

The woman's eyes flash from Miriam to the truck and then back again.

Inside the Subaru station wagon: movement.

And that's when Miriam gets it. Because she sees a small face, round and wide-eyed, peer over the dashboard. A boy. Young, maybe ten years old. Blue T-shirt with some red on it—the Superman logo, she realizes. Just the top of it. She's a mother protecting her kid. Right?

Miriam thinks to ask if everything's okay, but her gut clenches: *Just let it go. Don't get involved.* This is a trap. The Trespasser put her here—she doesn't even know if it works like that, but whatever gets her out of this situation and back at the motel where she can crack one of those little vodka bottles . . . But then her dumb mouth starts forming words, and those words somehow escape like parakeets from open cages, and she says, "Do you need help?"

"You got a cell phone?"

"I . . . do. You want me to call somebody?"

The woman leans forward like she's about to pounce. "I want you to give it here. I want that phone."

Miriam arches an eyebrow. "Yeah, no."

"I want the phone and the keys to the truck."

"I will make a call for you and I will drive you somewhere."

"Oh, I know where you'll drive me. You ain't taking my boy back." And then the gun comes out—a little thumb-dicked .380 revolver. Snubby, priggish nose pointed right at Miriam. The woman's thumb cranes forward, clicks back the hammer. "Keys. Phone. Throw them over."

"If I throw the phone, I'll break it."

That seems to stun the woman, like she's too panicked to

think clearly and this tiny little hangnail has snagged the whole damn sweater.

"Fine," the woman barks, irritated. "*Fine.* Just . . . just come over, and you can hand them to me. No nonsense. Don't mess with me or I'll put this in you." She thrusts the gun forward, as if to demonstrate. The woman doesn't look like a killer, but she looks desperate—pushed to the edge. Miriam knows that people at the edge will do anything. Any dog trapped in any corner is likely to bite.

Miriam creeps forward. Her body throbs. Even in the heat she represses a chill. No idea what's happening here. What's driven this woman to this? She tries not to care. But the carapace she's carefully crafted is cracked—makes Miriam weak. Her hand ducks into her pocket, pulls out the little burner phone and the pickup's key ring. She jingles them like she's trying to distract a cat.

Thirty yards.

Twenty.

"C'mon, c'mon," the woman says, impatient.

Miriam knows she's not going to give over the keys or the phone.

That's all she knows, though. What happens next, she's not sure.